A soft whirring came from Pplimz's body. Their arms, which up until now had been humanoid enough, began to sprout additional appendages. Sharp, deadly-looking appendages. Soon, both their arms resembled a devil prince's own multitool, with blades, knives, whirling saws, and laser swords sticking out all which way.

I'd been so focused on the weaponry sprouting from their arms that I hadn't noticed that Pplimz also grew nearly eighteen inches in height, bulked out horizontally, and now sported a countenance that would make the most hardened Brobnar giant run screaming home to their parent. I found myself scrambling back until I ran into the wall.

It was the teeth, I think. Far too many sharp teeth for one face…

Pplimz,
…or Hire
…Nehm

TALES *from the* CRUCIBLE

EDITED BY

CHARLOTTE LLEWELYN-WELLS

ACONYTE

First published by Aconyte Books in 2020

ISBN 978 1 83908 023 4

Ebook ISBN 978 1 83908 024 1

Cover art by David Kegg

Distributed in North America by Simon & Schuster Inc, New York, USA

Printed in the United States of America

9 8 7 6 5 4 3 2 1

ACONYTE BOOKS

An imprint of Asmodee Entertainment Ltd

Mercury House, Shipstones Business Centre

North Gate, Nottingham NG7 7FN, UK

aconytebooks.com // twitter.com/aconytebooks

CONTENTS

CONTRACT
Tristan Palmgren

I perched atop a widower tree, half a centimeter from a tangle of razorvines.

Sometimes the best place to hide is where anyone else would be foolish to follow. Not even a niffle ape, with their preternatural wilderness senses, would be up here. Sometimes preternatural wilderness senses come second to *common* sense.

I didn't have common sense, or I wouldn't have taken this job.

It's hard to miss a battle between Archons. Sure, there's the screaming, the chaos, the clash of swords and the hissing of a hundred different kinds of ray gun – but this is the Crucible. That kind of nonsense happens all the time. It's easy enough to find if you want it. I don't. No, what really sets these things apart is the spectators.

Some of them come in person (or in energy-cloud, or in spirit, or in whatever-corporeal-or-incorporeal-embodiment they call their own). They set up their picnic mats or gambling booths, and, *maybe,* if it looks like they're about to get vaporized, move out of the way. But most vaultheads watch from afar, where the only (admittedly, considerable) danger is the postgame riots.

Anywhere would have been safer than here.

Before I'd left Hub City, I had not waited for the head of my shadowguild to find out what I was up to. I went to her office, tucked inside an old æmbrew warehouse, to tell her myself. Better that she heard it from me.

"You accepted a contract against Ponderous Url." The first sign of danger was that she was already showing her markedly chilly elvish smile. "The Archon."

"No other Ponderous Urls," I replied.

She said, "You could have found a simpler way to announce you had a death wish."

"I'm not afraid of Archons," I said. Fear would mean that I had something, anything, I wanted to hold onto.

"You're new to the Crucible," she said. "You don't understand." *Everyone* knew Archons couldn't get killed. But I didn't believe in immortality.

I looked her squarely in the eyes. "I understand."

"Then telling me this of your own free will is just as suicidal," she said. "I can't countenance this bringing attention back upon us."

The death threats had come out before I'd even told her that it was a demon of Dis who'd offered me the contract.

She tried to kill me, of course.

It was all expected, all *pro forma.* It was polite, even in an assassins' guild, for an employee who had announced they were leaving to stay for an exit interview. I had just given my interview and would have been a fool to go in there without my escape route set. Her blade swept through empty air as the dazzling lights of my stolen Star Alliance teleporter swept over me.

"It would have been a mercy," she said, as I dematerialized.

It had not been the first time I'd given up everything, but it *was* the first time I had done so by choice. It almost felt good.

For two hours now, the spectator drones had been swarming above the widower trees, dodging the lashing razorvines. I figured the vaultheads knew something I didn't. I was right.

Sudden movement focused my attention. An azure halo of plasma fire crowned the foliage. Widower trees screamed as they caught fire.

Opening salvo in the contest.

Judging from the tenor of the screams – not all from the trees – first blood as well. As one, the drones flocked toward the chaos.

I braced for impact, and dropped. My widower tree, somehow stirring from the botanical soporific I'd administered, shrieked. It lashed a razorvine at me.

Panic, dull and distant, coursed through me. The other widowers' screams must have jarred it awake. I landed, rolled, and sidestepped, but too late. The razorvine struck through my boot sole. A crimson flash of pain lashed through my foot.

I ran, hobbled and bleeding. I'd been lucky. I'd lost, at most, a toe. It could have been a foot, an Achilles tendon, or worse. My sense of balance compensated with elvish alacrity, keeping me nimble in spite of it all.

I'm what most beings on the Crucible would call a Svarr elf. I had the ears, the gold eyes, and the conniving, at least, to blend in among the assortment of gangs and thieves' guilds who called themselves Shadows. But blending in isn't the same as *fitting* in.

I didn't come from the same world as anyone else in my guild. I'd been ripped from my home. Years ago, in a flash of alien magics, my city had been transported from my world and reappeared in the Crucible – another victim of whatever power was stitching the Crucible together out of patchworks of stolen worlds.

Things made sense where I came from. I knew what I was. I was Vira Tirandel Agrulikhan – executioner, enforcer, third niece of the Lord Mayor, and god-aunt of the heir to the city. After we arrived on the Crucible, my people and I tried to hold to our center. But the Crucible might have been better named Centrifuge. It'll rip you apart. Nothing you had before can last. No belief, no ideal, no self-conception.

Until we arrived, my people had thought we were alone in the universe. Just coming here was violence enough to us. But that had been just the start. We'd materialized on the border of martian territory. It hadn't taken the martians long to sense our disorientation and weakness. In hard-fought battles, we turned away their saucers and tripod walkers, but not a single one of our buildings was left standing. By the time the Brobnar decided to hold one of their (literal) death concerts atop the rubble, we scattered.

It's been years since I've seen anyone from home. I'm not sure we would recognize each other if we did.

A flock of silverwings erupted in the far distance, and fled skyward. Silverwings were deaf birds, apparently evolved on a world awash in tremendous thunder. The foliage would have hidden movement. Those birds would have budged for one thing only: vibration. Big, ground-churning, root-snapping vibration.

Ponderous Url was a mammoth of an Archon – an adamantium-skinned golem even heavier than he looked. Ponderous Url was not reputed to employ any Brobnar giants or other creatures that could shake the earth. I had to gamble that Ponderous Url's opponent didn't, either – or that they themselves weren't as large as Ponderous Url.

Everything's a gamble when it comes to Archons. The Archons can be small as a faerie, or so big as to be mistaken for some dead king's vainglorious monument. But they have a few things in common:

One – they're all interested in cracking open vaults of ancient knowledge, treasures, and secrets left behind by the Crucible's even-more-mysterious Architects. They will fight each other, and recruit retinues of the Crucible's inhabitants to help them, for the privilege of opening a vault. Two – Archons all have the power to take care of their private armies. They heal traumas. They raise the fallen. But bystanders, let alone infiltrators like me, get no such guarantees. Sure, sometimes you'll get lucky with a do-gooder Archon who will expend their precious energy resurrecting those caught in the crossfire. But Ponderous Url wasn't that type of Archon.

Three – they never explain where they came from, their relationship to the Crucible's Architects and what they ultimately want. Not under any level of duress. Most people believe that they *are*, somehow, related to the Architects, but they will never say so.

The bulk of the fighting seemed to have shifted up a shallow crater ridge, where an ironwood forest bordered the widower grove. Ironwood was one of the few species of tree strong enough to resist the widowers. I wouldn't have been surprised if someone planted them here to contain the widowers.

I bolted into the borders of the ironwood forest, ducking the errant swipe of a sentry widower's razorvine. The razorvine gouged a hole in the soil behind me. Plasma smoke and the coppery scent of spent æmber rolled down the ridge. The pain in my leg had faded to a background scream.

My elvish instincts took over. I leapt from a boulder to an ironwood branch to a trunk bent at just enough of an angle to offer good footing. I was moving too fast, counting on the chaos of the battle to protect me.

A sword cleaved into the trunk just behind me.

I was already mid-leap. In the fraction of a second of instinctive panic, I jabbed my good foot out and smashed into the helm of an armored knight.

Smoke curled from the ironwood's trunk. The knight's sword flared like a sun. The wood glowed red-hot. But all that power wasn't enough to saw through ironwood. I bounced off the knight, flailed through the air, and landed hard on my bad foot. But, even stumbling, I still moved faster than the knight could free his sword. I left him snarling some very unchivalric curses behind me.

Ponderous Url employed a mix of untamed barbarians, martian soldiers, and a handful of demons. The knight had to belong to Ponderous Url's competitor. The two Archons' armies had been drawn from every corner of the Crucible. Good. More chaos. The more chaos, the more opportunities. The only thing you can trust on the Crucible is chaos.

Something *will* happen, but you can never predict what.

I don't think creatures like us are *capable* of understanding the Crucible. We're bacteria flattened underneath a microscope slide. We don't have the tools to process what's happening to us.

I have no place here. I don't *want* a place here. Everything I had is gone. There's no ground – no stable ground, anyway – worth standing on. For years, ever since I'd arrived on the Crucible, even the brightest colors only render for me in shades of gray and ash.

That was why I'd taken the contract.

The towering, silver-eyed demon who'd offered me the contract on Ponderous Url's life hadn't given me any information about it. It had just handed me the page.

Glimmerings of shadowy magics whorled over the lettering. Contracts like these have power beyond their wording. I had no guarantee the demon was even acting of its own accord – though I couldn't think that anyone would trust delivery to a demon.

I couldn't find any loopholes. I signed. It was what I wanted, anyway.

The Crucible's Architects need to pay for ripping me, and so many others, out of their homes. But they're beyond my reach. The next nearest thing to them are the Archons.

A ray gun bolt sizzled through the air in front of me. I ducked and, trying to dodge, picked a direction at random: the wrong direction. The ray gun hadn't been aimed at me.

I stumbled directly between two combatants. Now their weapons *were* aimed at me. The first: some kind of hypertuned Logos massacre-rifle, loaded with scopes, underslung grenade launchers, and stabilizing gyroscopes. The second: a drawn bow and arrow held by a hide-clad barbarian with a beard and mustache so stained with filth I couldn't even tell what its original color had been.

In the space of an instant, I realized that the only way I would escape would be to pretend to be on one side or the other.

It was no choice. I ducked toward the barbarian.

A fraction of a second after the barbarian released the bowstring, his arrow shimmered. With a *pop* like a cork flying out of a bottle of æmbrew, and the distinct guano-and-pine-needles stink of druidic magic, the air fractured. Colors spun like a broken kaleidoscope. There were five – no, ten – no, thirty – iron-tipped arrows in the same space.

They struck simultaneously. Even some of the arrows that visibly missed shattered. Quantum entanglement can get a little messy when you're pulling from parallel universes. But not as messy as the results. The kinetic energy of those dozens and dozens of arrows, and surely more, was focused on a single point in space in *this* universe.

The simultaneously unleashed energy ripped both the Logos rifle and its wielder apart. A searing hot shockwave knocked me flat on my side. My head struck dirt.

I lost myself for a while.

The first thing to learn about the Crucible is to leave your prejudices at your world of origin. If you see someone facing down military tech with a flint spear – be *very afraid* of that spear.

The second thing to learn is to keep your thoughts about what's better than what to yourself, because they will get you killed, expelled, or put on trial by half the factions in the Crucible. The other half will evangelize you until you *wish* they were killing you. Everybody has their own opinions, and the ones who are sure about them are the worst.

When I take contracts, I don't ask questions. Sometimes the answers come anyway. "Sanctum Prelate Kyranos betrayed our fortifications to the demons of Dis, and though his death is mandated by justice and righteousness *it must be kept quiet.*" "Martian Supreme Warcommander Xot, Slayer of a Hundred Thousand Pacifist Protesters, Conqueror of the Seven Broken Cities, has been sneaking through the front lines to attend Brobnar death concerts. He must be made an example." And so on. They say it for themselves more than me. Those who are more secure with their reasons for hiring an assassin tend not to say anything.

I reassembled my wits fast as I could. The man with the bow still stood above me. He wiped soot from his bow, grinned, offered me a hand. I accepted, and, in exchange, helped him pat out the fire still smoldering somewhere under his beard.

Then I smashed his head into an ironwood trunk. He flopped to the ground, limp as a gorged snufflegator.

No "friends." No risks. I couldn't take the chance that he would tell his friends about me and realize I shouldn't have been there.

No doubt some vaultheads, watching through the drones, were going ballistic right now. But it's a rule of honor among vaultheads to never interfere with the matches.

The ironwood forest was a safer place than the widower grove, mostly. But it also offered less ground cover. The foliage was thick as sheet rock. The surface layer might as well have been a cave. Nothing besides mold, fungi, and the creatures that fed on them – and the creatures that fed on *them* – lived down here.

Once my eyes adjusted to the darkness, I saw that the ironwood trees grew in bundles, their limbs locked together, a frozen frame of a centuries-long battle for dominance as they tried to shove each other out of the way of the sunlight. I could not help but stare as I ran.

More free advice: don't let yourself get lost in the "grandeur and majesty" of the Crucible. In my moment of distraction, my ankle snapped through an invisibly thin tripwire strung between two trunks. In a burst of stinking druidic magic, I found myself surrounded by a glimmering of faeries.

(Yes, I know the proper collective noun for a group of faeries is a glimmering. I studied plenty of the Crucible's languages. I said I didn't fit in here, not that I didn't *try*.)

I instinctively reached for my dagger. I could cut a swath through faeries, but there were too many of them. More than dozens. Hundreds. The largest among them was smaller than my palm, but faeries were as ruthless as they were tiny. They could cut me to ribbons.

So I held up my hands, and took a step back. Surrender. Simple mistake. We were all on the same side. Friends, yes?

Friends, no.

Their short, but wickedly sharp daggers came out. I laid my hand on my knife's hilt, but, in the space of another instant, there was a sound like a distant chime of bells.

At once, the faeries scattered. They vanished behind a curtain of whatever magic had summoned them. Before I could take two breaths, I was alone.

There was no sign of whoever, or whatever, had made the sound.

It's a mistake to try to understand the Crucible's chaos. Looking for reasons for everything that happens to you is how you end up ripping out your hair and marching off to join the Untamed. It's why the Logos, who *did* try to understand everything, were so unbalanced. The whole incident still left me unsettled.

There were two more tripwires in my way, taut and humming with faerie magic. I stepped over them. Then, ahead, I caught my first glimpse of something huge, shiny and silver. It was Ponderous Url.

I couldn't be sure if his skin was organic or artificial. Or both. Ponderous Url's flesh was shiny and smooth like metal, but supple. Flexible. Muscles rippled under his shoulders. Even after he tromped through this forest, felling widower trees and scraping past gods-know-how-many ironwoods, he was unblemished. No scrapes, no tears, no bruises. Not even any tarnishing. A Star Alliance handscanner might have been able to tell me more, but more likely it would have just raised more questions.

I'd done plenty of research before hunting Ponderous Url. Not even the most dedicated vaultheads could tell me what his body was made of. Archons were reputed to be able to control how they appeared. This was how Ponderous Url wanted to be seen.

Well, he had his secrets, and I had my surprises.

I sucked air through my teeth, picked up speed. All the pain had left me, submerged underneath a tide of adrenaline.

This was the only thing I really chased after now – this

cocktail mix of panic and exhilaration. Good and bad chemicals swilling together in my brain. They buried everything else. It wasn't much to keep me going, but I wasn't prepared to give it up. It was the last thing I had, and so it was the only thing I couldn't part with.

I'd seen plenty of people who *had* given up their last thing. New arrivals who couldn't handle the culture shock. Adventurers, monks, and mystics who'd learned one secret too many. Logos scientists addled by the Crucible's absolute refusal to be studied, probed, prodded or understood. Knights who'd betrayed their vows. In some parts of Hub City – the kind my guild trafficked in – you could hardly move without stepping over the wreckage of what used to be a sentient being.

The Crucible is, among other things, a place for people with strong beliefs and high ideals. For the rest of us, well… There's just this feeling. Adrenaline. Panic. Terror. Exhilaration. All mixed together.

Ponderous Url turned. His eyes were solid white with cherry-red irises and no pupils. No veins, no discoloration. Nothing, anywhere on his face, of the minor asymmetries that marred beings who had grown naturally.

I would have sworn, to any god that was listening, that he looked right at me. And then he turned away again, uninterested.

He must have noticed me. Some of the adrenaline dripped away. The pain came back. He couldn't have made me any smaller if he'd stepped on me.

A barbarian witch with a flaming red peaked cap stood near him. She held up her hand. Something in her palm glowed gold. Even from this far away, I recognized æmber. There was enough of it there for Ponderous Url to shape into a key, one of the three he needed to unlock his vault.

Was this Ponderous Url's first key? His third? I had just gotten here, and already I might be too late.

I drew my prism knife.

The flat of the blade gleamed red, then gold, then a hot white-blue, like a sun. Hints of intangible depths swam beneath its surface.

Don't ask me to explain the prism blade. It was an artifact, stolen from the vaults of a saurian senator who had, until now, been my most challenging target. The saurian left no information about it. The only thing I knew for sure, with a deepness and surety I couldn't justify, was that it was ancient. The Saurian Republic was the oldest civilization on the Crucible, with a history stretching millions of years.

The knife was the size of a dagger… most of the time. Its edges were indeterminate. It wasn't an object as much as it was an absence. It was a hole in space, a gateway to other places. It only "rested" in its scabbard because the scabbard was a magnetic field generator, keeping the hilt – the only physically real part of the weapon – suspended.

I recognized the bow-and-arrow's interdimensional magic because it hadn't been the first time I'd seen it. The prism knife, too, was a gateway.

Instead of bringing things in, it gated them out. Slice by slice. I didn't recognize any of the places on the other side, but I had never seen one that looked hospitable.

It did not matter what Ponderous Url's skin was made of. I was going to pierce it. I was going to *make* him notice me.

Only a few dozen meters past the Archon, a battle raged. Plasma bolts blasted trunks apart in great clouds of razor-sharp ironwood chips. A four-winged angel hovered over the horizon, almost certainly a magical illusion meant to draw fire (sure enough, a few of those plasma bolts passed harmlessly through it).

I hardly noticed the fight. I had learned my lesson about distractions.

Ponderous Url stooped to pluck the key. Assuming he was vulnerable in all the places a normal humanoid was vulnerable, that meant I had a plan. A leap to a stout rocky prominence – to the crook of an outstretched ironwood limb – onto Ponderous Url's back – scramble toward his neck...

But the second after I took my first jump, pain lanced up my leg.

The shock overcame the adrenaline. I did not have a chance to register seeing the iron-hard ground before I crashed into it. My prism knife slipped from my palm. I curled my two smallest fingers around the hilt, retaining just enough control to smash it into the ground.

The agony in my leg grew in urgency until I could think of nothing else. I fought against it, scrambling forward on my hands and knees. Something sharp dug even farther into my leg, yanking me back.

This time, the pain splintered my mind. The agony made me light-headed. It took real effort to keep from fainting. I twisted around, trying not to move my leg.

A bony whip, molded in the shape of a spine, had lashed around my leg. The whip coiled past my knee, up to my thigh.

Spines ran down its length like vertebrae.

As if this all were not dramatic enough, flashes of red ran down the spine's length, either magic or electronics or both. The spines had not actually gone very far into my skin. No blood marred my leggings. But the red pulsing was obviously the point of this production. Pain jammed through me in sync with the lights.

This whip was unmistakably of demon manufacture. Sure enough, at the other end of the weapon stood a cloaked, red-and-black-armed demon. It stood three times as tall as me. It gripped the whip's handle with seven-fingered hands that were, even for its size, grotesquely out of proportion.

I had not seen a demon since the creature who had offered me this contract. The demons of Dis are among the Crucible's many mysteries, and best not looked into. No one who's found any answers among their subterranean warrens has returned to the surface.

There are only a few things worth knowing. They thrive on eliciting emotions from other beings. Most of the time, this tends to come from pain and torture – but they've also been sighted lingering on the sidelines of parties, weddings, and Brobnar concerts. They'll even join an Archon's retinue, apparently to feast on all the chaos and carnage and high emotions.

The other thing to know is that demons never, ever communicate. Autopsies of dead demons have shown that they have fully formed vocal cords, adapted for speech. But they've never used them. Same goes for their guts and digestive tracts – in autopsies, they're always empty. The only things they seem to consume are the emotions of others.

The pain was a snake coiled around my leg, biting into the base of my spine. A spasm of agony ran up my back like an electric shock, jamming my nerves. But if I had not already had my hand around the prism knife's hilt, I wouldn't have been able to draw it.

My instincts alone were kicking me along. I plucked the knife out of the ground and, in one swift stroke, I severed the whip between its vertebrae.

The lights along the whip died all at once. I fell into the dirt, and was left only with the "mundane" pain of the lash wrapped around my leg. Steel glinted around the base of the whip. Shiny little filaments had extruded from the bony vertebrae and wrapped around my leg. They kept the whip tightly bound to me.

That alone was enough of a shock to keep me from standing until, in three long strides, the demon had closed the distance between us.

Its outlandishly oversized fingers wrapped around my chest, dug into my skin. My ribs *popped* as it grabbed me, and then lifted me.

When I say that demons do not communicate, I don't mean in just language. It also did not snarl, or hiss, or growl, or make any noise that I might have been able to imbue with some kind of meaning. My weapon hand was pinned. I had just enough freedom of movement to drive the prism knife into its palm, but it gave no indication that it even noticed.

Then it tossed me toward the still-raging battle.

I've leapt from rooftops to passing trains, shimmied across the sensors and telescopes above Logos laboratories and danced through the brawling pits of a death concert without getting injured. But agility can only see you so far. Once I was in mid-air, there was nothing I could do. There was no way I could twist or contort myself except to curl up.

I landed hard. I tumbled across the packed dirt, accumulating scrapes and bruises, and rolled into an ironwood trunk.

For several seconds, I could not breathe. Only after I forced air into my lungs did I realize that I was not resting against an ironwood trunk.

It was a Brobnar giant's leg. Its ugly, ogreish face looked down at me with something between amusement and annoyance. Ponderous Url's opposition *did* employ giants, after all. I had been lucky that the silverwings led me in the right direction.

This giant held a club, scarred and pitted from numerous ray gun and plasma bolts. The moment I looked up, the giant raised its club.

I used to get angry very often. I can be ruthless, and I can be cruel, but those are calculating. Anger is a symptom of attachment. It had been a long time since I had felt strongly enough about anything to rouse myself to rage for it.

I was angry now.

It was almost refreshing. There was a real point to my being now. And that point was to hurt. I was tired of everything I faced being larger than me.

The prism knife was small, too, but it still penetrated deep into the giant's ankle. I twisted the knife and yanked upward. The prism knife flared colors, greedily absorbing parts of the giant and removing them from this world.

I rolled out of the way. I didn't see the giant fall. I just felt the impact reverberate through the packed earth. I staggered to my feet. The whip still dragged with me. I must have gotten disoriented in mid-air. I couldn't see any sign of Ponderous Url or his demon.

If the demon had wanted to kill me, it could have crushed me, or tossed me into a tree. It should have pursued me. It wasn't even here to feed from me.

A trio of violet-skinned Brobnar goblins bolted past me, running from a torrent of ray gun fire. Rage overcame me. Without thinking, I swiped my knife across their path. I struck one of the goblins. They folded backward, almost casually. None of its companions seemed to notice. In another flash of battle-chaos, the remaining goblins were gone.

Ordinarily, I prided myself on not harming anyone but my targets. The goblin and the giant would be healed at the end of the battle. If they died, they would be resurrected. But that was rationalization. Not justification. I had only thought of that after the fact. Back home, I had often been angry, but never uncontrolled. The part of me that had attacked that goblin was not a part of me I had met before I'd come to the Crucible.

A growl welled deep under my throat. Up ahead, a tall, crouched silhouette had taken cover behind an ironwood root. In my battle-rage, I hallucinated Ponderous Url. It was not until I'd climbed onto it and dispatched it with my prism knife that I saw that, no, it was just another of those cursed giants.

I was doing a good job of clearing out Ponderous Url's opponents for him.

The ogre had been digging. No doubt searching for æmber.

Ironwood roots were attracted to æmber deposits. I'd already seen Ponderous Url collect enough æmber to forge one key. The battle couldn't last for much longer.

Hobbled by the weight of the whip still bound to my leg, I staggered on.

A blast of green-white light blinded me. It overwhelmed all of the plasma bolts and martian ray guns. It was so bright that, for a moment, I didn't realize I'd been deafened, too. The noise of the blast had been too loud to hear.

When the afterimage faded, half of the martian ray guns had fallen silent. Whatever the blast was, it had silenced a large part of Ponderous Url's army.

Not wanting to see, I turned.

The six-legged mechanical titan stood just underneath the next layer of ironwood foliage. It must have been built to order, made just for this particular place. The bits and knobs grafted onto it reminded me of the rifle I'd faced down minutes ago. It could only have been Logos technology. The Logos loved to tinker and redesign. Their robots and cyborgs were hyper-specialized. Every part had its specific purpose.

Any of its pincer legs could have trampled a martian tripod walker. There was nothing on the battlefield of any size capable of opposing it. When I looked where it was headed, I saw a familiar glint of silver skin.

Point of professional pride: a kill was not a kill unless I performed the deed myself.

I bolted after the walker, fast as my bad leg would carry me. That was just fast enough, as it turned out. The walker's size was its biggest weakness. Though its spiky legs surmounted roots and ruts with ease, it had to navigate around the thickest bundles of ironwood trunks.

A plan trickled into place. Whether there were other huge vehicles around or not, I would be a fool to assume Ponderous Url had no other defenses. All of Ponderous Url's retinue and remaining weapons would be directed at the walker shortly. They would not notice me until I was ready to *make* them notice me. All I had to do was make Ponderous Url's job a little easier, make sure the walker didn't *actually* harm him…

I ducked between the walker's pincer legs. A point-defense gun mounted on the walker's side swiveled toward me, too slow. My prism knife flashed, afterimages of colors behind it. Some kind of defensive shield flared over the walker's skin. Not enough. The prism knife passed through it like air.

The tip of the walker's pincer legs dug into the ground as it walked. The next time the walker tried to lift the leg I'd struck, it ripped off as if it were paper. My ears were still ringing, but even through that, I could hear a terrible metallic screeching.

The walker fell to one of its many knees. Perfect. It was an open target. And if any of Ponderous Url's allies had seen me, they would think I was on their side.

All I had to do was get out of the way fast enough.

That was too tall an order. It was not the pain that caught up with me. It was exhaustion. I was winded. My vision blurred. My body felt like it was at a great remove, and I could not move like I needed.

One of the titan's remaining pincer legs thrust into the small of my back. It propelled me forward, slamming me into an ironwood trunk.

My vision mottled red with agony. The pincer leg pinned

me against the trunk for a moment, and then withdrew. I fell.

Scores of plasma bolts seared the air, all aimed at where I'd left the walker. From where I lay, I could not see what had become of it. All I knew was that the pressure had lifted. But I could not breathe. I could not raise myself to twist around and look.

Eventually, the plasma fire stopped.

I could not hear anything besides a deep-abiding hum behind my ears. It was not even ringing. The malfunction was deeper than that, in my brain. Millions of neurons, overwhelmed with pain, misfiring.

I had had my breath knocked out of me plenty of times. This felt different. I was not fighting with my lungs. I could not feel them at all.

The red blotches had not gone away. Now they were piling in from the fringes of my vision, racing to fill up the center.

I drove my fingers into the dirt. Pulled myself forward. If I didn't force myself to focus on something, I was going to be lost.

Somewhere, at the far end of the red tunnel, I saw Ponderous Url. The foliage-dappled sunlight glinted across his silvery skin.

There was the demon beside him, still holding its half of the severed bone whip. It should have been over here. It was missing out on an emotional feast. It was offering something to Ponderous Url. Æmber glowed between its claws. A vault key.

The demon's hood fell as it raised its head.

I was not so far gone that I did not recognize the demon – it was the same silver-toothed demon who had offered me the contract on Ponderous Url's life.

I still couldn't breathe. I was quite beyond laughter.

The rest of my vision disappeared into the tunnel. I wished I could have convinced myself that I was hallucinating, but I was still lucid enough to know otherwise. One more way the Crucible was laughing at me. One more mystery I would never be able to solve.

I still felt the soil under my fingers. I clung to the feeling as long and as hard as I could. Eventually it, too, faded away.

Of course, I didn't stay dead. I'm here talking to you.

I woke with a cool feeling emanating from deep in my chest, spreading through the rest of my body. The bow-wielding barbarian stood over me, his torn fingernails aglow with strange magic.

I gasped and coughed, more from the shock than because any of my revived parts were working incorrectly. I rolled away, forced myself to stand on shaky legs. I reached for my prism knife, but only grabbed air. In fact, the whole magnetic sheath had been taken from me.

There was no pain. I wasn't dragging a severed half of a whip with my leg. Even the damage the widower tree had done to my foot was gone. I could see my unbroken skin through the boot's torn sole.

The barbarian grinned, but gave no sign that he recognized me. I *had* hit him on the head pretty hard. Or maybe, and more likely, he just didn't care. It had all been in the spirit of good fun.

He moved on to his next patient. A line of dead and wounded fighters was arrayed next to me. There was no guano-and-pine-needles stink of druidic magic this time, so I doubted the magic was his.

We were still under the gloom of the ironwood foliage, though I didn't recognize this part of it. I must have been dragged here. All around, Ponderous Url's fighters wandered amongst the fallen. Their hands glowed like my barbarian's.

Ponderous Url himself was not difficult to find. He sat with his back to a bundle of three trees, his legs folded. Luminous strands of magic emanated from him to his healers. As if he had called a council of war, he sat with a golden-skinned elf, a martian war-commander and a cloud of faeries. The demon who had hired me lingered nearby too – no doubt soaking in the ambient emotional energies.

I didn't care. I charged toward Ponderous Url, scattering the faeries with a wave of my hand. "This was a set-up," I told him. "You hired me – you wanted me to try to kill you."

Ponderous Url considered that for a long time. He hadn't gotten his name for nothing. Finally, he raised a silver finger. "I wanted you to fight," he said.

For all his size, Ponderous Url's voice was incongruously small. No deeper than an ordinary human or elf's. He even spoke in an accent that tickled an ancient memory. It was the accent of my home.

I was aware of the demon abandoning its meditations, stepping closer to me.

For the rest of Ponderous Url's retinue, even intense fighting was all in a day's work. Acclimation dulls emotion. But my rage and despair were boiling over.

Once again, and now not for the last time, the Crucible had bested me. At least if I had died it would have been over.

It was no accident that I had tangled mostly with his opponent's fighters, or that the demon had tossed me at the Brobnar giant and the goblins. I had, in some twisted sense, been doing Ponderous Url's work.

"If you had taken a moment to consider," Ponderous Url said, with another weighty pause, "then you would know demons can't communicate with your species. Not even in the form of the written letters of a contract."

Ponderous Url held out his hand to the demon. In a blaze of green fire, the contract I had signed appeared in the demon's hand.

I said, "*You* seem to have no trouble communicating with it."

"Archons are special in that way." He took the contract. "Among others."

No doubt now – that *was* the accent of my home city. I wondered if the others here heard the same thing, or if they heard their own childhood tongues.

If this was how Archons communicated, no wonder even the demon got along with Ponderous Url. "Are *you* part of what made the Crucible?" I swiped at my eyes, clearing the blurring away. I fought to stabilize my voice. "Are you part of what brought me here?"

He considered that question very carefully. For longer than even usual.

Then he shook his head. "You already know I cannot answer that question."

My hands trembled. I had never hated anything like I hated Ponderous Url. Never experienced this much rage, not even when I'd thought I was dying. I summoned all of my sense of authority – the voice of the executioner, enforcer, and third niece of the Lord Mayor, and more. "I demand that you tell me."

But it was a hollow voice for a hollow threat. I had no power to enforce anything. The person I'd been no longer existed. Even if I'd had my prism knife, I was now under no illusions that I would have been allowed to draw it.

Ponderous Url scanned the contract.

The letter of the contract stated that I would try to kill Ponderous Url until either he or I fell. That had seemed much simpler when I'd thought I'd still stood a chance of killing him, and certainly before I knew he intended to resurrect *me*.

By the contract's terms, I would be following Ponderous Url forever. Or until he decided to stop raising me.

"Do you mean to enforce that?" By which I meant to ask: *are you going to enslave me?*

For once, he did not hesitate. "No," he said, and the contract evaporated in a burst of multi-hued fire.

It happened so quickly that I did not have the time to avoid the ashes as the wind caught them. They stung my eyes.

Relief was, in its own way, more debilitating than pain. For a long time, I could not speak. I did not know what I had done to deserve the awful things that had just happened to me – or to have just been released from the contract.

"Why did you do this?"

"You're a skilled infiltrator and assassin. I would think that your value in an Archon's retinue would be obvious. You disabled a Logos titan."

"You could have *asked*."

"You would have said no."

That was true. I hadn't quit my old guild just to sign up for another gang. I wasn't about to be tied down to anything on the Crucible. "You didn't have the right."

Silly thing to say, and we both knew it. Ponderous Url did not dignify it with an answer. "It could have gone much worse for you," he told me. As if for punctuation, he dusted the ashes of the contract off his palm.

"If you're asking me to thank you, you can–"

"You made a mistake," Ponderous Url interrupted. "You did not take the time to think through all of the outcomes of accepting a contract with a demon. You only focused on what you wanted."

"And what do you think I wanted?"

"To give up," Ponderous Url answered.

I took a long time to answer, and not because I was pondering. The demon was hovering closer.

I said, "Contract or not, I could try to kill you again."

"Did you expect to be able to?"

Stupid question, and the answer made me feel stupider.

Ponderous Url said, "If you had, by some twist of circumstance, assassinated me, do you think you could have taken your pay and retired?"

That had never remotely been a possibility. If I had somehow, miraculously, killed the Archon, millions of vaultheads would have watched me do it. The rest of whatever life I'd had would have been spent hiding from fans, bookies, and any other unknowable vengeance that would have been coming my way. Even if I had been left alone with just myself, I still could not have found any peace.

"Either outcome would have been the end for you." Ponderous Url raised a gigantic finger to tap his head. "You people do not take the time to think about why you make the choices that you do."

"Whatever it was, it should have been *my* choice," I said, with a snarl. "You took it from me."

"If you're ignorant of both the causes and outcomes of your choices, did you really make one?"

"We can't help being 'ignorant.' We have no idea why anything happens in this place."

"If that's what you need to go on," he said, "then I would give up now."

He shifted his bulk. With great slowness, he began to rise. I saw, at the back of his waist, a magnetic-suspension holster with a familiar hilt. The prism knife looked outlandishly tiny on his body.

Had he tricked me into this because he wanted my services? Had he been after the prism knife all along? Even now, years after, I couldn't say.

The other members of his war council were already gone. He was leaving. I was running out of time. I had a thousand questions, but only one that could make it. I hated the way I sounded. "Then what do you think I should do?"

He paused, and once again turned to me.

He said, "The Crucible is the opportunities you've been given." After reflection, he added, "I *can* tell you that's as true for me as it is for you."

I let him walk off. This time, he did not look back. His council of war followed him, and, once I was out of earshot, resumed whatever plans they were hatching.

Like an ironwood tree slipping down a mudslide, I fell to my knees.

Minutes later, still feeling the vibrations of his footsteps in my bones, I stood. His retinue had finished their healing rounds. They were already striking camp.

I had no guild to return to. I was *persona non grata* in Hub City. If any one of my guild's numerous spies found me – not even I could avoid them all – they would report me to my old boss. My life would be over. She would kill me.

If I followed Ponderous Url, I could wait for an opportunity to steal my knife back. But even if I succeeded, my life would still be over. I would have been, at best, back where I started. More likely, I would have just been dead.

Not a life worth continuing.

Ponderous Url chose his words very carefully. No matter what I did, I would have given in, or given up, to something. I couldn't keep trying to be who I'd been before. That had been taken from me. It was never coming back.

There are no right choices, not in a place like the one where I'd ended up. The hardest thing I ever had to do was force myself to make this one.

Once I'd come to the Crucible, no path I took was going to end with me keeping my life – whether I was alive in body or not.

What I chose shouldn't be any great mystery. I'm still here to tell you about it, aren't I?

I had to run hard to catch up to Ponderous Url and his retinue.

I've learned a few more things since I joined him. He was wrong about at least one thing – the Crucible *is* more than a sum of its opportunities. Much, much more. But the opportunities are a good place to start.

I had to let go of the smallness of everything I'd been, to seize what I'd been given.

And so do you.

Welcome to the Crucible, outsider.

THE APPRENTICE
Cath Lauria

"Who built this thing?" Roz muttered, as she jammed a finger down into the depths of the jetpack, feeling for the catch-release that *should* be there. Every jetpack came with a catch-release for the æmber tanks – if something went wrong with the firing system, you needed to be able to cut the fuel loose so you didn't end up strapped to a fireball. But try as she might, she couldn't feel anything remotely like a switch down there.

Maybe the goblin who wore it was a lefty, maybe it was on the other side. Roz turned the pack over and looked for a likely spot. Nothing. Perhaps it was remote-controlled? But what goblin trusted a remote control over his own sturdy hands? They were often brilliant engineers – sometimes crazy ones too – but they liked being able to feel what they were working with.

Roz checked her tool belt for her telescoping extension light. Nothing.

"Arg." She was already ensconced in her workstation – a half-dome of flickering holoscreens, work tables, and failsafes she could trigger at a moment's notice if a client failed to mention a little "enhancement" that turned out to be dangerous. Roz glanced at the nearest screen thoughtfully. If she activated Grizl's Deep-Down scanner, she could get a three-dimensional image of the jetpack and find what she was looking for. But the Deep-Down scanner used a lot more power, and that meant spending more æmber.

Every job was a balancing act: to turn a decent profit, you had to spend around half as much on the repairs as you charged. Grizl Crustic was a popular mechanic because he offered flat rates for most fixes, but when the problem turned out to be complicated, that could mean taking the ledger from black to red in the quest to solve it. Every time Roz did that, Grizl took the difference out of her pay. Never mind that she'd been doing this for almost eight years now, twice the length of the normal goblin's apprenticeship, and could handle jobs that even her master preferred to avoid.

Honestly, Grizl preferred to avoid most jobs these days, letting Roz handle the shop while he spent his days betting on his favorite Archons or reliving famous matches at the local Shrine-O-Vault stadium.

Roz sighed and blew a strand of dirty blond hair out of her face. "TRIS," she called out, "can you bring me my extension light? I think I left it on the table by the door."

She heard her old guardian robot creak into action, slowly levering herself up from where she slumped on the floor and shambling over to the door. Roz bit her lip, trying not to feel guilty about making TRIS get up. The robot liked to be active, after all, despite how hard it was for her these days. TRIS was a treasure bot, designed to be able to follow explorers anywhere on the Crucible their journeys took them and protect whatever marvels they discovered. Once, TRIS had been top-of-the-line, and Roz remembered riding safe in TRIS's internal treasure vault as they followed her parents over mountains, across deserts, and into dilapidated ruins.

TRIS was the only reason she was alive, already tucked away safe when her parents accidentally triggered an ancient Wrathtar booby trap. A wave of radioactive fire had burst forth from a sacred temple, destroying everything – and everyone – in its path. TRIS had encapsulated Roz, curling around her and absorbing all the damage as they were thrown violently from the ruins. It had taken hours for TRIS's exoskeleton to cool enough to let Roz out, and all Roz saw when she emerged was the wreckage of everything she knew and loved. Her life as an explorer's child was over, but at least she still had TRIS.

Every extra bit of æmber Roz earned went to repairing TRIS. Right now, the bot was worth more for her valuable vault parts than she was for her ability as an actual, functioning treasure robot, but that would change. As soon as TRIS was fully fixed, Roz would become an explorer herself and leave all the mess, mire and noise of Hub City behind. It was her dream, and with TRIS's help it would become a reality.

But first she had to figure out how to fix this dang jetpack. The tip of her extension light poked through one of the holoscreens, momentarily blurring it. Roz could just make out TRIS's glowing yellow eyelights beyond it. "Thank you," she said, taking the light, then reaching out and laying her hand on the side of TRIS's arm. TRIS hummed a brief, fractured version of an old lullaby she used to sing for Roz as a child before lumbering back to the wall and sliding down with another noisy creak. Roz winced. Next on her robot repair list: æmber-vescent shocks.

Roz activated the light and stuck it down into the depths of the jetpack's harness. Where, where, where... *ah*. What the – who even put a catch-release so close to the openings of the engines? The goblin who owned this thing must wear asbestos gloves. Roz reached up beside the heat-tarnished mouth of the right engine and triggered the catch-release. The æmber tank fell onto her work table. "Now we're getting somewhere," she murmured with a nod.

Servicing the jetpack took all morning, and Roz barely got it done in time for its owner to pick it up. A delay would have meant giving a discount, though, and she'd be darned if she was going to take yet another cut to her pay when she was so close to affording the next round of parts for TRIS. "Just a couple more years," she said to herself after the goblin who owned the jetpack departed, a dubious look on his face. *Yeah, yeah, little human girl fixed your jetpack. Why don't you try it before figuring me for a fraud?*

Honestly, Roz knew enough at this point to open her own shop if she wanted, but she needed Grizl's reputation to bring in customers. Goblins were some of the best in the business – why go to a human mechanic when you could get cutthroat prices from someone like Grizl? And speaking of Grizl...

Roz blinked in surprise as the master mechanic himself sidled in through the front door of their little shop. What was he doing back so early? He usually didn't return to the shop until well after close. Was he checking up on her?

"I got the full fifteen æmbits for the jetpack job," she said before he could start complaining. "And I'm going to start on the gasket repairs for the elf's hovercar next. It should be finished before the end of the day."

Grizl shut the door behind him. "Uh… Roz…"

"And I don't want to hear another lecture from you about how to prioritize my workload," Roz continued. "I'm not kicking your friends' jobs to the head of the queue, no matter how much they beg."

Grizl took his leather hat off, a shock of bright orange hair expanding like a flower around his head. He wrung the hat in his long-fingered hands. "Roz, look–"

"They never pay on time either, have you noticed that? The next guy I have to threaten into turning over the æmbits just because he thinks he can take advantage of a human, I'm gonna–"

"Rozelyn!"

Roz stopped speaking, shutting her mouth so fast she nearly caught the tip of her tongue in her teeth. Grizl never called her by her actual name. He hardly ever used Roz, either – it was always "kid" or "girl" or "newbie," even though she'd been his apprentice for almost half her life. Him resorting to using her first name could only mean one thing: trouble.

"What happened?" she asked as calmly as she could.

Grizl looked down at the ground, his purple skin flushed darker than usual around his sharp cheekbones. He was… embarrassed? Nervous? Ashamed?

"I, uh… look, maybe we should talk over a drink, do you want a–"

"Just. Tell. Me."

Grizl sighed. "I made a bad bet today. Shoulda been a

sure thing, I mean, Argus has won the last five rounds and the rosters haven't even changed!" Roz recognized the name of Grizl's favorite Archon to watch. "Sure, some of his guys might have taken a drubbing last time, but they were rated as fully healed! But they, uh… they didn't do as well as they should have."

Roz pursed her lips. "So you made a bet and you lost."

Grizl winced. "Something like that."

"What did you wager?" Anger began to flare in Roz's chest. "You didn't wager my work contract, did you? Because that's against the *rules*, and I know you don't care about them all that much, but *I'm* not going to go work for a, a Shadow or a Whispered Walker and help them commit *crimes* while you–"

"No, no!" Grizl held his hands out placatingly. "No, it's nothing like that!"

Roz pushed to her feet. She was short for a human, but still taller than Grizl, and right now she felt like she needed every advantage she could get. "Then what *is* it?"

"I kind of… maybe… promised 'em… your bot."

Roz's anger cooled into icy dread in the space of a heartbeat. "No," she breathed. "She's mine."

Grizl sighed. "Technically she's mine, actually. You don't own anything other than the clothes you're wearing, kid."

"No, no, because – because she came here with me! You found her with me, she's *mine*, she belonged to my family!"

"The rules of an apprenticeship state that everything the apprentice brings with them becomes the property of the master, as collateral against the money the master outlays for their upkeep, until they move on," Grizl said quietly.

Roz's eyes filled with tears. "But I earn you money!"

"You do, but that's a side-effect of your training."

"What are you … ? I'm the *only* person here earning money!" She pointed around the grimy little front office. "You haven't taken an appointment here in *weeks*. What will the guild say if they learn that I'm doing all your work for you?"

"They'll probably congratulate me, honestly." Grizl shook his head as Roz growled. "I'm not sayin' it's fair, kid. I know it's not fair, but that's the system. It was either lose the bot, or lose the shop. You want both of us to be out on the street?"

Roz clenched her fists so hard it felt like her knuckles were going to pop right through the skin. "Or you could just not bet at all."

"Nah," Grizl said, sounding a little sad. "I never know when to quit. And now it's too late, and I'm sorry for this, Roz, I really am, but there's no way out of it. A bet's a bet."

"No." Roz reached up to wipe her traitorous leaky eyes, then realized she still hadn't cleaned her hands from the jetpack job. "No, I want to talk to this person first," she said, sniffing as she grabbed a fresh rag and dabbed at her cheeks.

"Roz…"

"No! Grizl, you *owe* me this." She put so much menace into her tone that the goblin actually shrank back a little. "You took me in when I needed help, and I'll always appreciate that. But I've more than paid you back in blood, sweat, and tears, and I'll be damned if I let you gamble away the only thing I have left of my family without at least *trying* to cut a new deal."

"A new deal?" Grizl narrowed his eyes. "What kind of deal are you thinking of?"

"The kind you don't get to know anything about until we

get there." Roz looked down at herself. She was still wearing protective leathers over her simple blue overalls, was covered in grease and soot, and smelled like jetpack fuel. *Oh well.*

"Take me to them. Now."

To say that Roz was surprised when Grizl took her to a saurian bar was an understatement. saurians generally didn't have much to do with vault matches – they considered themselves too refined for base entertainments like gambling. Roz became even more suspicious when Grizl hustled her around to the back of the establishment. "What, you're good enough for them to fleece but not good enough to let inside?" she snapped at Grizl.

"That's exactly what I'm saying," Grizl replied. "'Course, the guy I made the bet with isn't allowed inside either. His brother owns this place, I think. He's kind of a … *renegade* saurian. He's got an apartment in the back."

"A renegade saurian?" Roz's voice rose in disbelief, making Grizl turn and *shush* her with one long finger pressed to his lips.

"Don't go announcing it to the world," he hissed.

Roz resisted the urge to pull on her hair in frustration. "Where did you even *find* this guy?"

"Just – can you be quiet for one minute? We're here." He stepped up to a small, rather plain-looking apartment at the back of the building, lifted his hand, and knocked respectfully.

A moment later the door slid open on its own, and a deep voice called out, "Come in, Mr Crustic. Bring your apprentice."

Roz jumped. "How does he know about me?"

"How do saurians know half the stuff they know?" Grizl asked, morosely. He wiped his feet before stepping inside, and gestured for Roz to do the same. She walked into the apartment and–

This was more like what she expected of a saurian. The temperature was warmer than outside – set to saurian comfort levels, no doubt – the walls were eggshell blue, the furniture was soft and wide and suited to a carnisaur's body, and all the fittings were made of gold – or at least, something that looked too close for Roz to tell the difference. The Saurian Republic was one of the oldest civilizations on the whole Crucible, and they had a commensurate amount of wealth, knowledge, and prestige. *Not to mention arrogance,* Roz thought. She hadn't met many saurians – they didn't tend to mingle with the lower echelons of society – but those she *had* met had condescended to everyone around them as easily as breathing. This apartment might be modest by their standards, but to Roz it was fancier than anything she'd ever set foot in before.

"Heya, Mr Tsaagan," Grizl said, inclining his head toward the saurian resting on the central room's couch. He – judging from the brightly colored feathers around his head, he was probably male – was reclined in a position of ease, with a reader in one claw and a drink in the other. He wore a plain black jumpsuit, atypically drab for the species, but it looked tailored to his long, lean form. His eyes were the color of polished æmber, and his narrow snout was filled with needle-sharp teeth.

"Mr Crustic." Mr Tsaagan looked from Grizl to Roz. "I

assumed you were coming to pay your debt, but this doesn't look like a treasure robot to me."

"No, this is–"

"Your apprentice, I know." Mr Tsaagan stared at Roz. "Why are you here, girl?"

"First off, you can call me Roz, not 'girl,'" she said. Grizl sighed despairingly, but the saurian just quirked his head to the side.

"Very well. Why are you here, Roz?"

"Because you can't take my bot." Once she started speaking, the words just flowed out of her, almost as though they had a mind of their own. "TRIS is the only legacy I have of my parents. They've been dead for almost a decade now, and without TRIS, I…" *I don't know if I'd be able to remember their faces, or the way my mother tucked me into TRIS's treasure vault at night, or the lullaby my father sang to me.* "I need it. I came to ask if there's another way for us to cover Grizl's debt to you."

"Hey, don't drag me into this!" Grizl protested.

You dragged me in first, Roz wanted to say, but didn't. Hierarchy was very important to saurians, and she wasn't going to embarrass herself or shame her master – even though he wasn't much of one – by badmouthing him in public.

"Hmm." Mr Tsaagan put his drink down and stroked his scaly chin thoughtfully. "An interesting proposition, although not one I'm inclined to accept. If word gets out that I can be swayed into changing my mind about a debt, then everyone will try to renege."

"This wouldn't be reneging," Roz promised. "I want to get you a fair-value trade. I can fix almost anything–"

"I have no personal need for a mechanic or engineer," the saurian interrupted her.

"I could do work for your family, then!"

"My family doesn't acknowledge me." Mr Tsaagan smiled sharply. "At least not publicly. No."

Roz bit her lower lip. "There must be *something* you want," she said. "Something I might be able to get for you that you can't get for yourself."

Mr Tsaagan stared at her for a long moment, his expression impenetrable, and Roz felt a surge of despair well up in her chest. *If only I'd fixed TRIS sooner, we could make a break for it. There's no way right now, though. We wouldn't make it a mile.*

"There might be something," Mr Tsaagan said at last.

Roz exhaled in a *woosh*, the sense of relief almost knocking her over. "That's great," she managed. "What is it?"

"I have a personal interest in the history of the Saurian Republic." Mr Tsaagan turned his reader over and activated its hologram mode. A picture sprang up in the middle of it, hovering about a foot over the device. "Particularly in its ancient transport chariots." The chariot displayed by the hologram was a two-seater, blockier and less elegant than the modern ones Roz had seen, but there was a certain elemental *ferocity* to it, somehow.

"I have a client who owns the hull of one of these chariots, and is trying to find replacements for its missing parts," he went on. "There are rumors that some of the oldest chariots of our people, lost in conflict with the smilodon barbarians, have ended up buried in the vast trash piles of Hub City." Mr Tsaagan caught Roz's eyes over the hologram. "Have you ever seen anything like this in there?"

Roz didn't bother to deny that she ever trawled through the trash heaps looking for spare parts – it was a part of every apprentice mechanic's job. And, in fact… "I have, actually," she said. "It was about six years ago." She'd been so much smaller then, able to wriggle through the tightest tunnels in the heaps, where even the cyber rats couldn't get to her. She remembered seeing the gunky chariot, surrounded on three sides by piles of rusted metal slag but still somehow uncrushed. "It won't be in the same place now, of course," because the dumps were mobile beasts, shifting minutely but constantly, "but I'm pretty sure I can find it again."

"Excellent." Mr Tsaagan nodded. "If you do, and if you retrieve the part I need, then I'll consider the debt expunged."

Roz smiled gratefully. "That's wonderful, thank you! I'll start looking first thing tomorrow, and–"

"You have twenty-four hours, beginning now."

The smile fell off her face like her personal gravity had just multiplied by a thousand. "What?" she asked faintly.

"Twenty-four hours." Mr Tsaagan seemed slightly remorseful, judging from the way his topmost feathers flattened out, but his voice was firm. "That's all the time I can afford you before I have to leave the city myself."

"She can do it," Grizl put in confidently while Roz was still processing. "If the kid here says she's seen it, then she's seen it. Roz doesn't tell tales."

"I'm sure she doesn't," Mr Tsaagan agreed. "Is this deal agreeable to you, Roz?"

Roz straightened her back and stiffened her knees. This was the only chance she'd get to keep TRIS. It was a long shot, but she had to take it. She'd never forgive herself if she just let her robot go. "It is," she said. "We have a deal, Mr Tsaagan. Give me the specs for the part you need, and I'll be back here with it in twenty-four hours." She held out her hand, pleased that it hardly trembled at all.

Mr Tsaagan extended his own hand and carefully shook, mindful of his claws. "I look forward to it."

Acid-proof overalls, check. Æmber ash-filtered ventilator and goggles, check. Compact tool field kit, check. Zap blade, check. Roz stuffed a protein bar and another pouch of water into the pocket on the back of her pack, then shouldered it and fastened it firmly around her torso. She secured the zap blade in its sheath at her hip, checked her boots for holes for the fifth time... and finally admitted that she was stalling.

You can't stand around waiting forever, Roz reminded herself, and forced her feet to head toward the Nexian junk heap, one of the biggest, oldest piles of trash in all of Hub City. It wasn't a long walk, even with thirty pounds of baggage, and she was there in fifteen minutes. The smell was enough to have her strapping her ventilator on before she could even see it.

All right, here we go. You've got a chariot to find and not a lot of time to do it in. That was true, but... it was a lot easier to be brave about entering the dump when she was in a well-lit room in the middle of the day, instead of alone at the edge of the pile at twilight just as the cyber rats were starting to become active. One of them, a big, scarred critter with a bionic eye, scuttled out of the heap in her direction. It stopped a few feet away, looking Roz over like it was assessing her for parts.

"Come any closer and I'll zap the tail off you," she warned it.

The rat stared a moment longer, then yawned, showing off its shining, metallic teeth, before scurrying back into the pile.

"Rats with fangs. Great." Roz sighed and shook her head to clear it. She could do this. She'd trawled the pile enough to know which way the shift was progressing, and even though she hadn't seen the chariot in six years, she could extrapolate where she expected it to be.

She tapped her finger against the holo-projector built into her left-hand glove, and her personal map of the dump sprang a few inches into the air.

Roz had spent years compiling this map – it was only smart to mark down where the best hauls were, or spots where you might have hidden some raw materials to come back for later. Sometimes the caches were found, but the dump was so huge that there was space for everyone who wanted to trawl it. That didn't mean it was without its dangers, though. Apart from the rats, there were several gangs of looter goblins who tried to lay claim to the dump, constantly fighting with each other and either scaring off or shaking down anyone else they found in it. They didn't like direct confrontation, preferring to set traps for unwary dump-divers, but Roz had gotten good at recognizing those over the years.

As for the gurgle pools… well, that was what the ventilator was for. Roz just hoped it would buy her enough time to get out of the way if she ran into one.

"Okay." She tapped the map, lining it up with where she was about to enter. "I probably need to go… a little over a mile in," she muttered to herself. It didn't seem like so far out in the open air, but she'd need every second once she got deep into the trash. "You can do this." *You have to do this.*

Roz squared her shoulders, double-checked her straps, then walked over to the edge of the pile and began to climb. Her favorite entrance was halfway up the heap, and she wanted to get inside while she still had some light. After about ten minutes, she found her personal mark – a small, stylized *R* – on a rusty metal sheet, and lifted it up. Beneath it was a small, jagged-edged tunnel leading down at a forty-five-degree angle. Roz crept inside, slowly lowered the metal sheet back down, and began to crawl.

Watch for the rebar on the right... little dip here... gotta bring something to sop that oil up, I slip in it every single time. The first hundred yards of this was old, familiar territory for her. She looked for signs that someone else had been in her tunnel and saw a few – mostly rat droppings, *ugh* – but there weren't any thread-wires or fresh, flat pieces of metal that could be pressure plate-traps left by goblins, so that was good. It was dark, but she'd rigged her goggles with a night-vision setting that lit everything up in shades of orange and green and gold, depending on their temperature.

Hopefully, Roz would see anybody coming her way before they noticed her, and have time to hide.

Roz's tunnel filtered out into a wider one, tall enough to walk in as long as she hunkered down. She carefully picked her way along the floor of it, avoiding anything that steamed, crackled, or looked too sharp for her boots to handle. The refuse of a hundred different civilizations and cultures lay in fractured, brittle piles all around her, ninety-nine per cent true trash, one per cent genuine treasure.

Was that part of a martian blaster? They guarded their weapons jealously, she could probably sell that for – but no, she already had a goal. *Don't get distracted, Roz. Eyes on the prize.*

She pressed on into the heart of the dump, lifting holey hydraulic tubes out of her way and checking every pile of metal shavings she passed for pawprints or fresh gang signs. Nothing. Before an hour had passed, her map showed that she was already almost halfway there. *This is going to be easy!*

Clink... clink... clinkclinkclink...

Roz turned her head toward the strange, pattering sound. What on the Crucible was–?

"Ah!" She dodged to the side just as a pair of huge cyber rats leapt from the top of the tunnel at her. The *top* of the tunnel, how had they – what were they–?

Magnetic paw *implants?* Whoever was modifying these rats had *waaay* too much time on their hands.

Roz drew her knife as the rats flanked her, their alloy claws digging viciously into the refuse as they stalked closer. "Stay back," Roz said, trying to keep the tremble out of her voice. She didn't want to yell – no need to bring more trouble down on herself – but she didn't want to fight if she didn't have to, either. Sometimes you could back a rat off with your voice.

The one on the right side snapped at her, narrowly missing her foot and biting through a piece of sheet metal instead. Ok*aaay*, there would be no talking these rats down. She flicked the button on the bottom of her zap knife to change its range, then pointed it at the closest rat.

Zzzzaappp! A hundred thousand volts of electrical energy shot between them, crackling as the beam encountered the rat's gleaming, upturned nose. The cyber rat leapt into the air with a squeal of pain, jumping so high that it bounced off the ceiling. It fell down into a heap on the tunnel floor and lay still.

Roz didn't have time to check it – the other rat leapt onto the wall, scuttled up beside her head, and swiped at her with its claws. A sharp pain radiated from the side of her head – it had *scratched* her! Roz snarled under her ventilator mask and swung her zap knife around, straight for the rat. It dodged, but not fast enough.

Shnict!

The rat squeaked with dismay as it looked at its severed paw twitching on the floor, cybernetic ends still sparking with electricity. Roz brandished the knife at it. "I'll go two paws for two if you don't back off!" she hissed, prepping her knife to send out another stunning bolt. The rat looked between her and the knife and, after baring its teeth for a few seconds, turned and fled back down the corridor of refuse.

Roz made sure it was out of sight before checking on the first rat. It was knocked clean out, twitching faintly but still unconscious. Roz decided she could afford to ignore it while she checked out how badly she'd been scratched. She checked the ambient levels of gas on her ventilator – the air should be breathable – then slipped it over her head so it rested around her neck.

"Augh." It smelled *foul* in here, like battery acid if it was capable of rotting – Roz always forgot how absolutely disgusting the miasma could get in places. She quickly pulled off her backpack, unzipped a side pocket, and pulled out her mirror and medkit. She activated her glove's flashlight and took a look. "Dang it." It was a nasty cut, arcing from above her ear over to her temple and deep enough to send an oozing sheet of bright red blood down the side of her face. Roz didn't think it needed stitches, but she definitely couldn't leave it open either – if she got an infection down here, it could turn into something that even the best mender couldn't fix.

She splashed a dose of disinfectant across her head, wincing at the burn, then rummaged through her field kit until she found her super glue. This stuff was goblin-made and would bind almost anything together, but it was specially designed to release skin after a few days, just in case the user made a mistake.

She looked at herself in the mirror and grimaced. "Lovely." Her hair stuck straight up on one side, her ear was still sticky with blood and she needed to wait until the glue dried to put her ventilator back on, which meant she got to bask in the scent of chemicals, crap, and rusty metal for at least a few more minutes. "Just another half a mile," she told herself, glancing at her map. She could be there in a few more hours if she hustled.

Roz replaced her medkit but decided to leave the ventilator around her neck while the glue dried. Then she strapped her pack on and headed down the tunnel again. She didn't have the benefit of night vision now, but the flashlight from her glove was more than enough to light the way until she could–

"*Aaaahhh!*" The floor suddenly gave way beneath her feet, one side of it swinging open with an ominous creak she barely heard as she plunged through the gap. She tried to grab for the edge, but she was too far away. A second later she hit the ground and fell over flat onto her back, all the wind knocked out of her and her right ankle throbbing dangerously.

Roz stared up at the hole she'd fallen through, too stunned

to think straight. A trap. She'd fallen into a goblin trap. That was bad, that meant that looter goblins would be heading to check on what had set it off. She needed to get out of here, she needed to...

"ggGUurrrgllle..."

Wait, what was that? Roz stared blearily around the cavernous space she'd fallen into – it was surprisingly big, given how the refuse tended to fill any voids – and looked for the source of the sound. She couldn't see much beyond the general shape of the hole. Why weren't her night-vision goggles working?

Because you're not wearing your goggles, genius! They were built into the ventilator, and she hadn't put it back on yet. The light of her holographic display had turned off, too. Groggily, Roz slapped at her left glove until the light came back on. Okay, there was the ceiling, maybe... ten feet up? Ow, no wonder her ankle hurt so bad. She tested it with a grimace. She could move it, but it sure didn't feel happy about the process. Not broken, though – that was good.

"ggGGGUUURRRGgllleee..."

That noise was *not* helping her headache any. Roz turned her head to the left and–

"GGGUUUUURRRRGGGGLLLEE!"

Roz rolled away from the edge of the hungry gurgle pool, which seeped toward her in a steady, bubbling green wave. She managed to keep it from touching her – if it did it would immediately start doing damage – but even as she rolled, she inhaled the telltale stench of the pool's psychic fog. It was rank, the smell of moldy death, like a blighted orchard or a...

... a delicious slice of cherry chocolate cake...

"No!" No, it was trying to mess with her head! Roz needed to get out of this chamber, before the smell overwhelmed her. She groped at her neck for the ventilator, but there was no time – the gurgle pool was coming on fast, faster than she'd ever seen one flow before. She crawled backward until she hit the wall, then flashed her light desperately around the room, hoping for some refuge that wasn't through the ceiling.

Nothing. No new holes, no tunnels, no escape hatches other than the one she couldn't reach. Maybe she could jump up to it… Roz tested her foot again with a wince. Not likely. She might be able to climb, but not before she…

… come over to the pool to find what you're seeking – we know where it is, we know everything in the dump…

Roz shook her head to try and clear it and looked around for a place out of the pool's reach. This one was moving pretty fast, but she doubted it could climb a wall. She'd find a place to hole up, and then–

Crrruuuunch! One of the walls began to move. Roz pushed to her feet and dashed for the first likely place she could see – a little triangular ledge just to the right of the gurgle pool, a few feet off the ragged floor.

She did a staggering hop around the edge of the pool, which sent a tentacle out toward her but couldn't quite make contact, and crawled up onto the ledge. It was partially covered by a rusty metal sheet, and as long as Roz tucked her feet in tight, kept her breathing slow and steady and didn't move, maybe…

… maybe you can find what you're looking for right over here… come, look closer, bring your little light and look…

Oh no, the light! Roz turned off her projector just as the

shuddering crunch of the mobile trash door came to a halt.

"Back up, you!" a harsh voice called out. "Back up now!"

"Use the fire on it, Snart," another voice suggested. "Damn pools only respect one thing."

The other voice didn't reply, but a second later a jet of white-hot fire shot into the cavern, right into the center of the gurgle pool. It shriveled around the edges, collapsing in on itself with a guttural cry. A moment later a looter goblin stepped into view, the flamethrower it carried still lit and ready at the muzzle.

"What set this thing off?" he said with a grunt, staring curiously around the room. Roz couldn't look away. One more step inside, maybe two, and then he'd see her for sure. Would they take her captive and try to ransom her, or just steal all her equipment and turn her out at the edge of the dump? Or even worse, would they cut their losses and burn her to slag right where she crouched?

"Nothing in it, then?" the other goblin asked. They both once had bright blue hair, but where most goblins were fastidious about keeping their vibrant colors visible, these ones had let gunk and oil settle in, dulling most of their locks to a dirty blue-gray. Their gear was solid, though – they had on tougher overalls than Roz was wearing, and heavy spike-tipped boots.

"Not a thing, Brikt. But *something* set it off, and – wait." The goblin took another step into the room. "What's that?"

"What's what?"

"That thing on the wa–"

Squeak! Whatever the goblin had been about to say was interrupted by the clatter of a cyber rat – maybe the very same cyber rat that Roz had stunned – crawling into the chamber through the hole in the ceiling. It clung to the ceiling easily with its magnetic paws, and bared its shiny, sharp teeth at the goblins.

"Those rats again!" The goblin called Brikt swore and threw a heavy lug nut at it. The rat danced out of the way, then crawled casually back up through the hole. "This is the worst bunch yet, I swear! They set off a trap three tunnels over yesterday, the same way! Didn't catch one of them, thanks to those nasty paws of theirs."

"A rat." The goblin Snart nodded his head, like he was convincing himself of something. "Of course."

"Come on, let's leave the pool to regenerate and see if we can't catch that little bastard." Brikt stomped off, and after another moment Snart followed. The hidden passage closed with another groaning *crunch*, and a minute later the room was empty except for the sad, burbling croon of the wounded gurgle pool and Roz, still clinging to the ledge like a spider, eyes wide and unseeing in the darkness as she slowly pulled herself together.

By the time the psychic fog of the gurgle pool had completely worn off, Roz had recovered a little of her gumption. Of all the dumb ways to die, getting dissolved by a gurgle pool was close to the very top. Even worse than being eaten by cyber rats.

"That's enough of that," she murmured to herself, as she pulled her ventilator back on. The pool wasn't emitting its chemicals any more, too concerned with healing itself to bother with her, but she needed the relative freshness of her rebreather after the time she'd just spent bare-faced. How much time had passed since she'd crawled in, anyway? Roz checked the clock function in her glove.

Nine hours! How was it possible that she'd been in here for nine hours already? It didn't feel like more than half of that. She tried to straighten her legs out and groaned. Okaaay, maybe she had been sitting in one place for a little longer than she'd realized.

Roz sighed and lifted her ventilator just long enough to pound a protein bar and a sachet of water, then carefully slipped a numbing patch down her overalls and stuck it to her ankle. Relief flowed through her, and when she stood up, her legs held.

Okay. Time to get out of here. Roz sprayed a layer of Stik-Tite onto the palms of her gloves – it was something that Spire climbers liked to use to improve their grip strength – and grasped the nearest length of pipe jutting out of the wall. She was going to pull herself out of this hole, find that darn chariot, and make it back to Mr Tsaagan before time ran out. No excuses.

Her pep talk was easy to think, much harder to do, but after ten minutes of grunting and straining, Roz finally levered herself back into the tunnel above the trap. She left it open – the looter goblins might notice if she tried to close it – and reopened her map. "All right, show me the way." Two hundred more feet in this tunnel, then up and through into a different section of the dump.

Roz moved slower than before, more cautious now – not to mention her ankle still hurt, despite the numbing patch. But she was making it, she was getting there. She avoided more traps, went silent at the first hint of scratching or squeaking and kept her ventilator on even when her cut began to itch beneath the strap. No more fooling around – she was on a mission, and she wasn't going to fail.

By the time she got to the projected location of the chariot, Roz's energy was starting to flag, so it was a relief to finally stop moving. "It should be… here." Roz shined her light on the dump in front of her. Nothing but gutted waste barrels.

Clearly time had taken its toll on the layout of this section of the dump. Roz had an ace in the hole, though. She'd brought along – after arguing with Grizl for almost half a precious hour – the electronic brain and imaging arm of his Deep-Down scanner, attached to a special battery pack that would give her enough juice for a thirty-second scan. It would penetrate deep into the junk pile and give her a three-dimensional view of whatever was behind the outer layer up to ten feet back, but she wouldn't have long with it.

"From here…" she looked at the section in front of her, one of the barrels sporting a bright orange hazmat symbol "… to there." She pointed at a broken pipe about thirty feet away. It was a decent swath of metal – the odds were good that she'd catch at least part of the chariot with a scan, as long as it was still here. *Please still be here.*

"Okay." She aimed the arm of the scanner at the wall in front of her and took a deep breath. "Here we go." She flipped the switch, and immediately felt the battery inside her pack begin to heat up.

Move, move… Roz stepped slowly but steadily down the tunnel, careful not to trip or slide or do anything else to mess with the picture she was taking. Three feet… six feet… ten feet… The battery was really starting to heat up now, leaking its uncomfortable warmth through her overalls and into her skin. Twenty feet–

The heat dropped off instantly, the battery completely exhausted. It didn't melt down, thank the Architects, but she wouldn't be getting any more use out of it, that was for sure. Roz took off her pack and set the battery aside, connected the Deep-Down's brain to her glove's hologram setup, and began to review her images.

"What a mess," she muttered as she examined the first few feet of data. She'd tried to hold the scanner steady, but there was plenty of noise in the picture. Still, it was good enough to give her a general idea of what was back there, and so far – no chariot.

"C'mon." She kept searching, her heart sinking with every new foot of distance displayed. Plenty of junkyard scraps, a few pieces of ships here and there, but nothing strikingly saurian like the chariot. "C'mon, don't do this to me." Nothing… nothing… all the way at the end now, and her heart was down in her boots. "Please, please, ple–" *Wait.* There, at the very edge of the scan. That was the start of an elegant scalloped curve, the material extremely high-density compared to the stuff around it. Roz fumbled up a comparison picture that Mr Tsaagan had given her. Yep, same base.

Yessss. Now, to get to it.

That part was surprisingly easy, actually. A little judicious use of her field kit's pocket blowtorch, and Roz had burned herself a path through the barrels. There was even a little alcove back by the ship that she could fit into if she hunkered down. *Perfect.*

Roz stacked a loose barrel in front of the hole she'd made, just in case, then crawled through the narrow gap and shimmied her way out right onto the chariot's platform. It was oily, and a little hard to get a purchase on, but Roz dug her toes in and pulled up the original picture again. She needed one of the front hubs for an antigravity generator – Mr Tsaagan already had one himself, and he was looking for a perfect match for it. That meant taking the one with the least damage.

"All this work for the sake of authenticity," Roz murmured, as she reached for her blowtorch again. She would just cut away an entire front section in order to avoid potentially damaging the hub with a prybar or magnetic screwdriver. It was bizarre to her that the saurians would go to so much trouble to get something that they could probably replicate in minutes. But then, they *did* have one of the oldest civilizations on the entire Crucible. Perhaps it made more sense to a species used to treasuring its past to also treasure its sense of age. "Good news for me, anyway." She edged over to the side of the platform, raised her blowtorch, and–

It went out. Roz frowned. "What the…" She checked the fuel bottle – still half full. She tried to re-light it, and it sparked up with no problem. "Okaaay…" She leaned forward again and–

It went out. Again. This time, it didn't spark when she tried to re-light it. Roz sighed. "Of course." Why would anything at all go smoothly? "Fine." She reached into her field kit for her magnetic screwdriver. It could find and attenuate to the fastenings in the hub, and while it was slower, it would get the job done. She reached over the edge and–

The screwdriver flew out of her hand and stuck to the far

side of the alcove. Roz stared.

"What?" That shouldn't have happened. That wasn't how the magnetic field in the screwdriver worked, it didn't just *leap* toward any old piece of metal. She gritted her teeth. Something was wrong here, seriously wrong, but Roz couldn't just leave, no matter how much she wanted to. Prybar it was, then. She jerked the thing out of her kit, gripping it tightly with both hands, and crawled to the edge of the platform. She looked down at the antigravity generator and–

"Whoa!" This time Roz knew *she* was responsible for losing the prybar, but she couldn't help it – the chariot's antigravity generator just below her was glowing with light, looking like it was a few seconds away from blasting her head off. "What the hell?" It was impossible. There was no way the chariot still had any sort of active power source after so long, this had to be a trick of some kind. Another goblin trap, maybe, or… or…

Or maybe, it was something else entirely. Roz remembered her parents talking to a creature made of pure light once, that lived in an ancient temple. A spirit, they had called it. Could this be…

I might as well try. Roz coughed to clear her throat, then gingerly pulled off her ventilator. "Um… excuse me?" she said softly. "Is there anyone living here?"

There was no reply, and she began to feel stupid. *Maybe I'm just seeing things.* She leaned over to reach for her prybar–

And found it floating in the air right in front of her, inside a cloud of pale light. Roz gulped, then took hold of the prybar very slowly. It released easily into her grasp. "Uh… hello."

"Hello, little one."

Roz grinned despite herself. She *knew* it! It was a spirit, an actual spirit! She'd only seen one from a distance before. "Hi! Wow, are you – are you really a spirit?"

"I am," it replied simply.

"That's..." She shook her head helplessly. "That is so amazing. I'm so honored to meet you."

"Why is that?"

"Why? Because... because I've never met someone like you before," Roz said, after a moment's consideration. "I thought spirits were usually associated with religious places. Temples and churches and things."

"Many of us are. Many are not. We are not a monolith."

"No, of course not." That would be dumb – like saying all goblins were engineers. "I didn't mean to offend you."

"I am not offended."

"Great! Great. So, um..." Roz bit her lower lip, then regretted it as she tasted her own sour sweat. "What are you doing here?"

"I like to explore this place. There are many potential containment suits within it, but I have not yet found one that entirely suits my needs. When I am not searching, I come back here to rest."

"Oh. So, the chariot is like... your home, then?"

"It is as close as I can come without a containment suit." The light seemed to waver for a moment. "Some spirits go without, but I prefer to be enclosed."

"I see." So basically, Roz was going to be prying a piece off a spirit's home. Lovely. "I don't mean to cause you trouble, but I really need a hub off one of the antigravity generators down there."

"You wish to… to diminish my place of rest? In doing so, you diminish me."

That was definitely offense in the spirit's voice. "No! No, I'm not trying to diminish you, I promise. I just really, desperately need that part, and I didn't know you lived here when I made the deal for it, and I've tried *so* hard and it's been a pretty terrible trip so far, and…" Roz fought back the quaver in her voice. "I need it, or I'm going to lose my best friend."

The spirit was silent for a moment. "Who is your best friend?"

Roz resisted the urge to wipe her eyes – her gloves were foul. "Her name is TRIS, she's a robot that belonged to my parents. They're gone now, but when I was little, TRIS took care of me when they weren't around – she was my nanny, my friend, my teacher… even when I slept at night. TRIS is damaged, really damaged, and she'll be scrapped for parts if I don't give the people who own her now this hub in the next…" She checked the time. "Seven hours."

"There are some robots here and there in the dump," the spirit related quietly. "They're mostly in pieces. Some were treated very poorly."

"Well, that's not gonna be TRIS if I have any say in it," Roz said. "Which, uh… *do* I have any say in it? Will you please let me have a hub?" She held her breath as the spirit seemed to consider her request.

"Sometimes I think I would like to leave this place, but moving about in the open is… disturbing to me."

"Oh." Roz wasn't sure what the spirit was trying to say, but she waited it out.

"I need containment to feel safe, but I would enjoy seeing more of the world. Do you think TRIS would allow me to join her?"

"You want to live... in my robot?"

The light wavered a little. "If that is unacceptable, I understand. Robots are their own people, after all."

"No, it's not that." Roz thought of how TRIS had so little purpose right now, how she sometimes patted her empty treasure hold as if mourning the fact that it was empty. "I think TRIS might really enjoy having you with her. She always loved carrying *me* around, after all. It's worth finding out, at least." And if something in TRIS's programming rebelled at the idea of having a passenger riding alongside, then Roz could bring the spirit back to the chariot. "I'd be happy to take you along with me. What, um, what's your name?" She couldn't keep using "spirit" if she wanted the other being to be comfortable.

"You may call me... Stella."

"Stella. That's lovely." Roz grinned. "I'm Roz."

"Very pleased to meet you. Is that the correct greeting?"

"That was perfect," Roz assured her. "Stella, if you want to ride in the battery in my backpack, you should feel nice and safe while we're moving around."

"I will do so. But first..." She floated Roz's screwdriver back over to her, then with a barely audible *ka-chunk*, detached a hub and handed that over as well. Roz happily inspected it. It was almost pristine, just a few scratches here and there that an expert could buff out in no time. Surely Mr Tsaagan would like it enough to forgive a little wear and tear.

"Thank you," she said wholeheartedly. "You don't know

how much this means to me."

"I don't. I've been here so long that I've forgotten many things. But I hope to relearn them soon."

"I hope so too."

The moment Roz staggered back into Mr Tsaagan's apartment, Grizl whooped so loud she almost had to cover her ears, and punched the air with one bright-blue fist. "Ha! I knew she'd make it in time! Pay up, pal!"

Roz scowled at him. "What does that mean?" she demanded, pushing a strand of gunky hair out of her face. Good grief, had he been here lounging around the whole time? She'd only gotten out of the dump half an hour ago, and hadn't even stopped at the workshop to change – she still had a few hours left on the clock, but if there was ever a day not to take anything for granted, this was it. What if a street had collapsed? What if a fire broke out? Roz wasn't going to lose this damn bet on a technicality, not when she was so close.

"Your master wished to lay a bet on whether or not you would make it back in time," Mr Tsaagan said from where he was still reclining on the couch. He was wearing a different jumpsuit this time – not black, but a dark, shining bronze color that complimented his skin tone nicely. "In addition to another bet on whether you'd make it back at all."

Roz whirled on Grizl, so affronted she could barely keep from shouting. "Are you serious?" she demanded. "You wanted to make a profit off me *disappearing*?"

"It was just a back-up bet, like – like life insurance," Grizl said quickly. "I woulda used the æmber to put a memorial plaque up for you in the shop."

Roz scowled. "Half of whatever you get for my return goes straight to me."

"Hey," Grizl protested, "*I'm* the one who made the bet. Who's the master and who's the apprentice here, after all?"

"*I'm* the one who *won* the bet, *both* of them, so I guess that makes me the master when it comes to getting things done right, doesn't it?"

"Excuse me," Mr Tsaagan said, breaking the stony silence that had fallen between the two of them, "but whether or not you've fulfilled your end of our deal remains to be seen. Where is the part?"

"It's here." Roz took off her backpack, opened it up, and pulled out the hub. She paused to gently pat the battery Stella was resting in before straightening up. "As requested." Mr Tsaagan took the hub from her, careful not to touch her mucky hand, and ran his claws over it reverently.

"Perfect," he said. "Quite perfect. Is the rest of the chariot still there?"

"Yeeees…"

"I may have more orders for you, depending on how well this one is received. Would you be amenable to that?"

"Hey," Grizl protested. "I'm her master, you've gotta go through me if you want to put her to work."

It was true, Roz reflected. Grizl was still the guardian of her time, and he would be until she had enough æmber to repair TRIS. Although… if things between TRIS and Stella worked out, then maybe the repairs wouldn't even be necessary. Stella could improve TRIS's functionality, and TRIS could be a safe, secure containment suit for Stella.

"You two work it out," Roz said after a moment. "I'm going home. I need to shower."

"Yeah, you do." Grizl waved a hand in front of his nose. "Uh… you need me to call up a mender for you too? I'll even cover the charges, just this once."

How generous. "Maybe later," Roz said, testing the wobble in her ankle. "For now, I just need to get clean and get some sleep." *And introduce Stella to TRIS without you looking over my shoulder.*

"Sure, yeah, okay."

It was a slow walk back to the shop, but a surprisingly easy one – turns out people gave you a lot of space when you were as odiferous as Roz. She got inside, then locked the door behind her – no work today, not when she could barely keep her eyes open. She really did need a shower, some food, and a lot of sleep, in that order. But first…

Roz walked into the workshop, all the way back to the corner where TRIS was slumped, her battery ebbing low even though she probably hadn't moved since yesterday. Roz knelt down in front of the robot. "Hey," she said gently. "TRIS."

Her eyelights slowly brightened, curving in a way that always reminded Roz of a smile. Her vocal apparatus was still shattered – Roz hadn't heard the robot speak clearly since she was a child – but TRIS found ways to communicate nevertheless.

Roz took the battery out again and laid it on the floor in front of TRIS. "I brought you a friend," she said. "Really, I think I brought *us* a friend. Stella, are you ready to try?"

A golden glow hovered over the case of the battery. "I am."

"Okay." Pinching her lips together, Roz moved back a little.

"Go for it."

Stella rose up into the air, a beautiful, amorphous cloud of light, before gliding over to TRIS and slowly, carefully, sinking inside her. TRIS's eyelights flickered, then dimmed. The battery lights shut down all together, and the robot's head sank against the wall with a *clunk*.

Oh no. What had happened? What had she done? "TRIS?" Roz called anxiously. "Stella? Are you okay?" What would she do if they weren't okay? She had worked so hard, it couldn't all be for nothing, it *couldn't*...

All at once TRIS's eyelights blazed like torches, illuminating the entire workshop. Her body whirred to life, all systems go for the first time in over a decade. TRIS stood without a single creak, and when she spoke, her voice was a perfect mix of what Roz remembered and Stella's own airy tones.

"We are so happy to be with you, Rozelyn."

Roz started to laugh, and to cry a little, too. She swiped her hand over her filthy cheek. "Not nearly as happy as I am. It's... it's working, then? You can live with each other?"

"We think we will work well together. And with you." The TRIS/Stella being tilted her head. "What should we do first?"

"First is cleanup. For me and for you," because TRIS was a little dingy still, and Roz –well, she wasn't getting any cleaner just standing there. "And then..."

And then, they could do anything.

EXTERMINATION EXAMINATION
Robbie MacNiven

Professor Longaard was, according to his own academic profile on HubU, a ninety-six point seven per cent nonorganic. The nature of the remaining three point three per cent was a point of fierce debate among the student body of Hub University, though it wasn't apparent from a glance what it might be, unless it accounted for the æmber that made up a large part of his cranium. As one of his students, Nal'ai had been asked on more than a few occasions whether the most senior member of the Martian Studies faculty ever glitched or froze out during tutorials. Nal'ai had never seen anything like that, but she was certainly hoping the professor's systems would be in the midst of a reboot right now. She was late.

"Good morning, Nal'ai," the professor's vocal grille buzzed as she let herself into the office. Longaard was plugged in behind his powerbank desk, a bulky wedge of polished chromium plates and system panels clad in a suit made of Harrian tw'ee. His head – if head was the correct expression – was a small box of optic clusters and communication devices wired into a glassy sphere that glowed and pulsed softy with the golden aura of pure æmber. He wasn't, despite Nal'ai's silent prayers, rebooting.

"Take a seat," the professor's vocals crackled. Nal'ai hurried to do so.

"I'm sorry I'm late, professor," she began, but Longaard cut her off.

"Normally I am deeply perturbed by unpunctuality, Ms Nal'ai, as well you know. However, in this case, you are a lesser sinner. There remains no sign of your assessment partner."

"Assessment partner," Nal'ai repeated. The young krxix student had thought this was going to be a one-to-one discussion, a review of her results in a case study on cultural markers adopted by martian exile enclaves living in Hub City.

"Indeed," Longaard droned in a heavy monotone. "Did you not read about it in the meeting circular prior to coming here?"

Nal'ai decided that, given the start to her day, it was best to avoid admitting she hadn't read the circular. She had been kept up for most of the night nursing her roommate, Kolli, after the party-elf had stumbled home from a three-day post-exam blowout. Nal'ai had left her still groaning and semi-comatose after spending nearly half an hour digging through the room's jumbled belongings, hunting for her own clean clothes beneath Kolli's mess. Needless to say, elf garments didn't exactly fit a six-limbed insectoid-species like Nal'ai. Somehow, though, she doubted Longaard would consider that an excuse.

"Have you any idea where your partner might be?" the

professor pressed, one of his systems beeping away quietly in the background.

"I'm not sure," Nal'ai replied, as terrified now of getting caught up in lying to her academic supervisor as she was of her actual assessment results. What partner?

"We shall give them five more par-cycs," Longaard huffed. That seemed to be that. The office settled into silence. The professor's optics lit up blue while he conducted digital lit reviews, the only sound the low hum of his charge units.

Nal'ai shifted uncomfortably in her worn leather seat, her compound eyes turning a deep shade of maroon. The office space surrounding her was a disconcerting blend of digi files and raggedy-looking tomes, banks of power clusters and stained old wood paneling, bathed in the lights of Longaard's systems. The discordant decor certainly lent credence to the popular belief that Longaard hadn't always been majority cogs-and-circuits.

Just what species he'd belonged to before his mechanical metamorphosis remained unknown. Some said he was an Archon in disguise, others that he'd angered one and forfeited his body (or at least ninety-six point seven per cent of it) in order to survive the being's wrath. Still others said the martians had done it. Nal'ai suspected that was the closest answer to the truth. He was the head of Martian Studies at Hub University, after all. Nal'ai didn't know of any non-martian who had written so many celebrated studies of the infamously insular natives of Mars. He was an inspiration, in his own cold, bot-like way, and that was why Nal'ai was cursing herself for being late. In desperation she'd spun a multiweb to get across campus faster, swinging – in defiance of university protocol – between the Arts and Cultures block. Broodmother alone knew if she'd been seen or not.

She tried to think about something else. Who was her partner supposed to be? She only knew of two other students under Longaard's tutorship – Sorus the saurian and Gryk, a goblin. They'd already had their results back though. Surely he wasn't going to make them re-evaluate with her?

Just when she was considering asking to be excused so she could go and cry in the nearest chute cubicle, there was a hasty rap at the door. Nal'ai twisted in her chair and Longaard deactivated his review scanner.

"Enter," he intoned.

The door opened, and Nal'ai let out an involuntary flurry of shocked ticks with her lower mandibles.

"Sorry I'm late, professor," Kolli said, dropping down into the empty seat next to Nal'ai.

"A far from ideal beginning," Longaard droned. "But let us not waste any more time on your lamentable tardiness, Ms Kolli. I believe you and Ms Nal'ai know one other already?"

"She's my roomie," Kolli beamed. "Uh, I mean my roommate, professor."

"Then we can dispense with the introductions," Longaard began to say, before Nal'ai did something she never thought she would do in all of her darkest nightmares – she interrupted him.

"Professor, there must be some sort of mistake," she blurted. "Kolli isn't even in the School of Societies and Culture, let alone the Department of Martian Studies! She's… she's just a correspondence and communications studies student!"

"Was a C and C student," Longaard corrected, his machine

voice carrying a hard edge. "Ms Kolli's results this past trimester appear to have been less than satisfactory. However, pending a two-semester re-sit, she has successfully applied for a school transfer. I have personally reviewed her application concerning the working relationships established between martian exile communities and the bartering networks of Lower Hub traders. It is a commendable piece of research – perhaps you should ask Ms Kolli to share it with you? It would likely compliment your own studies."

Nal'ai didn't trust herself to speak. That had been her research. She'd dumped it after deciding it didn't fit with her broader argument about the malleability of martian phobias beyond the bounds of traditional Nova Hellas hierarchies. Why in the name of the Great Web had her roommate stolen it, let alone used it to put in a transfer request?

Next to her, Kolli was clearly struggling to maintain a serious academic exterior. A few years before Nal'ai would probably have marveled at the fact that the sick, grubby, intoxicated student she'd quite literally tucked into bed had reappeared clean and dressed, with only slightly hollow eyes and the faint scent of stale alcohol to suggest she'd been throwing up in a waste chute two hours previously. But Nal'ai had long since become accustomed to the seemingly supernatural powers of resurrection possessed by the student community's serial partygoers. Kolli's ability to endure no sleep and a thumping hangover knew no bounds, especially when twinned with the elf's natural biological capacity to process intoxicants rapidly.

"I'm really so grateful for this opportunity professor, believe me," she was saying. Nal'ai decided there and then that she was going to kill her. Literally, physically, kill her. The realization that Longaard's optic clusters were focused on her snapped her thoughts away from turning the professor's office into a crime scene.

"I suppose you are wondering about your end of year review results?" he asked.

"Yes," she managed to say, unintentionally adding a clack of her mandibles. Her eyes had turned a deep, dark russet color, almost black. Longaard made a buzzing noise before his vocal units kicked back in.

"Your first trimester work has been commendable, if ultimately incomplete. Based on your initial literature review and chapter by chapter breakdown, I will not be recommending that you continue with your studies."

Nal'ai's world dropped away underneath her. As she fell, she heard Longaard's damnable drone, as though from a great distance, dragging her back up again.

"However, I believe there is still time to salvage something of worth from the data you have compiled thus far. Your greatest shortcoming is your lack of fieldwork to date. I propose a way to rectify that."

"How?" Nal'ai asked, feeling lightheaded. She was glad she was already sitting down.

"I am sure you have both read my work on the integration methods of the Borreal enclave? I count myself a friend of their chief elder, Orix Veyy, though some of their subordinates are less than thrilled with my research. I have requested that Veyy welcomes you for the duration of a single week's study, and provides you with limited interview access to both the enclave's facilities and its members. Needless to say, this is a privilege rarely afforded to those outside the martian species. Do not waste this opportunity to further your research, Ms Nal'ai."

"And what about me, professor?" Kolli asked. Longaard's systems burbled for a second before responding.

"As excellent as your application was, Ms Kolli, I must warn you that transitioning to Martian Studies is no easy thing. The cultures of Mars are an exceedingly complex subject. Like Ms Nal'ai, you will benefit a great deal from personal contact with your subject species. Therefore, I am recommending that you accompany her on her research trip to the Borreal enclave."

Nal'ai was still struggling for words when Kolli responded.

"That sounds like an amazing opportunity, professor! I can't tell you how delighted I am!"

Nal'ai shot her a look as venomous as her mandibles.

"Tact is a must," Longaard said, his machine optics apparently oblivious to Nal'ai's silent fury. "I am sure even novices such as yourselves understand that martians, including rogue enclaves such as the Borreal, are deeply distrustful of outsiders. Even with my personal assurances, it may take them some time to trust you enough to communicate openly."

"We will certainly take our role as ambassadors for Hub University with the utmost seriousness, professor," Kolli said.

Ambassadors, Nal'ai snarled mentally. *You weren't much of an ambassador for Hub Uni last night, Kolli, unless the negotiations were being carried out with barmen or scrumball center forwards on a post-game night out!*

"I will draw up the necessary permission forms and see funds transferred to your department accounts within the next cycle," Longaard said. "It will be down to you to draw up your own research questionnaires and decide on a line of inquiry. Once you have made first contact with the enclave you will report to me at a scheduled time via uplink tablet. With it we can establish a vid connection and I will know your exact location. After that we can make a final decision on your future on this program."

Nal'ai couldn't help but feel as though the professor's optics had focused on her as he spoke.

Meeting over. Nal'ai stood up, feeling dazed. "Thank you so much for this opportunity, Professor Longaard," Kolli was repeating effusively as they both backed towards the door. Nal'ai wasn't listening to the response – they were barely out into the corridor before she snatched Kolli by her collar and rammed her up against the wall.

"What in the name of the Great Web are you doing?" she hissed, antennas rigid with anger. Kolli smirked in that infuriating, smug elf way.

"Getting us through second year."

"By copying my research notes? Word for word?"

"You threw them out," the tall, pale elf pouted. "I was doing a service to the academic community by rescuing them from the garbage."

Nal'ai let her go out of pure exasperation, turning away before spinning back to face her again.

"I nearly failed this year because of you! I can't count how many hours of sleep I've lost because of you! Helping you to bed when you come home half-spliced, comforting you when your idiot ex dumped you, writing half of your essays. You never tidy the room, you rarely do the cooking, you've never once cleaned the pantry–"

"Nal," Kolli said, and embraced her. "Nal, Nal, Nal. I'm sorry."

Nal'ai tried to pull away, but found she couldn't.

"I'll make it right, roomie," Kolli said, patting the krxix's head softly, in between her antennae. "Promise. I'm just taking this cruddy course to get some breathing space and re-sit my NATs. Then I won't have to redo the year. Once we reach the enclave, I'll dedicate all my time to helping your research. Besides, I got us a trip to Martian town. Isn't that what you've always wanted?"

"It is," Nal'ai sniffed, breaking the hug and looking at her roommate. "You promise you won't mess this one up for me?"

"Swear it on the contents of every vault on the Crucible," Kolli said with a pretty smile, holding up her elongated first and third digit. "Elf fem-scout's honor. It's going to be the best trip ever."

They packed to leave the next day. Nal'ai woke early, too nervous and excited to sleep. With Kolli still snoring in her bed across from the krxix's webrest, she stole into the corridor's pantry and helped herself to some flesher grubs from the humid depths of the live food bin. Then, still wearing her pajama bottoms, she returned to the bedroom and went through her handwritten interview prep one more time. She didn't want to turn the desk lamp on for fear of waking Kolli, but she also didn't need to – with her compound, multi-hued eyes, her krxix eyesight was as good in the dark as it was in the light. Besides, dawn was starting to give the window blinds a silver lining.

Outside, beyond the student habitation high-block, she could hear Hub City beginning to wake up. The window frame rattled as hover traffic increased, the monotonous grumble of personal fliers and bigger cargo units coming down from the west stacks reaching into the cluttered, darkened room. She knew that right now the illumination strips would be automatically shutting down, and the first raw-eyed store owners and foot commuters would be making their way out into the street far below. Storefront security grids would be rattling off, shield protectors flashing away, diner stoves heating up, neon closed signs blinking to open. In the neighboring inner-city campus of Hub University, the morning crowd would be heading to lectures and the library, replacing those damned souls who had worked through the night.

She glanced at Kolli, sorely tempted to let the elf sleep through and leave her behind. There was no way she was serious about becoming a Martian Studies student. But if she did abandon her, Longaard might find out, and Nal'ai had already ridden her luck as far as she dared with the supervisor. Ticking her mandibles, she began to pack, making sure her personal uplink tablet was secured in the bottom of her rucksack before gently shaking Kolli awake.

"Today's the day," she said as the elf groaned and rolled over. "Your life as a Martian Studies student starts now – we've got a hoverbus to catch."

Only the public laws of Hub City prevented its martian inhabitants from fortifying their communities. Nal'ai had no doubt they would if they could – the zone surrounding the

Borreal enclave would've been blocked off by bastion walls and overlooked by automated ray cannons and intrusion deflectors. As it was, there was no immediately obvious way to tell that the hoverbus had passed onto the Borreal martian collective. For a couple of streets at least, it just looked like any other part of the downtown nexus, albeit unusually quiet for the time of day. Then they saw the domes.

While the full-on militarized zones favored by the peoples of Mars were forbidden within the bounds of the city, that didn't stop the enclaves from building the structures they were most familiar with. The looming residence blocks and grav-towers of the nexus area gave way abruptly to a cluster of sloping, circular structures, all an uninspiring shade of matt-gray. They grew rapidly from the size of a small detached habitational unit to domes as big as hangar barns. Many were stamped with martian script printed in blocky letters, though the hoverbus was traveling too fast for Nal'ai to be able to decipher them. She glanced at the route map holographic on the headrest of the seat in front of her. Only a few minutes until their stop.

"When we get off, you let me do the talking," she said, turning to Kolli. Her roommate had spent most of the journey with her legs up, chewing popgum and flicking through the latest copy of Hub Scandal. She grunted, not looking up from an article about the break-up of Solstice 5 on the eve of their supposed comeback tour.

"And remember, don't call them little grays, or greenheads, or warmongers, and don't call the enclave 'Martian town,'" Nal'ai added sternly.

"Gotcha," Kolli said, turning the page.

"Final stop, Borreal enclave," chimed the hoverbus's automated announcer. End of the line. Nal'ai gave Kolli's legs a kick and they both got up. The transporter's doors squeaked open.

Before them the enclave's dome primus squatted like a gargantuan, gray-shelled crustacean clamped to a rock. Nal'ai recognized it from the research she'd done before the trip, though it was hard to mistake it for anything else – it was the largest of the martian structures surrounding them, a towering semi-sphere of armored plates, stamped with great blocks of text that Nal'ai now recognized as an independent variation of the martian creed of Nova Hellas. Six purple and green banners with more script fluttered on either side of the main concourse leading to the dome's large portal hatch.

The building's sheer size, impressive though it was, wasn't the most surprising thing about the whole scene. What was shocking was the total lack of a single living being or intelligent construct in sight. The rockform boulevard lay totally deserted before them.

"This is quite the welcoming party," Kolli said.

As though to underscore her words, there was a hum followed by the rush of anti grav boosters as the hoverbus turned in the street behind them and swept back along its route, leaving them in its wake.

Nal'ai didn't say anything. She felt the first stirrings of panic. This wasn't what she had planned for, and she was very much a planning kind of person.

"What now?" Kolli asked.

"Well, we could knock..."

The two students exchanged a glance.

"You're the expert," Kolli said. "You first."

Nal'ai clenched her mandibles, checked her antennae were straight, and began to walk towards the hatch port. The banners rattled and fluttered against their poles on either side, a counterpoint to the distant, muffled grumbling of the city. The dome loomed ahead, its bulk stark and gleaming in the morning light. It felt as though they had stepped through into a different dimension. Nal'ai wondered briefly whether they actually had.

The hatch towered over them – up close it was even bigger than it had seemed from the street. She came up short in front of the flush metal surface and, after taking a second to quell the churning in her stomach and the rigid krxix lockdown urge in her limbs, reached up and knocked.

There was no response, besides a very faint whirring noise. Nal'ai looked around for evidence of a monitoring device hidden in the dome's curvature above them.

"Think they're watching us?" Kolli asked, reading her mind.

"Professor Longaard said he was friendly with this enclave," Nal'ai said, glancing back down the boulevard towards the deserted street. "He said we'd be made welcome."

"Maybe the enclave is deserted," Kolli suggested unhelpfully. "Maybe they've all gone back to Nova Hellas? Perhaps they've been abducted by–"

"Martians," Nal'ai finished sarcastically.

"Hey, I don't have to be a fancy Martian Studies second trimester student to know graylings don't like their own kind going rogue," Kolli said. "Perhaps Nova Hellas has sent a strike force to round them all up and take them back? Or maybe they're all dead."

She said the last word with undue, morbid relish. Nal'ai clicked irritably.

"You read too many bad terror novels, Kolli. Nova Hellas would rather pretend rogue enclaves like Borreal just don't exist, rather than waste time and resources bringing them to heel. The existence of independent martian communities outside the control of Nova Hellas is a source of unspeakable embarrassment to the loyalist elders. They're an unmentionable taboo."

"No need for the lecture, Professor Nal'ai," Kolli said. "All I'm saying is something's not right here, and we–"

A thunk stopped the elf in her tracks. Nal'ai's antennae twitched and she took a sharp step back as the iris of the portal in front of her slid open, exposing the darkness of the dome's interior.

In the gaping space a short, green-gray figure stood waiting. They had a bulbous, smooth cranium and eyes as large and black as jet. The creature was clad in a rubberized white vacuum suit overlaid with plates of purple blast armor. At barely half of Nal'ai's height, they didn't even come up to Kolli's slender waist.

They said something, too quick for Nal'ai to understand.

"My name is Nal'ai," she responded in her best Mars cant. "And this is my companion–"

The hatch portal slammed shut. Nal'ai found herself staring once more at gray metal.

"Well, that went well," Kolli said into the stunned silence that followed. "What time is the hoverbus back?"

"Hey," Nal'ai shouted, and began to bang on the hatch. The thought of failing her entire degree lent force to her blows –

she'd never be accepted back in the web nest if she crashed out. "I'm a student at Hub University! I'm top of my gacking class in Martian Studies! At least tell me why you won't let us in!"

"I don't think they care," Kolli said, lazily blowing a popgum bubble.

The hatch opened again. Nal'ai, still knocking, almost fell in. She froze, teetering, on the threshold, and found herself staring down the barrels of several dozen ray guns.

The first martian had been joined by a lot more, and they were all armed. Two had crackling green energy leashes too, grasped by their extra exo-arms. Straining against the bonds were half a dozen martian hounds, razor-muzzles slavering, beady eyestalks swiveling as their six-limbed, furless bodies twisted and jerked just a few paces from Nal'ai. The air hummed with charged weapon systems and feral snarling.

Nal'ai and Kolli raised their hands.

"Looks like they care after all," Kolli said, lips splattered with burst popgum.

The greeting party scanned them and their rucksacks before marching them inside. The hatch sealed with a thud that made Nal'ai shiver, thrusting them into darkness. Her eyesight adapted, just in time for her to be momentarily blinded when the lights blinked on. She felt something hard in her back – a ray gun, she suspected – and stumbled forward.

They were in a wide, curving chamber that arced away to the left and right, following the outline of the dome's outer walls. A tunnel leading deeper into the structure lay ahead, its own walls and ceiling similarly curved. The lights were recessed into strips underfoot, between smooth, glassy flooring plates.

The martian behind her said something. She kept walking. They were taking the corridor leading into the heart of the dome primus.

She snatched a glance sideways at Kolli. The elf was wide-eyed and clearly afraid, though she was trying to hide it. The martian party behind them exchanged a few quick-fire words among themselves, their hounds still yapping at their heels.

"We're just Hub Uni students," Nal'ai tried to say. "We come in peace."

"Xaybeen laey," snapped the martian behind her. She'd understood that one. Keep quiet.

She was already wishing they'd just gone back to the hoverbus stop after she'd knocked the first time.

The tunnel arced first left then right, passing by more portal hatches. Eventually the party halted outside one. A pair of the diminutive martians stepped in front of Nal'ai and held another quick-fire discussion. She could only pick out a few words, but it sounded like they were arguing – elders ready, intruders, orders, exterminate. Eventually one seemed to relent and, with their three long fingers, entered a flurry of digits into a keycode pad. The hatch iris whirred open.

"Ul-yex," one of the martians ordered her. Go.

She stepped forward onto what appeared to be some form of gantry, Kolli at her side. Immediately a spotlight fell upon them, and a great rush of voices swelled to meet them. Nal'ai flinched and raised her two right arms to shield her compound eyes as they adjusted.

They were in a greater chamber that the krxix took to be the heart of the dome primus. Its ceiling followed the curve of the outer structure, while its floor was tiered like a vast amphitheater, with hundreds of concentric rings occupied by a sea of little gray-green men. In the pit forming the chamber's center an oval platform hovered, raised up from the floor by anti-grav units. It was an air dais, rotating slowly, occupied by a half-dozen figures who stood apart from the throng of martians beneath them. From a distance they looked similar to those below, except they were altogether taller and more slender. Nal'ai recognized them as elders, the leader cast subspecies of the martian race.

The spotlight remained glaring down on the two captured students as the gantry underfoot shuddered and began to move. Nal'ai realized it was another hoverplate. She could feel the grav suppressors thrumming up through the soles of her feet as it carried them down towards the waiting dais. The chatter of the martian horde below redoubled, echoing around the chamber's lofty ceiling.

"How's this for a welcoming party?" Nal'ai hissed to Kolli.

"This is normal, right?" the elf replied nervously. "Like, they do this with all their visitors?"

"Totally."

The hoverplate docked seamlessly with the dais, and their guards ushered them onto the larger platform with more prodding. Nal'ai and Kolli found themselves surrounded by the elders. They turned in a semi-circle, looking from one haughty, black-eyed face to the next.

One of the martian leaders stepped forward. Like their kindred they were tall, taller even than an elf like Kolli, though that was partially due to the fact that their long, skinny neck-stalk accounted for a quarter of their height.

Their painfully slender body was clad in a form-fitting purple vacuum suit, along with a robe that hung lightly from clasps at their shoulders and elbows. The silken garment shimmered from deep blue to light purple, shifting beneath the spotlight. It was the only thing that differentiated them from the others.

"My name is Eyxyx," the elder declared in the standard tongue. "I am the current chief elder of the One True Independent Mars Enclave of Borreal. I require you both to identify yourselves, for the records."

"My name is Nal'ai Sho," Nal'ai said. "And this is Kolli Betan. We're–"

"Nal'ai Sho and Kolli Betan, you have been found guilty of conspiring to besiege the One True Independent Mars Enclave of Borreal. After a long and thorough trial, the Council of Elders have unanimously agreed on a verdict of guilty-as-charged. The sentence is death, to be enacted immediately."

Nal'ai and Kolli both began to shout, but their words were lost in the roar of approval that rose from the onlooking crowd. The dais shifted slightly, and Nal'ai caught a humming noise rising over the chaos. In a total panic, she looked down and realized the circular floor that constituted the base of the amphitheater was slowly levering open. Beneath it was a pit, dug into Hub City's bedrock and apparently filled with a sea of snapping, razor-sharp maws – a pack of martian hounds, chained beneath the amphitheater like gladiatorial beasts.

"We haven't done anything," Kolli was screaming. "We're just here for the course credits!"

"This is merely a sentencing court," Eyxyx rasped. "The judgment has already been passed, and it will not be rescinded.

We shall take 'we're just here for the course credits' to be your final words."

The part of the platform Nal'ai and Kolli were standing on began to retract. Nal'ai staggered and had to snatch onto her roommate to avoid falling.

"Longaard sent us," she shouted at Eyxyx, desperately. "Professor Longaard!"

For a second she thought the slender martian hadn't heard her over the noise rebounding around the chamber.

Then Eyxyx raised one bony hand. The retracting dais froze, the two women teetering on its edge.

"What... did you say?" the elder asked.

"Professor Longaard sent us," Nal'ai responded desperately. "We're students at Hub University! We mean you no harm!"

The chamber had gone deathly silent. The elders exchanged glances, sneers giving way to obvious confusion.

"Longaard the non-organic?" Eyxyx asked.

"Yes," Nal'ai said, still clutching Kolli. "He's my... academic supervisor."

Eyxyx said nothing. Then they uttered a single word, one which Nal'ai didn't recognize. There was a cracking sound, and a burst of white light. The elder abruptly clenched their fist. The remaining retractable section of the hoverplate shot away beneath them.

Screaming, Nal'ai and Kolli fell.

"Rude," Kolli said, scowling furiously as she tried to brush the static-induced tangles out of her long, black hair. "That's what that was. Totally rude."

"It could've been worse," Nal'ai pointed out. "They could

have dropped us without any electro-netting. Now that would've been rude."

Kolli grunted, giving up on her hair. The hatch they'd been waiting outside had opened. Wordlessly, a single martian solider gestured them inside.

Nal'ai half expected to find herself back in the amphitheater. Instead they entered an altogether smaller room. It possessed the same standard prefabbed Mars properties all martians seemed drawn to, from the curving walls and ceiling to the spartan gray surfaces. Its only adornments were two chairs, a desk and some shelves, the latter two stacked with data pads and a couple of strangely shaped ornaments. Incongruously, all the furniture was premade EKKA blackwood, the kind that decorated Hub Uni student blocks, stuff Nal'ai could've found in any downstack home-hab store or charity seller. It was a nod, she assumed, to the Borreal enclave's adopted home, a little statement of independence. No Nova Hellas loyalist would be seen vaporized with anything other than Mars-sanctioned and approved DIY.

Besides the martian who had ushered them in, the only other occupant of the room was Eyxyx. The elder was still clad in their vacc-suit and gossamer cape. While they might have been happy enough to use Hub City furnishing for the rest of their office, they clearly wanted something more familiar for their own chair – they were reclining behind the desk in a floater pod, its smooth, spherical underside pulsing gently. The elder leant back further and steepled their bony fingers as the hatch portal sealed behind Nal'ai and Kolli.

"Sit," they instructed, staring at the two students without

blinking. They both obeyed hastily, the cheap blackwood chairs opposite the desk creaking. A few seconds of silence passed. There was a slight squeak of vulcanized rubber as the martian soldier, who had remained by the door, shifted. Eyxyx still hadn't blinked. Nal'ai could make out her reflection in their glassy black eyes.

"You come into my enclave unannounced," Eyxyx said finally. They spoke in martian. "And you claim to have been sent by our old enemy, the non-organic Longaard."

Nal'ai wasn't sure which part to process first. She cleared her throat before speaking, carefully using the formal intonations of speech she had painstakingly learned over the past few years of research.

"Apologies a hundred times over, wise-valiant elder, but I fear you are recalling the wrong being. Professor Longaard is an academic at Hub University, an expert in the study of the glorious cultures of Mars. He is no enemy. In fact, I believe he has spent time at this very enclave, performing groundbreaking-research."

"Researching our weaknesses," Eyxyx said, their fingers still pressed together. "Finding every employable advantage in our defenses."

"What?" Nal'ai said, her protocols of address breaking down. "No. He's just a dedicated researcher. Why would he be researching your defenses?"

"To sell the information to our misguided kindred in Nova Hellas, for a start," Eyxyx snapped. "Or the Archons? Hub City's brutish Arbitrators? Insane Sanctum preachers? Logos tech-thieves? The Strixian Cartel? The Brotherhood of Five? The Black–"

"Professor Longaard hasn't shared anything classified with anyone," Nal'ai interjected. "He takes his non-disclosure agreements extremely seriously. I should know, he made us sign enough forms before sending us here."

"Sending you here," Eyxyx said, placing their palms flat on the desk and leaning forward in their floater pod. "Now we come to the crux of the matter, krxix. Just why did the robot send you here? Be truthful, and I might be able to convince the other elders to spare your lives … for a while longer."

"We are here to conduct our own research," Nal'ai said, trying to choose her words as carefully as possible.

"So you are his spies?"

"No! We're just students! I am interested in martian culture. My studies would go much better if I was able to experience it first-hand."

Eyxyx leant back again, as though assessing the truth of her words. Nal'ai got the strange impression that she was undergoing some perverse parody of an academic supervisor meeting. She wondered whether the martian had learned the style off Longaard.

"Your interests are non-hostile?" they asked slowly. "You do not intend to mount an invasion of Borreal or its inhabitants?"

"No," Nal'ai said firmly. "Kolli and I aren't an invasion force. We both respect your people and the Borreal enclave as a whole. We wish to understand your ways, so we can teach other species that same respect. We have no interest in your defensive capabilities."

Eyxyx watched them closely for a minute more. Kolli looking from them to Nal'ai, clearly not understanding a word that was being said, but sensing that their fate hung in the balance.

"How long would these studies take?" Eyxyx asked.

"A few standard day cycles," Nal'ai said. They'd been scheduled to stay at the enclave for a week, but she had no intention of pushing her luck. Only the fear of causing offense was stopping her from leaving the very next day.

"And the research itself…" Eyxyx left the sentence dangling.

"Interviews," Nal'ai answered. "With just a few subjects. Basic things about daily routines, attitudes towards other species and the wider Hub City community. Perhaps discussions about Nova Hellas."

Eyxyx's black eyes narrowed at the mention of the loyalist martian capital, but they said nothing as Nal'ai continued to offer a potted description of the research goals and interview questions she had agreed with Longaard. Eventually they held up one hand.

"I see you plan thoroughly, krxix," he said. "That, at least, is to be commended." He paused to allow Nal'ai to offer the proper thanks for the compliment before carrying on. "I am not fully convinced by your cover story, but your presence here may yet serve a … certain purpose. We will allow you to stay, for three days. I shall see you provided with quarters in the East Barracks. In turn, you will be allowed to interview a single member of our enclave."

The elder indicated the diminutive martian guarding the hatch, waving them forward.

"This one's name is Klixx," Eyxyx said, as though the soldier subspecies wasn't present in the room with them. "They will be available to answer all your questions. In fact, they will be at your side constantly. Is that understood, Klixx?"

The martian snapped to attention, but said nothing.

Nal'ai thought about arguing. The same suicidal urge that had gripped her in Longaard's office almost overcame her. But the precariousness of the situation eventually won out. She forced herself to nod her head, mandibles clenched.

"You have my thanks a hundred times over, wise-valiant elder," she managed to say. Eyxyx nodded magnanimously.

"Klixx, show these… visitors to their new quarters," they ordered. "You will both provide me with the results of your research before you depart, so that the council might review it. Until then, I wish you a prosperous campaign."

"And a prosperous campaign to you too, great elder," Nal'ai said, making eyes at Kolli as she stood and clasped a fist to her chest carapace, the traditional martian salute. Klixx ushered them out.

"What the great gack was that all about?" Kolli hissed as they returned to the corridor.

"Not now," Nal'ai responded as Klixx gestured to them both.

"*Ul-yex*," they said.

When the hoverplate's base had swept away from beneath her, Nal'ai couldn't exactly say that her life had flashed before her eyes. She was too busy screaming and imagining the wicked teeth of the martian hounds snapping up from below.

When she'd hit the electro-net engaged by the elder's gesture, she had assumed she was dead. The shock had knocked her out, limbs splayed in the air, rigid. She had come to in a sparsely furnished barrack room next to Kolli, and then been ushered to Eyxyx's office.

Now they found themselves in an almost identical-looking barrack dorm. It was a long, low, vault, ranked with row after row of metal bed bunks that were lit by the recessed floor lighting. Most didn't have any sheets or blankets, but Klixx led them to a pair that had been hastily made up.

"Where is everyone else?" Nal'ai asked the martian in a half-hearted attempt at brokering a conversation.

"Away," Klixx replied tersely. They were greener than most of the other Borrealians Nal'ai had seen, their skin almost an emerald hue. They wore the enclave's standard white vacc-suit and purple armor though, and kept a ray gun holstered at their hip. Their sharp features and monochromatic black eyes seemed perpetually drawn up into a scowl or sneer. Then again, that appeared to be the standard expression favored by most of the martians Nal'ai had seen so far.

"My name is Nal'ai," she began to say, but the martian interrupted her.

"I know," they said in a reedy, nasal voice. "You are a krxix from the Hub University. And your compatriot is an elf named Kolli."

"You speak the standard tongue?"

"I prefer not to," Klixx replied in martian.

Nal'ai and Kolli shucked their rucksacks onto their assigned beds. Nal'ai discovered a handful of sealed food bars beneath her pillow. She read the labels.

"Ration sticks?" she asked Klixx. The martian nodded.

"Dinner," they explained.

"Lovely."

According to Klixx, it was late evening outside. It sure felt like it. Exhaustion caught up with Nal'ai almost as soon as she sat on the edge of her bed.

"If it's all right with you, we can begin the interviews tomorrow morning," she said to Klixx, still standing in the aisle beside the bunks.

"As you wish," the martian said, without moving.

"Are you going to stay there all night?" Nal'ai asked. The martian's grimace turned even more severe at the suggestion.

"I have been told to stay with you at all times… I will take a bunk at the far end of the row."

They stalked off down the vault, vacc-suit squeaking. A few moments after they disappeared from view, the lighting dimmed to sleep settings. Nal'ai changed, hastily and self-consciously, into her PJs. Kolli seemed content to stay in the Hub Uni scrumball hoodie she'd stolen from the first team's center forward last semester.

Nal'ai chewed down one of the ration sticks and settled into the bed, turning uncomfortably. She struggled to sleep in anything that wasn't her own webrest. She briefly considered spinning a web above the bunk, but decided it would be too much effort. Besides, she didn't want to cause offense. Even after all her studies, nothing could have prepared her for how prickly martians were in person. And these were the liberal ones.

Every time she rolled over, the whole bunk frame rocked and squeaked. Eventually she heard the sound of feet on the ladder rungs, followed by a rustling noise as Kolli clambered in beside her. She'd brought her own blanket.

"Hey," Nal'ai said.

"Hey," Kolli answered in the half dark. They shared the

silence for a while before Kolli spoke.

"So, I'm guessing field trips aren't always this crazy?"

"I'm guessing not," Nal'ai said. "Today has been... interesting."

"That's an interesting word to use," the elf agreed. "Dropping us in a fang pit, then electro-webbing us. Not my usual weekday lecture routine."

Despite her words, Nal'ai could sense how tense and stressed Kolli still was. She put two arms round her shoulder, letting her rest her head against her carapace.

"I think they were just trying to intimidate us. See if we were really a threat."

"Well count me intimidated. And what was all that about back there? I'm guessing that lanky thing was the boss of Martian town?"

"It's called the Borreal enclave," Nal'ai said sternly. "And yes. They're willing to let us spend a few days doing research. Plus, presumably, spare our lives. You're lucky I paid attention during my language courses."

"A few days doing research," Kolli repeated incredulously. "We should be leaving, tonight. I almost got eaten alive earlier!"

"We both did," Nal'ai corrected. "But I don't think trying to leave straight away will do us any good. For a start it would likely cause serious offense, and an offended martian is a dangerous martian. Plus, it would seem to confirm Eyxyx's suspicions that we're some sort of spy team."

"Spy team," Kolli almost shouted. Nal'ai batted lightly at her face with a free hand, indicating for her to keep her voice down.

"How in gack's name do you mistake us for spies?" the elf whispered. "Are they all insane?"

"They're martians," Nal'ai said. "This is how they function, Kolli. They're a hyper militarized race. Their whole society is based on warfare. Add to that a dose of rampant xenophobia–"

"Xenowhatnow?"

"They hate outsiders. Anything non-martian is inferior. The groups that have deserted Nova Hellas, like the Borreal, are supposedly a little more easygoing, but their exile also makes them wildly suspicious. Eyxyx thinks Nova Hellas is out to get them, even though in reality the loyalists would rather just ignore rogue groups like this one. They seem to think we've been hired to spy on them."

"But if martians hate non-martians, why would Nova Hellas hire us – a krxix and an elf – to spy on a rogue faction like Borreal?" Kolli asked slowly.

"Exactly."

"They all seem super-dumb, just saying."

"There's an old saying that… well, to paraphrase, martians always seem super dumb until you see them on the battlefield, exterminating everything in their way. Then their dumbness tends to make a lot more sense."

"Let's hope we don't experience that, then."

"Agreed."

Neither of them slept well. At one point, Nal'ai woke to what she thought was the sound of a vacc-suit squeaking past the bunk. She peered over the edge, but saw nothing.

Next morning there was no sign of Klixx. After washing and getting dressed in the barrack's adjacent bathroom block,

Nal'ai discovered that fresh "breakfast" bars had appeared on the pillow of the lower bunk. She was still chewing unenthusiastically on one when their martian handler reappeared in person.

"I have been ordered to attend you," they said grudgingly. "I am to… answer your questions regarding the enclave."

Nal'ai already had a record-stick, notepad, scriber and translation box in each set of hands. Kolli rolled her eyes, swallowing the last of her ration bar and fishing in her baggy hoodie pockets for a fresh wad of popgum.

"Is there somewhere better suited to a Q and A?" Nal'ai asked. Klixx shrugged indifferently and led them to a side room off the main barracks vault. It looked as though at one point it had been a storage locker, though it had been mostly cleared out – only a few tape-sealed crates and cardboard boxes remained. There were a couple of low stools that the three of them squatted on – they were the perfect size for Klixx, and Nal'ai could just about manage, but Kolli looked borderline ridiculous, knees drawn up almost to her chest. She affected a distant, bored look as Nal'ai began questioning Klixx in martian.

"War," Klixx said, "is the natural state of all beings in the universe. It is the basis of existence which lesser societies attempt to cover with illusions of cooperation and charity. It is how all cultures begin, and it is how they all end."

Nal'ai was scribing furiously with two limbs on two pads at once – pop-out quotes and her own notes.

"You're quoting the philosophy of the revered martian elder, Hobyx," she said as she wrote. "But how does that mindset survive here on the Crucible? There hasn't been a major war in… forever, at least not one outside of the campaigns waged by Nova Hellas. A thousand intelligent species and subspecies, all living together in peace. Doesn't sound like the natural state of all beings to me."

"You don't see it out there?" Klixx asked, gesturing as though to the city beyond the surrounding dome. "Perhaps my use of the term 'war' was too complex for a… creature such as yourself. Conflict may be a better term. This city, this derelict, disorganized mess, is a place of constant conflict, constant tension. The struggle to exist in a place like this is, in itself, a form of conflict. Conflict in its endless different forms is the business Hub City wakes up to, and the reality that carries on even in its sleep."

ABSTRACT THINKER, Nal'ai was busily writing in her secondary notepad. She shot a glance at Kolli, but the elf appeared to have dozed off.

"How would you describe life as a martian soldier?" Nal'ai asked, deciding to change tack rather than risk a disagreement so early on.

"Solitary," Klixx said. "Socially deprived, vile, cruel, and brief. Not that any of my subspecies would realize it. We are the slaves of the elders: expendable, easily replaced."

Nal'ai paused for a second, taken aback. Nothing had prepared her for that level of frankness. Klixx returned her gaze levelly.

"Is that why your enclave left Nova Hellas?" she asked. "You realized the other elders didn't care about the majority of the martian race?"

"I wouldn't know," Klixx said. "I was not born into the enclave. I arrived here one month-cycle ago from Nova Hellas."

Another surprise – Nal'ai hadn't picked up that Klixx was a new arrival. She went back to her notes.

"So what was it that pushed you into abandoning your home and coming here?" she asked.

"There was... an infraction," the martian said slowly. "I do not wish to discuss it."

EXILE, Nal'ai wrote, underlining it. SELF-SUFFICIENT SOLDIER?

"Perhaps you can help me understand just how much the mindset of an independent enclave such as Borreal differs from the loyalist collective, then?" she went on.

"That is a question better suited for the elders. They are the ones who set policy."

"So even though you've described the life of a soldier martian in Nova Hellas as..." she glanced back at her notes, "... vile, cruel and brief, the elders still exert full control over the soldiers of this enclave?"

"You seem to be operating under a misapprehension, krxix," the martian said. "You assume that all those who abandon Nova Hellas abandon the core principles of what it means to be a child of Mars. I am not ashamed of who I am. I am not ashamed of the great empire my race has built. Be under no illusions: martians are the galaxy's supreme species, and one day all other creatures will know it. It is simply the case that those who claim the title 'Nova Hellas' are currently misguided."

"You think that a reunification is possible, then? That, unlikely as it may be, the elders of independent enclaves and Nova Hellas could one day reach an accord?"

Klixx smirked. "I very much doubt the likes of Eyxyx

would ever surrender their petty power. But as for the rest of us, who knows? If Nova Hellas repents, perhaps."

More frenzied notetaking. COMPLEX IDEOLOGIES. MORE INDEPENDENT-MINDED THAN MOST SOLDIERS. ALLEGIANCE ONLY TO SELF? Nal'ai paused for a moment.

"Am I right in thinking that Nova Hellas would rather ignore these free enclaves than try to reach out to them... or attack them?"

"Perhaps," Klixx said slowly, glancing at Kolli's sleeping form, then back to Nal'ai. "But I doubt the elders of Nova Hellas would wish to waste their strength against an enclave with a fully functioning defense data core. Borreal is still a martian community. It has soldiery, automated weapons systems and shielding to spare, most of it controlled from the core."

Nal'ai considered the answer for a moment before noting it down. It didn't seem like a subject she should press too hard on – she moved on to the next topic, interactions and relations with non-martian groups in Hub City. To her surprise, Klixx showed only minimal reluctance in their answers. Nal'ai realized it was likely few, if any, had ever bothered to stop and ask the opinions of a generic martian soldier drone before.

"Sometimes necessity comes first," the little soldier said when Nal'ai asked them how martians, with their culturally ingrained xenophobia, dealt with the many other species they were forced to interact with in Hub City.

"You mean like this interview," Nal'ai dared suggest, the shade of her eyes dipping to a dark amber. The martian actually smiled.

"Perhaps. I'm sure this interview will be of some use to both of us. Eventually."

"I hope so," Nal'ai said, struggling not to beam with excitement. Clearly, she really had perfected her interview technique. She could practically see the A-plus grade on the final paper.

"Are you two still talking?" Kolli asked. She'd started awake, and was now looking around the storage space blearily. "I'm hungry. Is anyone else hungry?"

"Perhaps now would be a good time for a break," Nal'ai allowed. Klixx agreed to leave them for long enough to source something that wasn't ration bars. They even started to speak in the standard tongue, so that Kolli could understand them.

"See," Nal'ai said brightly after the martian had left. "It's like my brood mother used to say. Even the most intractable species lighten up once you get to know them better."

"You krxix are just far too friendly," Kolli said dubiously. "It's that hive instinct, always helping and sharing with everyone."

"You say that like it's a bad thing."

"Hey, I'm the one who usually benefits from it."

Klixx came back with several trays of steaming sucrale, which both Nal'ai and Kolli devoured. The questioning resumed, focused now on standard martian foodstuffs, and carried on in a similar vein until a buzzing in Nal'ai's pocket made her jump.

"Oh gack, sorry," she said, cutting off Klixx as the martian described their clone mother's favorite pre-battle stew back home in Nova Hellas. "I lost track of the time! Kolli, can you take over?"

"Take over?" Kolli stammered.

"Just note down what Klixx is saying," Nal'ai said, fumbling with the alarm chip in her pocket. Klixx half-rose from their stool as Nal'ai made for the door, but she waved them back down.

"I'm going to stay in the barrack block, promise. I almost forgot, I have a scheduled uplink call with my supervisor. I need to check in and report my findings."

Klixx looked at her with narrowed eyes, but slowly sank back onto their stool.

Cursing under her breath, Nal'ai hurried along the rows of bunks and fished the uplink from her rucksack under their commandeered bed. The screen blinked to life in her hands. She cursed again, paused to check her antennae were straight, then perched on the edge of the bed and established the vid connection with Longaard's office. The professor appeared on the screen, still plugged in to his desk.

"I'm sorry, Professor Longaard," Nal'ai said, all in a rush. "I was conducting an interview and didn't notice the time."

Longaard made a buzz that Nal'ai took to be the robo version of a huffing noise.

"Well, at least you have begun your interviews promptly," the professor said. "I take it from that fact alone that you have been well received?"

"Yes," Nal'ai said, pausing. Longaard buzzed again.

"My systems detect hesitation, Ms Nal'ai."

"Our initial contact was… difficult," she said slowly.

"Describe 'difficult.'"

"Apparently the chief elder viewed myself and Kolli as some sort of threat. They thought we were… attacking the enclave."

Longaard made a buzzing sound that Nal'ai took to be surprise.

"The chief elder is still Orix Veyy?" he asked. She shook her head.

"If it is, that's not how they introduced themselves. They call themselves Eyxyx."

Even over the fuzzy screen, Nal'ai saw the professor's optic units refocus.

"Eyxyx is now the chief elder of the Borreal enclave?" he demanded, his words chopped by the uplink's distortion.

"I believe so, yes. Why? Is that a problem?"

"Listen t… Nal'ai, this is v… clear?"

"Professor, you're breaking up," Nal'ai said, giving the side of the uplink an exasperated tap. The connection continued to deteriorate. Longaard's picture had frozen. A blurt of words came through, all scrambled up. She only caught one. "Danger." Then the screen went blank, replaced by a small, circular icon. Connection lost.

"Piece of junk," Nal'ai hissed, her eyes going violet as she smacked the uplink once more. It made no difference. She snapped it shut and stuffed it back inside her rucksack.

When she returned to the storage room, she found Klixx gone.

"Said they were tired," Kolli said with a shrug, offering her the pad she'd been digi-scribing notes on. They consisted of a quarter-page of illegible scribbles and a doodle of a bug-eyed martian hound.

"Did they give you any trouble?" Nal'ai asked. "I assume me suddenly disappearing didn't go down well."

"They made sure they could see you hadn't left the dorm

from the door," Kolli said. "But that was about it. You know they have seventeen siblings? And half of them are clones? Apparently that's, like, standard."

"The things you know," Nal'ai said, the violet hue of her changeable compound eyes giving away the sarcasm she'd tried to hide. Kolli didn't seem to notice.

"They're actually a pretty chill little tyke," she said.

"Martian datemate confirmed," Nal'ai smirked, eyes shifting to magenta. Joke-shade, as Kolli called it.

"Oh shut up, Nal. They're too short for me. And that's just for starters."

"And probably too fond of exterminating non-martians," Nal'ai pointed out. Kolli shrugged.

"Well they're definitely a lot less aggressive than the lanky one. So, what did the prof say?"

"Oh, he seemed impressed with the start we've made."

"Really? What about the whole 'found guilty of besieging the Borreal enclave' thing?"

"Just a classic martian misunderstanding," Nal'ai lied. Now really wasn't the time to be worrying Kolli with the professor's apparent unease over Eyxyx. The first interview had gone far too well for her to back out now. It was surely nothing more than some old academic tiff.

"Looks like we've really turned this trip around," Kolli said.

"Yeah," Nal'ai replied with a smile. "Looks like we have."

Nal'ai felt like she had barely closed her eyes before she heard the door to the barrack vault hiss open, followed by the clatter of dozens of armored feet invading the long, echoing space.

"What's going on?" Kolli said blearily from below.

Nal'ai didn't get a chance to answer. Figures were rushing between the rows of bunks, stab-lights probing the half-dark. She heard barked orders ringing out.

"Nyy ix!" Find them!

She threw aside her blanket and leapt down into the aisle, just in time to be lit up by one of the search beams. She raised her right limbs, cringing as the glare hurt her eye lenses. She got an impression of a cluster of armed martians pointing an assortment of ray weapons in her direction. Eyxyx stood among them, towering over the smaller soldiers.

"You," the elder rasped, pointing one long, accusatory finger at Nal'ai. "Caught in the act!"

"The act of sleeping," Nal'ai demanded, confusion warring with dismay. Kolli stumbled out of bed and into the spotlight next to her, groaning, hair an unkempt mess.

"What time is it?" she murmured.

"Bring them," Eyxyx snapped to the swarm of martian soldiers surrounding them.

It took Kolli a while to grasp exactly what was happening, but when she had woken up enough to realize they'd both just been thrown into a martian prison block, she really began losing it.

"I knew I should never have switched courses," she sniveled, eyes red, clutching her knees as she rocked back and forth in the corner of the featureless, metallic cube-cell the two students had been consigned to. "Only crazy people do martian studies. Really crazy people, or boring people."

"Thanks," Nal'ai said tersely, eyes black, pausing her back-and-forth prowl along the edge of the cell. Rather than a door, they were sealed off from the corridor outside by a row of crackling green energy bars. Their jailer paced outside, mimicking Nal'ai's movements. It wasn't a martian, but it was one of their hounds. Its stalk-eyes swiveled as it looked at Nal'ai hungrily. She felt as if the beast was staring into her soul.

"I hate martians," Kolli snapped.

"Please be quiet," Nal'ai said, doing her best to keep her own tone level. "I'm trying to think."

"Why?" Kolli said. "Your thinking is what got us in here in the first place!"

"I'm thinking about how to get the keys from around that thing's neck," Nal'ai answered, exasperated. The martian hound wore a heavy lock-collar, studded with activation chips. If only she could reach it...

"I'm sure it would be happy to swap one of your arms for the collar," Kolli said, unhelpfully.

Nal'ai didn't respond. She'd just heard the sound of a hatch levering open. Moments later a trio of figures appeared on the opposite side of the energy bars. The key-hound shrank back, tail down, whining.

"You," hissed Eyxyx. They were flanked by two other lugubrious-looking elders. "Tell us where you've hidden it!"

"Hidden what?" Nal'ai asked, all four hands on her hips.

"The enclave's defense data core," Eyxyx snarled, almost snatching hold of the crackling energy bars. "We know you've taken it for Longaard! Where is it?"

"We don't know anything about a defense data core," Nal'ai said. "We spent the whole of yesterday in the barrack block you provided. We haven't left–"

"You think you can circumvent our defenses so easily,"

Eyxyx said. "That we are blind and deaf to your cunning infiltration? Not so! If I return here without the core, you will wish we had cast you into the Pit of Hounds when you first arrived!"

Nal'ai began to reply, but the trio of elders had already turned on their heels and stormed from the cell block. She sighed.

"I guess we're still in trouble," Kolli said, nonplussed after the martian diatribe. She'd reached into her pocket and was trying to work free another wad of popgum. "Hey, you want one?"

"No," Nal'ai said irritably, then paused. Her eyes flashed from black to orange. "Wait. Yes. I want the whole pack."

"Greedy," Kolli gasped, clutching the sliver of foil to her chest.

"Not to chew!"

"Yeah right, what else–"

"For once in your existence, K, please just do as I ask," Nal'ai said. Kolli hesitated for a moment longer, but she knew that tone. Her roommate had reached her tipping point. Slowly, she held out the popgum packet.

Nal'ai took it and stripped away the foil, exposing the whole stick. Ignoring a final half-hearted complaint from Kolli, she knelt on the edge of the energy bars, and whistled.

The key-hound had been sitting quietly since Eyxyx's visit, but now its head twitched. It snapped and snarled, and leapt onto its paws.

Slowly, Nal'ai began to feed her arm through the gap between the energy bars.

"Great gack, don't," Kolli cried out. "It'll rip it clean off!"

"I've got three more," Nal'ai said, mandibles clenched in concentration. Her eyes had gone black as jet.

The martian hound didn't need further encouragement. It leapt for her arm, slavering. She tossed the gum stick into the air and threw herself backwards into the cell.

The hound's hurtling jaws snapped shut over thin air. Nal'ai blinked, on her back, surprised to see her limb still attached to her body. The hound snarled and snapped again, muzzle inches from the crackling bars separating the cell from the corridor. Then it made an odd noise, like a grunt.

It half turned, shaking its muzzle, then made as if to snap at Nal'ai through the bars. Instead, though, it could only yawn its jaws half-open. Its terrible fangs were gummed up – quite literally – with a rapidly expanding ball of popgum. The beast snarled and struggled, but with every motion of its jaw the chewy snack was more furiously masticated, became more covered in saliva, grew more intractable. In a few seconds the stick had almost completely sealed the hound's jaws together, bubbles popping and oozing past its suddenly impotent fangs.

Nal'ai leapt to her feet and thrust three arms back out past the bars, gritting her teeth as she focused on not making contact with the vertical energy beams. The hound tried to snap at her, but all it could do was bump its muzzle against one forearm. With two hands Nal'ai snatched it by the collar and hauled its bulk, with all of her strength, up against the bars.

There was a crack and a yelp, and she felt the beast go limp, knocked for six by the power discharge earthed by the bars.

"Oh my great gack," Kolli said, staring at her roommate's handiwork. "That was amazing!"

Nal'ai was too busy reaching through the bars again to carefully free the hound's collar. It was studded with key chips. She had no idea which one belong to their cell, but it wouldn't take long to find out. She stood and reached round to the locking pad on the wall outside, inserting one after the other.

"We're getting out of here," she said as the chip pad beeped, and the energy bars flickered out of existence.

"Sounds like a plan," Kolli said, grinning from one pointy ear to the other. "Left or right?"

"Left," Nal'ai said on a whim. They made it as far as the hatch at the end of the cell block's corridor. The portal slid open in front of them. Two martian soldiers, coming in the opposite direction, stopped mid conversation and stared up at them.

"Oh," Kolli said as both pairs came to an abrupt halt. "Hi, guys."

"Run," Nal'ai said.

They went the other way, as ray beams and angry shouts pursued them along the cell block. Kolli yelped as one shot vaporized a section of wall beside her, and Nal'ai was almost blinded by another beam that passed a hand's-width to the left of her head.

There was a second hatch at the opposite end of the row of cells. This one, however, was locked.

"Hurry," Kolli pleaded as Nal'ai fumbled with the key chips, like she wasn't going as fast as she could.

"Not this one," she mouthed as more ray beams blossomed with furious *pew-pew* sounds in the air all around them. "Or this one, or this one, or…"

"It's this one," Kolli yelled, snatching the collar and pressing the last chip against the locking pad.

The hatch levered open. This time there was no one on the other side. In fact, it was the outside. They ran.

"There's the hoverbus," Kolli shouted. Nal'ai realized she was right. The cell block had been part of the outer structure of the dome primus. The open boulevard lay ahead, still deserted, and beyond it the street with its incongruous hoverbus stop. Nal'ai slowed down.

"What're you waiting for?" Kolli all but screamed.

"My notes," Nal'ai said. "I'm going to get my notes."

"Are you *insane*?"

"I'm not failing, Kolli! Get the bus. I'll find my own way out."

There was no time for an argument. Nal'ai took off left, towards the East Barracks Dome, praying to the Web in the Sky that against all odds that her rucksack was still there. After a few seconds she heard footsteps catching up with her. It was Kolli.

"I'm not paying the student rent for the whole damn room on my own," she panted as she drew alongside her. Despite herself, Nal'ai laughed.

A wailing sound broke out across the open space. Someone somewhere had tripped an alarm. Nal'ai pushed herself on, panting, past another dome to the deserted structure they'd slept in the night before. Nal'ai briefly thought her keys weren't working on the hatch, before realizing it was already open.

"This way," she said breathlessly, leading Kolli back to their bunk. Her rucksack was still there, though it had been turned upside down – its contents scattered across the floor and bottom bed. Nal'ai cursed, and they both bent to retrieving the notes spread across the aisle.

"Where's my uplink?" Nal'ai asked as she jammed several digi-pads back in alongside their charging cable.

"I don't know," Kolli said distractedly, scrambling to get as many loose sheaves of paper into her hands as possible. "Who still uses physical notes, Nal? This is what mem-space is for!"

"Not much use if I can't find the recorder," Nal'ai pointed out. "I need that uplink!"

A realization hit her, and she trailed off. The hatch to the closet space at the far end of the barrack vault – the room where they'd interviewed Klixx – was open. She put down her rucksack and began to walk towards it.

"Stay here," she called back to Kolli. "And finish packing."

Kolli protested, but Nal'ai wasn't listening. She could hear a sound coming from within the storage room. The squeak of a rubberized vacc-suit.

"Do not move," Klixx said, pointing a ray pistol at her face. They were bent over next to one of the stools beside a stack of crates at the rear of the room. On the stool itself was Nal'ai's uplink, active and unlocked. It had been physically hardwired to a head-sized, metallic orb covered in blinking red and green lights and node-switches. Slowly, Nal'ai raised her hands.

"It was you," she said. "You stole the enclave's defense overrides. And you knew the elders would blame us."

"I did," Klixx admitted, sneering at her. "Ever since arriving here I have been trying to conceive of a way to return to Nova Hellas. And what better means to prove my loyalty and annul my exile than by providing the loyalist elders with the key to destroying this pathetic rogue enclave? Once this upload has been completed, Borreal will be defenseless!"

"You honestly think they'll take you back?" Nal'ai said. "Whatever you did must've been pretty serious if they exiled you in the first place. And your race isn't the forgiving type."

"Well we shall have to find out, won't we?" the martian traitor snapped, indicating for her to step inside the room and keep her hands up. "A few moments more, and I can leave this miserable city and its pathetic infestation of lesser species behind forever."

"Nal'ai, they're coming," came Kolli's voice from beyond the hatch, just before she appeared in the room, both rucksacks on her back. "Nal, I– oh…"

"And there's the other one," Klixx said, switching his aim. "The gullible krxix and the spare-brained elf. You are both perfect. No one will believe you, especially not that Mars-traitor Eyxyx. And while they are throwing you to the hounds, I will be going home. To Nova Hellas."

They raised their voice, calling through the hatch.

"In here! I've captured them both! They've just finished uploading the enclave defense data!"

Nal'ai and Kolli exchanged a despairing glance as they heard the sound of more running feet. Martian soldiery crowded the hatch, weapons bristling. Once again Eyxyx was among them, their gaunt face contorted with rage.

"It's all lies," Nal'ai shouted, pointing at Klixx. "They've set us up!"

She knew it was useless. If there was one thing she had learned from the past day it was that they didn't trust outsiders.

Eyxyx never got around to cursing Nal'ai though, at least not there and then. A rumble became audible over the whining of the charged ray guns, followed by a tremor in the structure of the dome itself. It grew rapidly more violent. Klixx slowly lowered their sidearm and turned, just in time for the wall at the back of the storage room to come crashing in.

A cascade of shattered rockform and twisted girders came right down on top of Klixx and the stolen data core. Nal'ai and Kolli threw themselves back, almost into the midst of the martians crowding the hatchway. A wall of dust and debris crashed against them, making everyone cringe and cough.

Something had just slammed straight in through the side of the dome, wreathed in dust. It was an armored chassis, a little smaller than a standard hovercar, with an angled, ram-like prow and a little turret bristling with charged laser guns. In the top of the turret, still clad in tw'ee, was Nal'ai's academic supervisor.

"Longaard," Eyxyx snarled, an arm raised as he peered through the dust cloud. "We meet again."

"Hopefully for the last time, Eyxyx," Longaard blurted from a speaker grille in the turret's base. His robotic form had been hardwired into the personal armored assault unit, his eyes glowing in the gloom like target-identifiers as they zeroed in on the mass of martians just past Nal'ai and Kolli. "Put down the blasters, gentlemartians, or I vaporize you all."

After what looked like a fierce internal struggle, Eyxyx waved for their minions to comply. Grudgingly, the martians lowered their weapons.

"Professor," Nal'ai stammered. "How did you find us?"

"Your uplink contains a tracker," Longaard droned. "Or do you think I would allow my students to go on a field trip entirely unsupervised?"

Nal'ai shook her head hastily, trying to nudge Kolli out of the firing line.

"Did you really think I would spend so long with you and not note every weakness in your defenses, Eyxyx?" Longaard demanded of the assembled martians. "I knew the day would come when you would supplant Orix Veyy and turn on all of the work we did together. If I'd known sooner, I would never have sent my students here."

"Students," Eyxyx hissed. "More like your spies, you treacherous robot. No good ever came of your dealings with Veyy! No martian elder should ever submit for... interviews! Look where it leads to – your little minions have your prize, but no one will be leaving here alive if the defense core isn't returned!"

"We didn't take the core," Nal'ai interjected. "It was Klixx! They were trying to send it to Nova Hellas."

"Klixx," Eyxyx said, as though hearing the name for the first time. They glared at Nal'ai. "If this is true, they will pay for their treachery, right after the three of you!"

"I think they might have already," Nal'ai said, glancing at the mound of rubble Longaard's entry had created.

"My students are coming with me," Longaard declared. "You can dig your data core out from underneath my treads. On behalf of Hub University, I thank Borreal for your time. We will show ourselves out."

Longaard's personal tank reversed, churning up rubble,

leaving daylight streaming in through the fearsome hole smashed in the dome's shell. Nal'ai and Kolli both looked at Eyxyx – the elder was physically shaking with wrath, but neither they nor their underlings made any move for the weaponry scattered at their feet. Longaard's blasters were still trained on them.

Nal'ai and Kolli followed the professor out, both trying not to run.

"They're up," said Kolli excitedly. She was already sitting at the data hub in their bedroom, logging into her HubU account. Nal'ai had just gotten back from a wall-crawl and was still kicking off her footpads by the door.

"What is?" she asked.

It had been half a semester since Longaard has saved them from the Borreal enclave. The academic meeting Nal'ai had attended immediately after had been the longest and most stressful of her life. There had been a lot of forms to fill out, most of them involving the two students putting into writing the fact that they didn't want to press any sort of compensation charge against Hub University.

"He can be a very hands-on supervisor when he wants to be," Nal'ai had explained to Kolli after the meeting.

"Hands-on? He drove a tank through a wall, Nal! He threatened an entire martian enclave!"

"Very hands-on," Nal'ai had repeated.

Thanks to Kolli salvaging their rucksacks, both of them had been able to resubmit their papers on time. And now, apparently, the results were in.

"I got a B minus," Kolli said, staring at the screen. "That's…

that's the best grade I've ever had! Nal!"

She leapt up and hugged her roommate hard.

"H- how," Nal'ai managed to grunt, all four arms pinned around the slender elf. "I saw the notes you took with Klixx. I mean, no offense but–"

"Did you bother to read them though?" Kolli asked, beaming.

"–mean no, it was just a quarter-page of–"

"Elf hyper-script," Kolli said, finally releasing Nal'ai and patting her on the head. "A thousand permutations per symbol. And you thought I just never took notes in class."

Nal'ai laughed despite herself and reached past her roommate to scroll down the hub to her own grades. "I think our excellent fieldwork made it almost impossible to fail us. Ah, there we go. I got a C-plus. That's a pass!"

Kolli looked from the screen to her roommate, her dark eyes wide.

"Nal, I'm... I'm so sorry."

"It's okay," Nal'ai said, still smiling, her eyes a serene, pale blue. "I think there might be some better news inside this anyway."

She ripped the top off a form packet she'd picked up from the door on the way in.

"But I scored higher than you," Kolli said, still staring at the offending C. "That's not possible. You never score lower than an A minus... Hey, what's in the pack?"

"Success," Nal'ai exclaimed, waving it triumphantly. "My request has been approved!"

"What request?" Kolli asked, taking the packet and scanning it.

"After everything that happened at Borreal I decided Martian Studies can't be done just through grades and papers," Nal'ai said slowly, still smiling. "So I put in for a year as a research assistant with Longaard. And now it's been approved, there are plenty more martian enclaves in Hub City that need visiting."

She hugged Kolli again, as the elf began to laugh.

"Well I'm not coming with you this time! Unless you let me copy your notes…"

THE LIBRARIAN'S DUEL
M K Hutchins

Arash's library was not haunted. Ghosts were the remnants of dead things. Her daughter's soul, trapped in the walls of the library, was alive, *thank-you-very-much*. Given that two Sanctum priests, a witch, and one professor of spectral analysis had all barged or snuck into the library and then failed to exorcise little Marya, that really should have settled the matter.

Marya's phase state was just a little shifted from the rest of the world.

"Will you be back soon, Mama? Will you bring new books?" Marya asked. Her face had the same shape as before the accident – that small nose, those huge eyes, those long swirls of wild hair. But she looked like a moving bas-relief now, like brick brought to life. Today she was only strong enough to lean out a few inches.

Arash brushed Marya's cheek, the round stone gritty and cold against her fingers. It had been six months since Marya last asked if she could come along too. Arash had thought it would be easier when she stopped wanting the impossible, but somehow, it was worse. "Of course. I'll be back soon, my chickadee."

"And you'll come home with new books?"

New books in the library always revitalized Marya. Three months ago, when they got in *The Adventures of Quixo: Into the Everfire*, Marya had actually been able to lean out from the wall far enough to hold the book with her own hands instead of just sending her soul into the stack and reading it from the inside.

The more books they could store in this library, the stronger and more present Marya would be. Arash's annual budget was small – barely enough for upkeep. But the Central Hub City Library would pay her a small fee to deliver any of their books that had been returned to her branch.

"Maybe we'll be able to get a new dictionary. Or even a thesaurus."

Marya wrinkled her nose. "Let's not."

"What if it's *A Visual Dictionary of Flowers from the Base of the World Tree*?" Arash asked slyly.

Marya's hands squeezed into tight, hopeful fists. "Oh, I miss flowers, Mama. I'd love that."

Arash bit the inside of her lip. The library grounds used to have red æmberflowers and snow-in-summer that you could see from the windows. But she'd let that all go to weeds, spending all her time and æmbits on buying more books. When was the last time Marya had seen flowers? She could buy a potted plant instead of the dictionary... but what if Marya slipped entirely into the walls and never came back?

Books. Books were the most important thing.

Arash loaded the wagon that Marya had once used to pull around her rock collection. The Central Branch was only three miles away. Better to walk and save the price of a train ticket or hovercab fare.

There was the usual assortment of oddities to return: two clay tablets, four scrolls, one hologram book that was only solid when you squinted at it, three dozen cheap paperbacks with the covers falling off, a book with a rabbit fur cover that might actually be a shapeshifting rabbit (or, she supposed, a shapeshifting book, depending on your perspective), and a fat tome wrapped in oilcloth with a neat card pinned to it that read: *Only Open With Gloves. Read the Cautionary Preface Before Continuing.* Arash always heeded warnings like that, so she made sure the oilcloth was properly covering whatever was inside before stowing it alongside its fellows.

All fit neatly in the wagon. The sky was slate-gray out the window, so Arash covered her cargo with a tarp, in case it rained. Then she hauled the wagon to the front door and flipped the sign to *Closed.* With the door open and herself halfway outside, Arash turned back to look one last time at her daughter. Marya had moved up to the second story ceiling over the entryway, her texture changing from brick to white shiplap.

"And what do you do if any ghost hunters show up?" Arash asked.

"Hide in the stacks where we keep last year's tax laws."

"That's my girl."

Her daughter wasn't a ghost. But it didn't hurt to be on the safe side.

• • •

Halfway to the main branch in Hubcentral, Arash cursed her decision to walk. Of course, the spokes on a child's wagon weren't meant to haul this kind of weight. Or maybe it was the were-rabbit/were-book causing trouble again. Either way, one of the wheels had splayed to the side, making steering nigh impossible.

And, of course, it started to rain. For the first block, puddles collected in the sidewalk cracks, only to be thrown up by her wonky wheels. She turned into the Polytree district, which thankfully had slightly lower gravity and smooth streets of woven kevlar palm fronds. But Polytree was a tiny district, and she couldn't follow it all the way to Central. She had to enter the Cobblestone district, a place that mostly seemed to act as a buffer between Hubcentral and the Brobnar Clashzones. In Cobblestone, all the buildings were cheaply made and thus cheap to repair. Her own district, New Archton, had been developed as a low-cost place for humanoids to live, but even compared to Archton, Cobblestone had a slapped-together, temporary look – like the occupants expected that their homes and shops would get knocked down in a brawl or an especially enthusiastic celebration.

Arash yanked her load over the uneven street. The wagon was going to rust and fall apart any day now. All right, it was *already* falling apart. But she couldn't afford a new one. She'd sold her house and moved into the library – and that had only covered fixing the library's roof after the accident.

Arash was too busy tugging and swearing to pay much attention to what was happening at the roughly built wooden shops and pubs around her. She didn't even notice the pack of drunk Brobnar careening across the street until she ran right into one of them, knocking her shoulder into his knee.

She fumbled a few steps back and stared up and up and up at the giant in front of her. His gold hair and beard were tied up with gems that strobed red and yellow and orange. His brawny chest was bare except for an amulet and a bright blue tattoo of a niffle ape. Fur and leather clothed the rest of him.

"I… beg your pardon," she said.

Only then did his compatriots – six giants, two humans, a goblin, and a robot – turn and spot her. They laughed or sneered and talked raucously among themselves.

The giant she'd run into scowled and bent a little closer. "Your voice is so weak, little human, that I can't hear you over my own *footsteps*."

The reek of alcohol and fried food wafted off his breath. Arash tried to step back again, but her wheel had jammed. "I said," she called a little louder, "that I'm sorry. Excuse me."

She turned to go around him. He planted his foot in front of her. The man wasn't armed, but he could pummel her to a pulp with his bare hands, to say nothing of his companions.

"What a pathetic thing you are," he sneered. "Going to apologize and prance around me like a pansy?"

His niffle ape tattoo shifted from blue to burnt orange and silently roared, pounding its chest.

Despite the situation, Arash stared. She'd thought her daughter was the only one. "Is… is that ape trapped in your skin?"

"The *what?*" The tattoo shifted red and ran in agitated loops around the giant's chest.

She swallowed, and tried to keep her voice from quavering

as she asked again, louder this time, "Is that ape trapped in your skin? Is it phase-shifted?"

The ape suddenly turned blue again. The giant roared in laughter and leaned back to his compatriots. He cut straight over their own conversations. "The little maggot here thinks my moving tattoo's a real ape!"

"That's a good one, chief," said the giant closest to him – a woman with blood-red hair. She slugged him on the shoulder, which made him laugh again, releasing flecks of spittle and more of his potent reek.

He turned back to Arash. "Well, seeing as it's not fair to fight with stupid people, I won't answer your nudge with a little nudge of my own. I'll just take some of the loot you're hauling," he jutted his chin at her wagon, "and then we'll be on our way!"

Arash tightened her grip on the wet handle. "You can't have it."

"Ooh, is there a speck of fire in you after all?" Now the niffle ape was laughing, too.

She kept her posture tall. "It's public property. It's not mine to give. You can't have it. They're all books anyway. Nothing especially valuable."

"It's the principle of the thing! I have ethics, and my ethics say that you owe me, so I'm taking something. Are you going to raise a puny fist against me? Let's say this is a champion's ring, then. It's official. Stop me if you can, vermin."

The giant reached right over her, pulled off the tarp, and snatched a book. Arash dove. She was too late to save the book, but she yanked the tarp back into place before the others were damaged by the rain.

"Here's your little booky-book." He dangled it above her head. "Did you want to try to take it back?"

If she lost that book, she'd have to pay for it. At least it was the one wrapped in oilcloth; the rain wouldn't hurt it. Arash left her dignity behind and jumped.

Of course the giant pulled the book up and away from her, to the cackling laughter of those behind him.

"I'm afraid you're just a hair too short. I think I'm winning this duel. Is there even anything good inside? Stories of great champions?"

He started undoing the oilcloth.

"You'll ruin it! It's raining, you idiot!" Arash shouted.

He snorted. "You're an idiot. I at least know a *tattoo* when I see one."

The goblin behind him coughed. "Chief Goldenbeard. She's right, you know. Let's take it back to camp and open it there. If there's schematics for, say, siege equipment in there, it'd be a shame to get it soggy."

"It's my book, I'll sog it if I want to."

Arash jumped again, knowing she'd fall painfully short. "You need gloves to open it! It's fragile! Or possibly dangerous!"

Goldenbeard tossed the oilcloth to the ground. Rain splattered onto the exposed cover. "Bah. It's a book. It'd only be dangerous if I *threw* it at someone."

He flipped open the pages, getting them wet, too.

"Stop! Please! That's public property!" Where was a district watchman when she needed one? She should have paid for a blasted hovercab.

Arash jumped. And jumped again. In desperation, she did

something she knew was foolish: she kicked the giant in the shins.

"Oh no, I'm *trembling*," Goldenbeard said.

She aimed another kick. He side-stepped, then he cursed. "Ach. You made me give myself a papercut. Stop that, or I'll boot you back."

He popped the injured finger in his mouth.

And then he promptly collapsed onto the cobbles.

One of the humans – a man with a cybernetic leg covered in so many spikes it couldn't be anything like practical – ran forward and checked his pulse. "Twitch, I think–"

"Already here," responded the squat, humanoid robot. He laid a hand on Goldenbeard's chest. Filaments streamed from his fingers, crisscrossing over the giant in a web of shifting white, blue and pink. Then Twitch slowly retracted the filaments. "Revival efforts have failed. He's dead as a doornail, guys. Generating autopsy."

For the first time, the Brobnar crowd fell silent. They all stared at Arash as the rain pattered down. She had no idea what to say. Apologize profusely? Deny any wrongdoing? Remain silent until she found a lawyer? "I, umm, did warn him the book could be dangerous," she muttered.

And she couldn't just leave it lying there on the sidewalk next to a dead giant. She found a stick on the side of the road and used it to flip the book closed.

The cover read: "*The Hemlock Book of Hemlock Paper*. The paper of this book is made with samples of hemlock from all over the Crucible, including the extremely lethal hemlock that grows on the slopes of Mount Strond. This makes it a treasury of natural history and my life's work – and also very dangerous. Please proceed with caution, always wearing the thickest leather gloves available."

Arash's heart pounded, making her lightheaded. The cause of death… it couldn't be the book. It couldn't.

"Hemlock poisoning from the papercut," Twitch announced. "Our chief was defeated by the small human woman's weapon."

Arash swallowed and grabbed the oilcloth, using that to snatch up the book. "I warned him. I told him. It wasn't me. It's not my weapon. It's *public property*."

Inside, she was thinking, Architects and Archons, I've killed a man.

"I can pretty solidly confirm that your book did him in," Twitch asserted.

One of the giants at the back spoke up. "You were his second, Brunhilda."

The woman with the crimson hair shook her head. "The chief called for a champion's ring."

"Oh, stuff it," the same giant at the back said. "I didn't hear him say any such thing."

Twitch helpfully played back a sound recording in the voice of the dead giant: "Let's say this is a champion's ring, then. It's official. Stop me if you can, vermin."

Arash shuddered and stuffed *The Hemlock Book of Hemlock Paper* in the back of her wagon where it hopefully wouldn't get anything else wet. Should she stay until a district watchman arrived? Call for help?

She'd come to return books. To get money. To buy more books. To make Marya more solid in this world. Return the books. That's what she needed to do. Arash yanked on the handle, but of course the wagon was still stuck in the cobbles.

The spiky-legged man exhaled. "Well. I think that settles it."

He unhooked Goldenbeard's amulet. It was a massive thing, bigger than her fist, glowing orange-red from a chunk of æmber inside it. He strode right up to Arash and dumped the heavy thing around her neck.

It felt like he'd just marked her for death. Six giants, two humans, a goblin, and a robot. They could snap her neck faster than she could turn to run.

And she couldn't run, anyway. She couldn't abandon the books.

The giantess, Brunhilda, bowed to her. "Well, you're tiny. And not very fierce. But we Brobnar have nothing if not our ethics."

"Aye," one of the others echoed. And then all of them – even the robot – bowed to her.

The blood drained from Arash's face. "What… what are you going to do to me?"

"You defeated our chief in single combat in a champion's ring," Brunhilda said. "We're going to follow you now, that's what we're going to do, isn't it?"

The rest of the band let out a roar of approval that shook the sidewalk, knocked *The Hemlock Book of Hemlock Paper* back out of the wagon, and shattered the nearest glass window.

At least the roaring finally brought a district watchman. With Twitch's recording of the whole event, Goldenbeard's death was declared an accident of public drunkenness, and Arash was free to go.

Except, she was not exactly free. An entourage followed

her. Brunhilda gustily sung some ballad about battles fought in champion's rings, swinging her arms as she went, snapping a few branches off trees and startling more than one flock of feathered squirrels. Lamp posts bent as they passed, and cobbles cracked.

When the man with the spike-leg set off an alarm that sent a swarm of hornet-drones chasing them until they crossed into Hubcentral, Arash was done. She yanked the absurdly large pendant off. "Here. Take this back. And leave me alone."

All of the Brobnar shuffled back a step. One of them bumped into the nearest steel and glass building – the norm for Hubcentral – and was repelled back onto the street by a force field of some kind, toppling over two of his fellows.

Arash silently sighed. She stepped toward Brunhilda. "You were second-in-command, right? It's yours."

"That's not how it works, little one. We have our ethics, see. You have to wait at least a month."

"And then you'll take it?" Arash couldn't imagine a *month* with these walking disasters following her around. She didn't have time for this nonsense.

Brunhilda shook her head, long red hair swaying. "No. After a month, you can declare another champion's ring and fight one of us. Wouldn't be very sporting if you had to do two back-to-back, see?"

Arash stared up, rain streaming down her face. "I have to *die* to give up being your chief?"

"Well, no. champion's rings aren't always to the death. You might just get roughed up a bit. If you lose. Which you won't. Because you're the fiercest of the fierce! The bane of Goldenbeard!"

Arash rubbed her forehead. Even against the goblin, the smallest member of this group, she'd be lucky to leave a fight with all her limbs intact. She was a *librarian*, for goodness sake, and not one of those librarians that masqueraded at night as a vigilante of justice.

Brunhilda gave her a broad smile. Given the size of her face, all her smiles were probably broad. "You're already a dire fighter. You'll get used to the leadership part soon enough." The giantess picked the wagon up under one arm and bowed. "I'll take care of this. You just worry about leading the way, chief."

Arash managed to convince most of the Brobnar to stay outside while she returned the books, but they insisted on sending at least Tek with her as an honor guard. The goblin was dressed just as flamboyantly as the others, with crimson nose rings and earrings, a mess of wire-wrapped hair, and clothing that seemed more studs than cloth. But at least he was smaller than the giants.

Behind the front desk stood Mr Dantant, the head librarian himself. Arash silently swore while she plastered a smile on her face. Mr Dantant had more metal on him than Tek – most of it cybernetic – but it was all of the blue, stainless steel variety that gleamed with condescension.

"I was just about to close. Do you have returns in that shabby cart of yours, or another greasy little goblin?"

It was hard to keep smiling at him. "If you're about to close, we should get these checked back into the system right away, don't you think?"

Mr Dantant snorted and used his telescoping arms to toss

the tarp aside and gather up the books from where he stood. He stopped when he reached *The Hemlock Book of Hemlock Paper*.

"Ruined. Absolutely ruined." His hand split into two halves up to the elbow. He used those, not his biological hand, to flip through the pages. "Rain damage. Fresh. This was your fault. Your negligence."

"It's only a little wet. Surely a short stay in the nanobot restoration chamber–"

Mr Dantant waved her words away with his free hand. "Nonsense. This isn't ordinary paper. The nanobots aren't programmed to repair something like this. You'll have to be fined for its replacement."

His pulled up a holographic data screen and scrolled through it with a lazy flick of his steely fingers. "Ah. This volume appears to be out of print now, and quite rare. Replacing it will cost three thousand æmbits."

Three thousand? Arash gaped. For that much, she could buy a flying suit of armor. She didn't have that kind of money. "Mr Dantant. That book was damaged not due to negligence but the unavoidable hazards of transportation. The city budget for the library ought to cover this."

"Very well. If you cannot pay the fine, I will repossess books from your library to sell until the price is met. I will not have the grandeur of the Central Branch's collection damaged by some satellite establishment in *New Archton*, of all places."

What a pompous twit. Arash argued in circles with him for the next ten minutes solid with Tek standing next to her, arms crossed, trying to look menacing. An annoyed Mr

Dantant eventually got a city official on the holoscreen to corroborate that as far as running the Interdistrict Hub City Library System went, they were happy to leave everything in Mr Dantant's capable hands.

She trudged outside, pulling her decrepit cart behind her. It had stopped raining and was merely foggy now, making all the streetlights cutting through the evening darkness seem gray and cheerless.

"Your chief destroyed one of my books. I'm holding all of you responsible." It was a brash thing to say. But what would be left of Marya if Mr Dantant emptied half of their library to pay for that stupid hemlock book? "You owe me three thousand æmbits."

Spike-leg stepped forward. "See, well, *we're* not his heirs, now, are we? You are. So you inherit his debts."

Arash pinched the bridge of her nose, trying to ward off a headache. "Fine. Where are his assets?"

"Well, he broke his double-barreled axe-bow during our last run. We take jobs guarding merchant caravans, you see? But we didn't get paid much for our last gig – some damages we owed to repair one of the merchant's antigrav carts, that's a long story involving some golf balls, anyway – and then we came into town to drink away our sorrows at the loss of his axe–"

"He died broke? You're telling me Goldenbeard died broke."

"Aye! As mightily broke as anyone's ever been!"

They all beamed at each other like it was some kind of feat to be out of æmbits.

It wasn't, of course. It was all too easy to have nothing left.

"All of you. Leave."

Brunhilda spoke this time. "You're our chief. We can't–"

"Well, your chief is telling you to go away!"

They all blinked at her, like they didn't think she was capable of yelling. Arash stomped down the steps and stormed away down the sidewalk.

No footsteps immediately followed. But Brobnar never were the sneakiest of creatures. Every time she glanced behind her, she saw one of the giants standing behind a tree or lamppost, like those were actually good hiding spots. They chattered "softly" among themselves about who was to blame for the chief's bad mood.

By the time Arash reached her own library, she was done with the lot of them. She took off her amulet and threw it down the stairs. "Whoever grabs that first can be the new chief. I'd better not see *any* of you tomorrow morning."

Arash let herself in and closed the door hard behind her. She slumped against the wood, head pounding. Did she have anything left to sell? Her wedding ring had gone first. Then what was left of her husband's laboratory equipment. The furniture. Her hyper-carbon dulcimer. She'd pawned about everything except some sensible clothes, Marya's old toys, and one self-heating cast iron frying pan.

Pawning a few sentimental toys wouldn't cover a three thousand æmbit fine. But it would let them keep a few more books in the library.

"Mama?" Marya peered at her, ghostly white, from the shiplap roof. She floated across it, to the wall joint, and down the door. Her face turned to oak, almost the color it had been in real life. She leaned out, barely an inch. Barely there. "Did you get paid? For returning the books? Can we get the flower dictionary?"

"Of course, my chickadee. Everything's going to be fine. Let's put you to bed."

Arash had converted two of the offices into bedrooms after she sold the house and moved permanently into the library. Marya rippled up from the floor onto the coverlet, her face a cheery pink flannel. She didn't make much of an impression right now. The blanket looked like it merely hadn't been pulled straight, or had gone lumpy after too many washes.

Arash read her a story, sang her a song, and kissed her flannel cheek before heading into her own small, dark room. She crawled into bed, but she couldn't fall asleep.

How many times had she told her husband that his efforts to travel through subspace to other worlds was dangerous? He told her he would stop, for real this time, after Arash's favorite bookend got sucked into a void. But that had just been another lie. He'd moved his lab to the basement of the library.

Arash had been at the circulation desk when his experiment exploded straight through the roof. She'd seen him for just a moment, hovering in the air, half transparent as if he really were a ghost.

"Her body has blended into the library," he'd said. "She needs books to enjoy, or she'll fade into the walls entirely."

And with that, he'd dissipated into nothingness.

Arash had thought those words were the last, mad rambling of a disintegrating mind, until she found Marya sobbing bits of sand from her brick eyes. Marya had figured out he'd moved the lab and had brought him down a cup of tea. She hadn't meant to spill it into his interdimensional vortex. It was her fault, she'd said, that everything had gone wrong.

Arash hadn't been able to hug her, even though back then Marya had been a good half foot out of the wall. Of course it wasn't Marya's fault. Her father wasn't supposed to be doing those kinds of experiments in the first place.

It was Arash's fault for being fool enough to think he'd actually stop.

She needs books to enjoy, or she'll fade into the walls entirely. It was the first thing Arash thought every morning, before her eyes even opened. Immediately afterwards, she thought *A Sanctum city has fallen from the sky.* But then she woke up all the way and realized that the crashing, shrieking, and laughter that had woken her was not a falling city, or even a pit of demons rising to the surface of the world. She knew Brunhilda's singing voice too well by now.

Arash stepped out into the library.

Someone had turned the chandelier into a zipline, anchoring it between the ceiling and a structural beam on the first floor. Tek the goblin jumped off the second story balcony, screaming with delight as he careened into the pile of couch cushions below. The spike-legged man – whose name she'd gathered actually was Spike – stood at the ready on the balcony to crank the chandelier back up so he could have a go at it.

Two of the giants had rearranged the bookshelves into forts and were lobbing paper balls at each other – some of which were on fire.

"Stop that! You're destroying books!"

One of the giants – Grinkle, she thought she'd heard the other one call him – smiled at her. "Don't worry! We're only ripping pages out of books that the little miss said were boring. We're livening them up!"

Grinkle crunched another page out of something that looked like it might be *A Child's Guide to Obedient Living*, dipped it into a reeking bucket, and used it to catch an incoming wad of flaming paper. It burst to life brilliantly just as Grinkle threw it back. "See, the key is not to hold it too long, or you'll lose a finger, you will."

"Where's my daughter?"

Grinkle blinked at her.

"The little girl!"

"Oh. I don't know." The next wad hit him in the head, catching his hair on fire. He swatted it out loudly. "Not fair, Red! I was talking to the chief!"

"Marya!" Arash called, but she could hardly hear herself over all the commotion. Brunhilda wasn't just singing – she seemed to be conducting a rock opera commemorating Arash's defeat of Goldenbeard. Someone had nailed three books, spine down, to an enormous club so the paper flapped wildly every time it was swung.

"You've got to swing The Papercutter with more *feeling*!" Brunhilda coached the other Brobnar, a human woman with tattoos all over her face. Brunhilda glanced at Arash. "Hey, chief! Good morning! We let ourselves in. Well, Twitch let us in. He's handy at things like that."

How could anyone treat *books* this way? "You'll have to pay me for those. You've ruined them."

"Nah, the little miss said they weren't any good for reading. Unyielding and unforgiving and enough to make a person go mad, the tax codes are, she said. Seemed the perfect stuff to make a weapon out of. Also, you're our chief, so I'm pretty sure, ethically, you're responsible for anything we break. But this isn't broken. It's *improved.*"

"Where's my daughter?"

Brunhilda frowned and glanced about. "Hmm. I saw her with them, last."

She waved at the quietest group in the room – a pair of giants huddled around a book, guffawing at it.

Arash still saw no signs of Marya. She doubted the Brobnar could hurt Marya physically, but if they destroyed enough books, she could vanish. Arash ran to the small group.

"Marya?" she called uselessly.

"Hey, chief! Did you know that there are books with scandalous pictures?" one of the giants asked.

She didn't think there *were* any books like that in her library. She grabbed the back of the cover and yanked it down. It was a board book with an elf in a tweed jacket. "That's scandalous?"

"Ach, have you no sense of *style?* He's wearing tweed, chief, tweed! And he's not even wearing it *sarcastically.*"

Her head was pounding. "Have you seen the little girl in the library?"

The giantess responded. "Twitch couldn't find the kind of picture book he wanted. Y'know, the really exciting kind. He offered to download some for her. They're in the stacks over there."

Arash spun and ran down the nonfiction section. There sat

Twitch, holding a screen in his hand. "And this is a poleaxe." He swiped, turning the page. "And this is–"

There was Marya, her face looking like the spines of five different books. "A halberd!"

"So close. It's a glaive. This one was wielded by Ygg the Punctual at the second Battle of Mygnhal."

Marya turned and grinned at her. "Mama! I found another kind of exciting dictionary!"

Her daughter hadn't disappeared. Maybe it was just the lighting, but she seemed to be able to lean out an inch or two further than she had last night. Everything was fine. Arash exhaled, suddenly feeling weak and shaky. She managed a smile. "I'm… I'm glad, sweetheart."

"Can I have an antimatter claymore?"

"No."

"What about a jet-propelled bastard sword?"

"No."

Marya frowned. "When we get further along in this dictionary, I'm going to have more questions for you."

"No weapons." Arash combed her fingers through her hair. Breakfast. She needed something to eat and a cup of tea before she could even think about the damage to the library. It would take all day to fix what had already been done.

She wrote a note that the library was unexpectedly closed today for a conference and tacked it to the front door. Then Arash picked her way around the rock opera rehearsals, dodged the zipline, and skirted the flaming tax war and ducked into her small room.

It was not quiet inside. But it was quieter.

The door opened. Brunhilda crouched outside. "Hey,

chief. I kept this safe for you." She tossed that accursed amulet on the bed. "I know you were just testing our loyalty and all. You're crafty like that. But I promise, we'll stick by you."

"Why?" Arash demanded.

"You're our chief." Brunhilda said it like it was the plainest thing in the world.

"And what about Goldenbeard? According to you, I *killed* him. Weren't you loyal to him, too?"

Brunhilda gave her another one of those broad smiles. "He was like a father to me."

"You should be his successor."

She shook her head. "Dying in grand combat… it's the honorable way to go with our people. Revering you as a grand warrior, that's how we honor Chief Goldenbeard. You were that fierce, that clever, that brave. Don't you see? It would be an insult to him if you were just a spineless librarian. We need you to be more than that."

Then Brunhilda closed the door again.

Arash kept the library closed to the public all day and tried to put it back in order, but the moment she'd gotten the chandelier properly attached again, one of the giants snapped the banister trying to slide down it. Then, as soon as she got the bookshelves back in place, her unwanted guests all decided to play hide and seek, knocking over lamps, desks and most of the biography section.

At least Marya was laughing at their antics, rapidly rippling up and down the walls to keep up with what all the Brobnar were doing. By nightfall, the library was sort of, almost, presentable again.

When Arash tucked her daughter into bed, she was more present – the bed looked like maybe someone had left a few rolled-up towels under the covers. "I like them, Mama."

"Who?"

"Mama! The Brobnar! Who else would I be talking about?"

Arash sighed. "They're destroying the library."

And, in turn, they were destroying Marya.

"Well, maybe a little bit. But I like them, Mama. Especially Twitch."

"Because he showed you all those pictures of weapons?" Arash asked, stroking her flannel-pink hair.

Marya smiled. "I did like that. But didn't you see them all, Mama? Brunhilda is *huge*. And Tek the goblin is small and squishy-shaped. Spike's got one leg. And Twitch is made out of metal."

"They do make a motley crew, chickadee."

"It's nice having them around. Some people are big. Some are small. Some are made of metal. And some people are stuck in walls. It's all okay, though. We're all just people."

Arash swallowed, throat suddenly tight. "Yes, we are. You like having them around that much?"

"Of course I do, Mama."

That night, sore muscles protesting, Arash climbed into her bed. She hadn't heard Marya laugh like that in ages. Might it actually be worthwhile to keep the Brobnar around? Part of her couldn't believe she was even thinking about it.

The other part of her had no idea how to get rid of them.

Arash climbed back out of bed and headed downstairs. Twitch and Brunhilda were playing Nine Men's Morris, and the rest of them looked like they were about to fall asleep on the floor, on top of the stacks, on couches, or wherever they might be.

"All of you, out on the lawn," Arash ordered. "We're having a meeting."

Oddly enough, no one argued with her imperious tone. They almost seemed happy about it. The grass was cold underfoot, the streetlights a sickly yellow against the black of night.

"My daughter's soul is caught up in the library. Having those shelves full of books keeps her alive and present. There will be no more destruction – not even of tax codes."

Every last one of them managed to look solemn at that.

"Brunhilda. Tomorrow, you will take everyone but Twitch, Tek, and Grinkle out to look for odd work in the city. If we can't earn back the fine I owe for that book Goldenbeard destroyed, Mr Dantant is going to exact the price in books. Which, as I mentioned, will hurt Marya.

"Twitch, you seem very sharp. I want you to spend tomorrow looking at Hub City law codes and any loopholes we might use to get out of this fine. Tek and Grinkle, the library's in rough shape and we need to put it back together and keep it running. Any questions?"

"Good plan, chief!" Spike called out. "We won't let you down!"

"Well, *I* won't," Tek replied, and then they were off bickering about who'd do their work best tomorrow.

Hoping that this whole idea wasn't a horrible mistake, Arash headed back up to sleep.

• • •

The next three days went surprisingly well. Tek built a book catapult to help patrons quickly get the volumes they were looking for. Grinkle scared the hiccups right out of an off-duty Star Alliance anthropologist just by shushing him. And Arash got a number of comments from her hard-of-hearing regulars that they were glad she'd finally gotten some staff who could speak up properly. Even Mrs Erinad from two districts over, who usually had her feathers puffed in disdain, left with a friendly smile. And that dear boy Lelag, who lived in the very wet Gnarhome district, danced on all eight of his tentacles when he found that the waterproof books had all been piled into one spot. Twitch had wanted to try building a raft out of them.

But the best part was Marya, laughing. Marya, singing bits of Brunhilda's ridiculous rock opera. Marya, leaning out so far from the walls she could actually swing The Papercutter around in an overly dramatic fashion. She even did a drawing of the thing and captioned it herself, so Twitch could add it to his book of weapons.

Brunhilda came back every day with at least enough to feed all of them, even if the æmbits they earned weren't sufficient to make much of a dent in the fine Arash owed. Everyone sat around the lobby eating sourdough rolls drizzled with synthetic honey butter.

Mr Dantant had sent a message. He was coming tomorrow morning. Twitch had only been able to confirm what the city official had said: Mr Dantant had the right to fine their branch in the form of books.

Arash licked honey butter off her fingers. She and Twitch had spent hours looking for a cheaper replacement for *The*

Hemlock Book of Hemlock Paper. They'd even contacted both the author and the publisher, hoping to find a copy for a more reasonable price. But that had failed too.

She didn't want tomorrow to come. She wanted to eat sourdough and listen to Brunhilda's absurd rock opera and watch Marya, nearly popping out of the wall, designing a new catapult with Twitch and Tek.

"Worried about tomorrow, aren't you, chief?" Brunhilda asked, plopping down next to her and making the stacks wobble.

"More than a bit, I'm afraid."

"You're worried it'll hurt Marya. That librarian man coming to take away your books."

Arash nodded, her husband's words echoing in her ears. *She needs books to enjoy, or she'll fade into the walls entirely.*

How many books in this library was too few? Two thousand? Two hundred? Two dozen? Arash didn't want to know the answer. She wanted to fill this place so full to bursting with books that she never had to worry about Marya fading away again.

"Some problems are trickier than one brain can handle. That's why you've got a second-in-command. It's especially hard to think straight when it comes to matters of the heart."

Arash shook her head. "He'll be here tomorrow. There's no time to come up with another plan."

"Of course there isn't. But I've already got another plan," Brunhilda whispered conspiratorially, tapping the side of her head. "You leave everything to me, chief."

• • •

Mr Dantant showed up promptly at opening time the next morning, his stainless steel and red tie gleaming in the sunlight streaming in the windows. He'd brought two large hoverbins with him and a dozen assistants. "Well, well. I assume you haven't got the fine money ready?"

Arash clenched her fist around the few extra æmbits from the Brobnar's odd jobs. She glanced at Brunhilda.

The giantess stepped forward, arms crossed over her broad chest, and bent down to stare fiercely at Mr Dantant. "We've got a different deal for you, annoying central librarian man."

He stared at her like she was nothing more formidable than dust on a shelf. "This isn't a *deal*, and you don't get to change it."

Arash's throat tightened. This was it. Brunhilda had been a hired caravan guard for Architects-only-knew how long. She was going to cleverly save the library now with some brilliant negotiating tactic.

"Yeah. Libraries, they can be dangerous places. I'm thinking you should pay *us* to make sure that you and your lackies here don't get *hurt*."

Brunhilda pulled The Papercutter off her back and meaningfully gripped the handle.

Arash's gut fell to the bottom of her feet as she stared in horror. This was Brunhilda's master plan? "Brunhilda–" Arash began, but Mr Dantant cut her off.

"You're trying to threaten me? Extort city finances for your gain? I won't be moved by such ridiculous tactics."

"Well!" Brunhilda roared. "Maybe you'll be moved by this!"

Brunhilda pulled back to swing. Mr Dantant's eyes – both

the fleshy one and the cybernetic – went wide in shock.

If Brunhilda landed that blow, either Arash's branch would be fined for the medical bills, or she'd lose her post entirely and never get to see Marya again.

Arash dove, shouldering Mr Dantant out of the way.

She heard the crack of wood and the tearing of book spines before she felt it, a mass of pain across her shoulder radiating into her gut and making her want to throw up.

Then everything went black.

When she woke again, Arash was laying in her bed. Twitch was next to her. He retracted his stretched-out filaments back into his fingers. "I'm a fully certified doctor, I swear. It's what I do for this clan. You've been roughed up, but I've mended all the breaks and you shouldn't be concussed any more."

Arash ached all over, but she felt far better than she ought to. Whatever Twitch had done, he'd done it well.

Spike and Brunhilda were also present. Someone had laid The Papercutter, the covers to its tax codes all torn, next to her bed.

Brunhilda swallowed hard, head bowed. "This is my fault. I tried to make you something you weren't. And you got walloped because of it."

Spike patted Brunhilda's hand. "She knows you weren't trying to hurt her."

"But I still did. I hurt her. I didn't want to admit Goldenbeard died in an *accident,* and now I've made things worse." Brunhilda rubbed the back of her neck. "I'm sorry. Mighty sorry. This is my fault. This clan, well, we just don't belong in a library, now do we?"

Arash's throat felt like sandpaper. "What happened?"

Brunhilda and Twitch looked too ashamed to speak. Spike sighed. "Mr Dantant took a lot of books."

"How many?" Arash asked, painfully aware that her daughter was *not* in the room.

"About half."

Arash lurched to her feet. Twitch tried to stop her. "You need to rest! You really shouldn't be out of bed!"

Brunhilda shook her head, and gestured Twitch away. They peeled back and let her pass.

Hand on the doorframe for support, Arash hobbled into the library proper. "Marya!" The skeletons of empty shelves met her. "Marya!"

"Mama!"

Was she only a voice now? Still, Arash collapsed to her knees in relief. Somehow they'd find more books. Somehow. Someday.

Marya came running to her. Across the floor. Her feet and lower legs were still stuck in the library and she still turned the color and texture of low-ply rugs and oaken flooring – but she stood out three and a half feet. Marya crashed into her, and for the first time since the accident, Arash could put her arms all the way around her daughter.

"You're… you're still here," Arash exhaled.

"Don't be silly, Mama. You're the one we've all been worried about."

It was impossible for her to be this far out of the walls. Half the library had disappeared into Mr Dantant's hoverbins. "What were you doing? While I was lying in bed?"

"Oh! Tek has some really nice oil pastels. He was trying to

help me not be worried, so we sewed some papers together and I started drawing a book about a unicorn made of amethysts traveling to the Everfire Volcano! I used lots of red and purple."

With uncanny quiet, the Brobnar followed Brunhilda toward the front door.

She needs books to enjoy. Arash always thought that simply meant she needed an abundance of books. But Marya had improved as soon as Twitch showed her that weapons dictionary, hadn't she? And now, drawing her own book with Tek, she was better than she'd ever been.

Quantity of books, apparently, mattered less than the enjoyment. And over the past few days, there had been plenty of people for Marya to enjoy books *with*.

Brunhilda opened the door to leave.

"Do you think I'd let you off that easy?" Arash called in her fiercest voice.

Six giants, two humans, a robot, and a goblin stopped and stared at her, puzzled.

Using the wall for support, Arash made it back to her feet. "I didn't declare any champion's ring. I wasn't armed with my faithful Papercutter. Don't think I can't see what's happening here."

Brunhilda frowned. "What do you think's happening here?"

"You're all scared of me, of course! I'm too terrifying a chief, so you're sneaking off and trying to find someone less intimidating. I won't let you. You're my clan now, and if you don't like it, you'll have to challenge me to a champion's ring like any Brobnar with ethics when I get better."

Arash had always thought Brunhilda gave broad smiles, but she'd never seen one like this.

Brunhilda closed the door. And the Brobnar stayed.

True, Arash would have preferred to recover in peace and quiet. She did not authorize the bonfire of tax books, even though Marya assured her that she enjoyed watching Grinkle cook a whole cod snake over them. Arash didn't like it when Red and Tek made a maze out of the stacks. She didn't approve of the Brobnar using socks as bookmarks or trying to see who could make the tallest castle out of dictionaries.

But soon, it was hard to imagine her library any other way. There ought to be at least one library in Hub City, after all, that was welcoming to Brobnar and adventuresome children alike.

TO CATCH A THIEF
Thomas Parrott

If there was one thing Nalea Wysasandoral loved, it was luxury.

The purple-skinned elf ran her hand along the silken curtains as she made her way into the room. It brought a smile to her face. They were so smooth to the touch. The room was mostly dark. The only light was what leaked in through the window. That didn't bother her. She'd lived most of her life in shadowy places.

Furniture was just fuzzy shapes in the gloom. She ran her fingertips along the side of the bed as she passed it. Satin sheets. She stifled a yawn. It had been a long night already, but this was no time for sleep. There was still work to do. On into the heart of the chambers, there was a table. A golden goblet had been left out on it, and it went into her pouch. Fresh fruit was piled in a bowl in the middle, replaced daily.

Nalea sorted through them curiously. She hadn't even seen some of these before. She was pretty sure one of them was a bluestar that grew only in saurian lands. She scooped that one up and peeled it with nimble fingers, taking a bite. It was sour beyond reckoning, and she carefully set it back down with her mouth screwed tightly. An acquired taste, to put it lightly.

A number of portraits and tapestries hung from the walls. They were hard to make out in the dark, but she had seen enough in other manses to imagine. Stern forebears glaring down at their wastrel descendants. Or perhaps a landscape. The wealthy sometimes had things that had come from other worlds entirely. She remembered hearing about a picture that had gone for hundreds of thousands of æmbits. It had shown a soup can, as she recalled.

To think they called *her* a criminal.

Nalea strolled along them, her hand held over them as if feeling the heat from a fireplace. She had a certain talent that helped her to be the best at her job. A nose for value. A sixth sense, as it were. She didn't even bother to look, just closed her eyes and focused on the feeling. Four of them she walked right past, then she paused.

This was the one.

The elf opened her eyes and tapped her palm, triggering the illuminator built into her fingerless glove. Dull red light shone forth. It didn't allow much in the way of color, but she got the impression of what the painting showed. A meeting place between sectors, lava spilling over a cliff side into an icy lake. Steam arose in a great cloud, in which the vague impression of figures could be seen. Enigmas, caught between hostile extremes.

Nalea rather liked it, truth be told. With great care she lifted the portrait off the wall. It took a little maneuvering to work the corner into her belt pouch, then it all slid away. An onlooker would have found the process startling and inexplicable. Unless, of course, they were familiar with how dimensional satchels worked. She made it a point to never leave home without one.

As much as she appreciated the keepsake, however, what she was after actually lay behind it. Now that the picture was out of the way, she could see the safe. A dial was set in the center. She placed the fingers of one hand against the metal of the door and used the other hand to spin the lock slowly. She had carefully trained her sense of touch, one reason why her gloves were fingerless. One click. Two. Then the third, and the door swung open with the slightest of creaks. She froze for a moment, but the sound elicited no reaction. Relaxing, she began to rummage through the contents.

There were a number of things inside. Papers she cared nothing for, nor the data-cubes. Jewelry was appreciated and went into the pouch. At the back, however, was what had drawn her to this place from the start. A crystal no bigger than her fist. It glowed with a light of its own, as if a tiny spark of sunlight were trapped inside. The light reflected from her own golden eyes and revealed the smile of delight on her face.

Raw æmber, the most precious and useful substance in all of the Crucible. It lay behind any number of miracles and marvels. Sorcerers and scientists swore by it alike. People had killed for it. Not Nalea, though. Violence was so ugly and crass. She hated the very sight of blood. No, why go through all that sweat and mess of fighting when you could just stroll in and take what you wanted?

Once it was tucked away in her pouch, she tapped her palm again to turn the light back off. She took in the chambers again with a last wistful sigh then headed back for the window. Luxury. She was forever touching it but never quite able to truly *luxuriate* in it. It didn't seem quite fair.

Nalea was halfway to the window when the person on the bed finally coughed and began to stir. She sped up her catlike tread only slightly, a grin spreading across her face.

"Who's that? What's going on here?" called the man's alarmed voice.

The elf pulled her mask up over her mouth and nose and leapt up into the window right as he turned the chamber lights on. A human, with salt and pepper hair and distinguished features. He was staring at her with wide eyes as she crouched in the opening, his mouth working silently. The open window let in a chilly drizzle, cold wind billowing the curtains.

"Thank you kindly for your hospitality, High Councilor." She tugged her hood deferentially. "I'll leave before I overstay my welcome."

The councilor finally found his voice. "Guards! Guards!"

With a chuckle, Nalea slid out of the window and scrambled down the rain-slick wall with no more difficulty than a spider. By the time she reached the ground, lights were coming on throughout the house and shouts had begun echoing. By the time they actually came searching, however, she would be long gone into another district altogether. The smile stayed on her face the whole way.

Inspector Virdon held the shimmering device over the table. The fingerprints on the wood stood out sharply under the silvery glow. The human took his hat off and swept a hand along his crew cut with a frustrated sigh before placing it back on his head. Normally he would have had to capture images of the prints and send them for processing. Not these. He had seen them so many times lately that he literally knew them by sight.

One of the patrol enforcers, "hubbers" as they were known, that were bustling about stopped to give a sympathetic burble. They were an aquan, living in a pressure suit that kept them suspended in water.

"The Slip again?" they asked.

Virdon gritted his teeth. That damnable name. You couldn't pass a paperboy or turn on the radio lately without hearing it. "The elf thief," he emphasized, "is indeed the culprit again. Which is fine because sooner or later she's going to make a mistake, and then we are going to catch her."

"Sooner or later, Inspector?" The refined voice was sharp and came from behind him.

Virdon did his best to hide a cringe. The aquan hubber quickly found a reason to be elsewhere. Taking a deep breath, the human turned to face the speaker. High Councilor Learmont stood there with his arms crossed and his expression dark. They stood in his apartments, though the inspector had thought he was still being interviewed by other officers.

"I beg your pardon–" Virdon started to apologize.

Learmont cut the lanky inspector off. "I had rather hoped you might see to making it a priority to catch this thief *now*. Perhaps you have more pressing matters to attend to, than one of the members of the High Council being menaced within his own home?"

"We can be reasonably confident that you were in no danger, councilor. The thief has never engaged in any violence." A glance at the councilor's face told him it had been the wrong thing to say, and Virdon cursed himself internally.

"I can only assume you don't grasp the value of what was taken. Maybe if we took it out of your pay, it would sink in on a deeper level."

The value of what had been taken was the better part of a year's pay for Virdon. "I assure you, councilor, that is not necessary. Catching this thief is my absolute highest priority. I will see her in chains. I swear."

Learmont narrowed his eyes. "Forgive me if I find your assurances empty. This hoodlum has plagued our fair city for months now, and you seem to be no closer to catching her than when you started. This final outrage – this assault upon my own person! – is too much. It's past time we brought in outside help."

Virdon stifled a frown. "I have patrolled this city for a decade now, councilor. No bounty hunter from the world beyond will know its streets better than me. I beg you to reconsider."

The councilor snorted. "They may not know the streets as well, but they assuredly know how to catch thieves better than you. The matter is decided, the first payment already made." Learmont turned. "Inspector, allow me to introduce you to Talus."

The inspector stiffened at the name. The sight awaiting him beyond the councilor only confirmed it. A sylicate stood there. They were shaped, seemingly, from pure obsidian.

Deep within their core a white light shone, distorted by the translucent layers between. It eked out pure from the eyes and mouth on the creature's head. It was small and slender. They wore no garb save a top hat, which they doffed in greeting with a long-fingered hand. The other was wrapped around the handle of a simple but well-made cane.

Talus the Thief-Taker, undoubtedly one of the most famous hired detectives in all the known reaches of the Crucible. Their name was spoken in the same breath as such investigative experts as the duo Wibble and Pplimz. It was said they had ended the predations of the Leaping Bandit in Spiretown, and most recently tracked down the Portal Pilferer in Quantum City. The sylicate was truly a luminary of investigative work, said to have pioneered whole new advances in the field. Virdon was irritated to realize he was a bit in awe.

He was further annoyed with himself when he realized the detective was waiting for him to speak. "Nice to meet you, Master Talus. I am Inspector Jaym Virdon, in charge of the hunt for–"

"Formerly in charge," interjected Learmont. "I place him at your disposal. He'll serve as your liaison with the city's resources." The councilor turned cold eyes on Virdon. "I assure you, he will cooperate fully and make himself very useful."

The inspector cleared his throat uneasily. "Inspector Jaym Virdon, at your service."

"I am sure he will be a welcome aide in the hunt for this miscreant." The sylicate's voice was surprisingly high and reedy, not at all what Virdon had been expecting. They turned their glowing eyes about the room slowly. "She is an interesting quarry."

"You have observations about her?" Virdon couldn't conceal his surprise.

"To be certain. She has made her mark quite indelibly. In what she took, in what she *didn't* take. In choosing to plunder this place at all, in a city with such a variety of choices available to her." The detective motioned around with their cane. "Yes, a picture of her begins to form."

The inspector blinked. "Perhaps you could share some of your insights, then?"

"The painting – taken, not just removed. The goblet, missing. The jewelry. She longs for the finer things. She is displeased with her status in life. To come after a councilor, this is a statement, you see? But she is no anarchist agitator. Not enough destruction or vandalism. No, her actions stem not from resentment but from *envy*. She would not tear down the current order. She simply longs to be at the top of it."

Virdon scratched his jaw thoughtfully. "Even supposing that's all true, what good does it do you? She probably retreats to the Lawless Zone after each job, and we don't have the reach there to find her."

Talus chuckled and turned their glowing eyes on the inspector. "That is exactly why understanding her will be the key, my good sir. We are faced with the conundrum of a clever quarry that we cannot go after. The trick will be getting her to come to us."

Nalea awoke to the patter of rain drops on the glass ceiling above her. She was warm and cozy and for the moment extracting herself did not appeal. Her bed was actually a collection of lounges pushed together and covered with as many blankets and pillows as she could haul home. Getting all of it to the top floor of her abode had been a trick, but it was well worth it to have the sky above.

She held up a hand to the light above, the natural gray stained a dozen colors against her skin by the roof. A sigh and a stretch heralded the time to rise. Further procrastination was counterproductive. It would be evening soon, time to get to work. She burrowed out of her blankets and hopped down to the floor. It was cold beneath her bare feet, forcing her to do an odd dance on her way over to the rope. She scrambled down it to the next room, dedicated to clothes and gear.

Her home was a hole in the wall. That wasn't a joke or a metaphor: she had moved into the gap in the walls of a truly tremendous cathedral in the Lawless Zone. It was long abandoned, but it must have been built by giants considering the sheer scale involved. It made for a very vertical living space, even so. Each makeshift "room" might have been three hundred square feet, with about seven of them stacked. They were connected by ropes, ramps, and ladders.

Nalea pulled on the leathers that were her usual clothes, and threw a gray cloak with an incorporated hood and mask around her shoulders. Tools went on her belt and were hidden in pockets in her sleeves: lockpicks, a file, pliers, and a few other things beside. She added a ring of invisibility reluctantly; they were undeniably useful, but also unreliably usable. One never knew when the charge was going to give out. She hefted a knife with an even more reluctant grimace, but tucked it into the back of her belt under her cloak.

Violence might be grotesque, but the Lawless Zone was no place to be unprotected.

She hurried on down through her home from there, passing through the rest of the rooms with scarcely a glance. She had set herself up relatively nice areas for cooking and bathing. She even had a nominal area to meet guests, assuming she met someone someday who was trustworthy enough to invite to this place. Most of it, however, was given over to storage. Artifacts and items from dozens of trips into the city littered those chambers haphazardly. The portrait from last night was among them.

At last, she emerged into the city streets, raising her hood against the sprinkling rain. The Lawless Zone was just as multicultural, in its own way, as Hubcentral itself. Plantoid phylls rubbed elbows with clattering robots and everything in between. Anyone who didn't particularly care to live under the constraints of the city's law found their way here. No one knew why the ancient High Council had declared this place an anarchic pocket, but no one hesitated to take advantage of it either.

Least of all Shadows, the network of illicit guilds that had its fingers in criminal activity all across the Crucible. Nalea had never been much of a bower and scraper, but being a Svarr elf meant practically being born into the organization. Luckily, the guilds didn't feel much of a need to intrude into the daily lives of their members. That is, as long as you paid your cut of each take and didn't bring too much heat down on their heads.

It did come with its benefits, of course. Belonging to a guild meant people to watch your back, people to give you information, people you could rely on. To a degree. In Nalea's opinion, nobody in Shadows was about to put their neck on the line for anyone else. As long as you weren't likely to get them killed, however, they'd probably help you out in a pinch.

Such as, for example, when one had a batch of freshly stolen goods that they were trying to offload. She made her way along the street, nimbly weaving her way among the crowd. Most people didn't even give her a look. There was no shortage of elves in the Lawless Zone, and she had never been all that remarkable looking in the first place. A useful trait in her line of work.

Arriving at her destination, Nalea ducked within. It was a scarred set of wooden doors leading into a pawn shop. She pulled her hood back from her white hair as she looked around. Shelves lay all about, strewn with all the strange products of the cosmopolitan city. The clean lines of Logos tech, the rough pragmatism of klaxxron devices, and more besides. She moseyed up and down the aisles, casting her eye over what was on offer. Sometimes remarkable little treasures ended up here.

Someone cleared their throat pointedly. "I just want you to know I'm watching you, Nalea. Anything goes missing and it's going right on your tab."

The elf thief turned and flashed a winning smile, showing off her silver-capped canines to good effect. "I would never steal from you, Ruvyn. You're my favorite."

Ruvyn was sitting behind the counter of the store. He was an elf as well, though he had midnight skin that made his golden eyes stand out all the more. A newsholo was laid out in front of him, which he'd been reading until she came in. He was also significantly older than her, showing some lines on his cheeks and forehead.

"You don't have favorites, Nalea. Just people who are useful and people who aren't."

She sidled up to the counter and leaned against it. "Then it's a lucky thing that you're always so very useful to me, isn't it?"

He gave her a flat look and she laughed. Reaching into her pouch, Nalea produced half of the jewelry and the goblet. The fence just narrowed his eyes thoughtfully. When she pulled the chunk of raw æmber out, though, his eyebrows scaled his forehead.

Ruvyn got up quickly and went over to lock the shop door and shut the blinds. Then he hurried back to the counter to stare at the glowing crystal. "I knew you were the ambitious sort, Nalea, but by the Architects you have gotten bold. What did you do, rob a councilor?"

Her grin just widened.

The older elf stared at her. "You cannot be serious. They're going to throw you into a pit one of these days, girl, and count yourself lucky if they don't stretch your neck first."

Nalea shrugged insouciantly and started to gather the stuff back up. "If you don't want the goods, all you have to do is say so. I'm sure I can find another–"

Ruvyn caught her wrist to stop her and then released it with a sigh. "You know I'm going to take the business. I don't have the bits to hand for the raw, though."

She grinned at him again and put it all back down. "I'll take it in barts, then."

He mulled this over then nodded. "Barts it is. I'll take the guild's cut off the top, as usual." He slid her a pile of æmbits for the other goods, and went into the back to retrieve the barts. They were plastic disks, each threaded with hypercarbon in a unique pattern. Each represented a favor owed in the black markets of the underworld. They were also known for the peculiar trait of glowing when around ultraviolent emotional radiation.

Nalea swiped through the holo while she waited. The guild occasionally recruited for jobs, but most of the time she operated on her own. That meant keeping up with current events. She frowned a little to see that her escapade had been pushed to the third page, if only because they'd hidden whose house she broke into this time. The first page was dominated instead by talk of a huge auction that had been announced. One of the city's bigwigs had apparently passed with no heirs, and now all their fancy goods were going to be sold off to the good and worthy among the citizenry.

By the time Ruvyn got back the idea was already half-formed. Her fingers were drumming restlessly on the countertop, and he raised an eyebrow at her.

"That's the look that forebodes trouble for someone. Hopefully, not me."

Nalea chuckled at that and accepted the barts from him, tucking them away into a pouch. "Not you at all. I think I'll leave you to see to your business, though." She put her hood back up and headed for the door. "I have an auction to attend."

Hours later, Nalea made her way through the city. Night had fallen, but that didn't bring darkness to great swaths of the Hub. Even the Dark Districts themselves were often lit by the red light of forges all through the night, a burning glow under their sooty cloud. She passed into the Logos district, a gleaming wonderland of advanced technology. Holographic advertisements sprang to life around her as she passed, hawking wares in simulated voices.

Besides, she had only come to this district to reach a public transit station. Someone occasionally got the bright idea of trying to run a line into the Lawless Zone. It always ended the same: with the structure picked clean by scavengers. The tragedy of the commons played out with alarming speed.

The station lay ahead. Hub City never really slept. People were coming and going at all hours. Still, the traffic was down from the heights of the day. She could easily make her way to the gate into the station. There, a slot waited for an æmbit to allow her inside. The elf dutifully slotted one in… then tugged on the string looped through it the moment it chimed acceptance. It shot back out into her hand, and she slipped into the waiting area.

Nalea boarded the train that would take her to Hubcentral, the beating heart of the city. She wormed her way through those already on board to find a seat. The train chugged into motion, and she hopped up onto one of the seats to peer out the window. She loved the city, in her way. It was forever growing and changing. If you got bored in the Hub, you could walk a few blocks in any direction and the world would transform around you. Forest groves full of pixies coexisted beside unfathomable lakes and neon signs.

Soon the locomotive was pulling into the Central station. Hubcentral was marked by towering buildings and an overabundance of the city's great and powerful. Nalea was drawing looks the moment she stepped off the train, hardly an ideal situation for someone of her profession. Luckily, she didn't intend to walk the rest of the way at ground level.

Instead, she found her way into the nearest alleyway. Sure that no one was looking, she skittered up the side of the building with casual ease. The wallcrawling techniques were not isolated to Shadows, but they certainly saw plenty of use in their ranks. A mark might be alert for pickpockets on the street, and doormen kept a watch on the front of most buildings here. Nobody ever thought to look up, though.

The wind was brisk once she reached the top. It set her cloak to flapping and chilled her body. She tugged her mask up to keep warm if nothing else, and set out across the rooftops. Some of them were close enough that she could simply leap across to the next with a graceful bound. Others forced her to jump over, catch herself, and climb up to continue. At least one she had to actually climb down to a fire escape to jump over, the next building was so much lower.

One way or another, Nalea made steady progress. She was soon within eyeshot of the building she was after. She took a moment to step up to the edge of the roof and glance down. People in fine dress, the glamorous sorts, were all headed inside. They were being dropped off by hovercabs and expensive limousines. This was definitely the place.

There was about a ten-foot gap between this building and that one. The elf glanced around but there wasn't any easier approach than the direct one. With a deep sigh, she backed up and focused hard on that wall. It seemed uncomfortably distant in this moment, but she put that out of her head in a hurry.

She counted down in her head. *3… 2… 1…* She was off like a shot. Even now, her footfalls were barely audible slaps against the roof below. The edge came up swiftly. There was a slight rise. A step carried her up onto it, and she flung out into empty air. For an eternal moment she was over nothing but a fall of more than a hundred feet. She hit the far wall with a *smack* and started to slide down.

Nalea caught hold of a windowsill with a lightning grab, arresting the beginning of her tumble into oblivion. The impact had knocked some air out of her lungs, so she just let herself hang and wheeze for a moment while she recovered. Then she scrambled up to crouch on the lip of the sill. It was a precarious balance, but her gyroscopic belt helped her maintain it.

The next problem was actually getting inside. The room beyond the window was dark and seemed like a good place to start. It wouldn't open to mere pressure though, just rattled under her hands. Locked.

"How security-minded of them," Nalea mumbled to herself.

A gust of wind howled by, and she caught the sides of the window to steady herself until it passed. Then she fished her lockpicks out of their pouch and began exploring the seam. A minute or two of fidgeting later and a soft *click* announced her success. The window opened, and she slid inside, dropping to the floor without a sound. She quietly shut the window behind her and turned to survey where she'd ended up.

It appeared to be a conference room, to judge by the table that dominated the center and the chairs surrounding it. Nalea maneuvered around it all and made her way to the door. Light peeked through the surrounding gaps. She leaned lightly against the wood to listen and heard footsteps and chattering voices heading her way. With a deep breath, she waited for them to pass.

"...such short notice. They only told us yesterday. We've been cooking the food non-stop ever since."

"Well, you can't schedule a death."

"Sure, but what's the rush to do this right afterwards...?"

The voices trailed off into the distance. Nalea waited a moment longer, just to be certain nothing else would break the silence, then eased the door open and crept out. The hallway extended in both directions. To the left it went on to a T-intersection, while the other way led to bright lights and the murmur of conversation. Remaining cautious, the thief headed towards where all the people were.

She arrived at a railed walkway circling an open central area. Dozens of tables had been set up below, filling most of the chamber. The high and mighty sat, while the peons served. From this high they were all tiny figures. That gave her a small smirk. She turned her attention towards the front of the chamber where the auction would be held. A stage and a podium had been set up, but none of the items had been brought forward yet. That suited her perfectly. They must be keeping them in a back room.

Nalea followed the railing, staying low and near the wall to avoid any unfortunate glances from below. She could see a shadowed set of doors back behind where the stage was set up. That seemed a likely place to try for, but was there another way? As she came around to the far end of the railing, she could feel the æmber already. Even through the intervening walls, it was like warmth on her skin. Raw or processed, the energy came off it like the sun's rays.

The elf crept into the room at the far end of the level she was on. This one was someone's office, though it was empty given the hour. She swept around the room quickly, searching for anything that would let her head downstairs from here. There were vents, but unlike those in the serials they weren't big enough to get into. Not even for her, and she was relatively small.

There were doors and more hallways off her current level, and other levels besides. She could spend the whole night searching. It was just a matter of time until the auction started, however, and that could ruin the whole night. She was going to have to be a bit more aggressive to see this through.

She stepped up to the edge and looked down into the center area again. Below her was another railed walkway, and more beyond. One for each floor down. It couldn't be more than a five- or six-foot gap from the bottom of one to the top of the next. No problem at all, she reassured herself.

The trick, of course, would be avoiding sight while she did it. Reluctantly she retrieved her ring of invisibility and put it on. She twisted it to activate, and the æmber-infused properties sprang to life. In a way that some simply called magic and others called the very edges of science, it would bend light around her so that she couldn't be seen. In the process, it somehow also kept her from going blind.

The problem was how long it lasted, which was completely uncertain. The cloaking devices were an old favorite of Shadows agents, but in Nalea's experience they were best only used in extremity because of their limitations.

Nalea swung out over the railing. The fall would be no less lethal inside the building than from the outer wall if she messed this up. With a deep breath, she steadied herself and let go. Her stomach lurched as she dropped. She caught herself nimbly on the next railing, then dropped down to repeat.

She continued down, leap by leap. Her hands were sweating by the time she got to the bottom level, but the leather across her palms kept the grip steady. She was now ready for the drop to floor level. She let go and began to fall, only for someone to step out beneath her at the last second. With a stifled shriek she caught hold of one of the columns on the railing's balustrade.

The person below, a human male of middling height with a bald head, was dressed as one of the serving staff in simple black garb. Nalea had time to absorb all these details because she was dangling by one hand right above him, kicking in empty air just a matter of feet from his scalp. Her grip was awkward, bending her wrist painfully.

The server looked up and frowned. He must have heard her. There was nothing to see, however. He stared right through where she was. All she could do was hang there as the pain in her arm grew. She gritted her teeth and held on with all of her might.

At last, he turned and walked away. The moment he was beyond earshot, Nalea let herself fall the rest of the way to the ground. She landed heavily, her usual grace stripped away. The impact sent a spike of pain through her ankle, and she flinched. That was going to swell later, she felt sure.

There was no time to recuperate, however. The elf gathered

herself to her feet and limped towards the back chamber as fast as she could. She had moved around behind the stage when she felt her skin tingling and a faint burning scent wafted through the air. With a silent curse she checked her ring; the power was depleted. She was visible once more.

Nalea had come too far to give up now. One quick glance around to confirm that no one had seen her yet, and she put on a last burst of painful speed. She pushed through the doors into the back chamber. Once inside, she closed it behind her just as swiftly.

The original purpose of the room was no longer clear. It had obviously been cleared out for these festivities. Now it was a storage room for all kinds of treasures. They were laid out in glass cases, reminiscent of a museum and ready to be wheeled out for the auction. The thief's heart was practically singing as she took it all in. Fantastical jewelry, strange devices, curious statuary and more.

Nalea stopped at one in particular and stared. It was nothing much to look at – truth be told, it was somewhat difficult to see. It appeared to be nothing more than a key, though one carved out of pure midnight black. A Key of Darkness. She had heard of such relics mentioned in the guilds before.

Used properly, it was said that one could open any lock. It would be a perfect place to start here, to say the least. She set about picking the lock on this case through more mundane means. The moment it had clicked open, she lifted the glass and–

A brilliant flash strobed directly into her face, even as a thunderclap of sound sent her staggering backwards. She pressed her hands to her face and stumbled away, crashing into another of the carts. Through half-blinded eyes she could see the contents had vanished, mere illusions. The door slammed open and people dressed as servers and the rich alike rushed in, only now they were carrying ray guns.

A trap.

Terrified, Nalea pulled her knife and swung it wildly, trying to keep them back. Her vision was still mostly a dark blot, her ears still ringing.

"You don't want to do that!" called a particularly lanky human. "You're not a killer! Don't make this any uglier than it has to be!"

Nalea bared her teeth at him. "You don't know anything about me, hubber!"

She reared back and hurled her knife. The man who'd spoken flinched away, and one of the others opened fire. Nalea dove right before they did, hitting the ground and low-crawling blindly among the fake displays. Green rays splattered the surrounding cases, shattering them into smoldering bits.

The knife, however, whistled right past the lead man. It went on to hit its target dead-on, striking the light switch behind him. All the lamps in the room flickered out instantly, plunging the room into complete darkness. The elf's golden eyes adapted swiftly, though her vision was still blurry from the flash. It played havoc with her pursuers, though, who shouted among themselves.

A few broke out hand lights and others bumped around trying to find the switch to turn the lights back on. By the time they'd succeeded, Nalea had staggered back to her feet and made it to the window. There was no time to fumble it open and risk it being locked. As the light flooded the room once more, she wrapped her cloak over her face and hurled herself through the glass.

Luckily, she erupted through at street level and tumbled to the ground in a pained heap. Though she'd preserved her face well enough, her arm had gotten slashed in the process. Nalea winced in pain as she scrambled to her feet, just in time to get blinded anew by the headlights of a groundcar. She stumbled back towards the building even as the groundcar slammed on its brakes, tires squealing.

She fetched up against the side of the building with a wince. It had started raining again while she was inside, cold droplets splattering the walls and street all around. It mixed with the blood from her arm, fell to the ground in drops of diluted red. Hubbers were already climbing through the broken window after her, and running up the street from both directions as well.

There was nowhere to go but up.

Nalea began to climb the wall. She lacked her usual agile speed. Instead, each grasping handhold higher was a source of pain. She bit her lip against the discomfort and blinked away the tears. A glance over her shoulder revealed the hubbers gathered beneath her. One was aiming their ray gun up at her, but the lanky one knocked their arm down and was visibly chastising them. Their voices were swept away in the wind and the rain.

The thief reached the height of the other roof first. She was exhausted and the pain was becoming worse. The gap would have been impossible even fresh, however. It was one thing to leap in and seize the wall, another to try to push off the flat surface at that distance. All she could do was push on and try to reach the roof.

At last, wheezing and gasping, she heaved herself up onto the top of the great building. She curled up on the cold, wet metal there, desperately trying to catch her breath. She had to get up. She had to find somewhere to run to. They would be on their way up through the building now.

Then a dark shape stepped over her, and something stopped the rain from reaching her.

"A good effort, Madam Wysasandoral. I can see how you've evaded them for so long."

Nalea blinked up, frantically wiping water from her face with hands that were also soaked. A sylicate stood over her, their white core gleaming from within an obsidian form. They were holding an umbrella slanted to cover them both. The other hand was keeping their top hat from blowing away in the wind.

As bizarre as the tableau was, all she could think to ask was, "How do you know my name?"

The sylicate chuckled. "Ah, but I know a great deal about you. Such as your predilection for roofs, and the fact that not being on the front page would draw your attention." They tipped their hat. "Please, allow me to introduce myself. I am Talus."

The name startled Nalea, and she scrambled back right to the dizzying edge of the roof. The rain pattered against her head and shoulders once more. "You're the Thief-Taker? I'm not going away! I won't!"

Talus clucked disapprovingly. "Do mind the drop there. I'm afraid there is no way to avoid a visit to the prison at this point."

The elf glowered at them. "Don't come any closer, or I- I'll throw you off!"

The sylicate hmmed softly, the sound nearly lost in a rumble of thunder. "That would be uncharacteristic of you, but the desperate do wild things." They shrugged. "At any rate, I have no intention of restraining you, madam. I will tell you, however, that the Hub City enforcers will be here soon." The door slammed open at the other end of the roof, and figures began to pile out. "Ah, here they are now. A bit early, actually. Go-getters."

Nalea turned to the edge, her stomach in her throat.

"I do not suggest it," commented Talus with maddening calm. "You are hurt and exhausted, and they will simply be waiting for you at the bottom." They tilted their head. "Think. Your whole life lies ahead of you. 'What is one moment in the dark to avoid the shadow of death?'"

Nalea froze. That phrase. She looked back. "What did you say?"

The sylicate just smiled and stepped back as the hubbers rushed forward past him. "We'll speak again!" they called.

Dizzy and weary, Nalea allowed herself to be seized and carried off.

Hub City prison was spare, but not horrifyingly grim. At least, the one run by the High Council itself. Some districts maintained their own, and a few of those were better not spoken of. Assuming the octogrix took you alive for violating their Eight Edicts, few would enjoy the "re-education" that followed. These cells were well maintained and clean, lit by high barred windows to let natural sunlight in.

They came in a wide variety, suited to the panoply of creatures they had to be able to contain. Sealed tanks for holding aquans, soil-floored pits to allow phylls to root, and even extra-large chambers for Brobnars who got even more out of hand than usual. The Logos had been persuaded to set up a monitor system to track them all, making sure there were no breaches in security and that no one ended up in too bad of a way.

Inspector Virdon was watching one of those screens with a frown. The figure of the elf thief, once called "The Slip" and now known to be Nalea Wysasandoral, was curled up on the bed of her cell. Her wounds had been treated, and she'd been fed and allowed to clean herself. Now she slept fitfully.

"You do not seem pleased, Inspector," came that reedy voice from behind him.

Virdon glanced back with a sad smile. "Don't get me wrong, Master Talus, I congratulate you on your success. You live up to your reputation. I'm just sad to see such a free spirit caged, I suppose. I wish she'd chosen a different path." The human shook his head, dismissing the thoughts. "What brings you? I figured you would be off being feted, or on to your next case."

The sylicate hmmed softly and nodded. "I see. Well, I must speak with the prisoner."

"Why?" asked Virdon. "She was obviously the thief."

"No, nothing like that," replied Talus. "She has requested to speak to me, and I am curious what she could have to say."

Virdon frowned and scratched his jaw, glancing to where the day guard sat.

"If you prefer, I could have Councilor Learmont arrange–"

"No," said Virdon hastily. "That won't be necessary. I'll take you in to see her now. I'll escort you myself."

The sylicate smiled and nodded. "Thank you kindly, Inspector. Your presence will be reassuring."

Virdon returned the smile and gathered the keys, guiding Talus within. They continued down the corridors past various other prisoners until they reached where the elf was being held.

The inspector tapped on the bars of the cell. "Wysasandoral, you have a visitor." As she stirred, he stepped off to the side.

The elf rolled over and frowned blearily. "You–"

"Yes," Talus interjected. "You wished to speak with me?"

The thief frowned and rose to her feet. "I suppose I did. I have questions." She glanced uneasily towards Virdon.

"What makes you think I have any answers for you?" asked the sylicate scornfully.

The venom, however restrained, startled the inspector. It seemed to do the same to the elf. She withdrew a step.

"Who are you?"

"Talus. They call me the Thief-Taker. I would think it a name they'd know well in the dark circles of your ilk." The remark was dry.

The elf tilted her head. "What would you know about me and mine, bounty hunter?"

"Enough to catch you. More than any daylight person in their right mind would want to. They go through their routines, blind to your machinations. Not me."

The thief looked to Virdon again. She seemed less worried now. He could have sworn she had even smirked for a moment, but it was gone before he was sure.

"Just the best at what you do, huh?" she asked. "No way out once Talus is on the case."

"Better than you have tried to escape me. Never say never, but I have seen it all. Traps and tricks." The sylicate shrugged. "Even outright violence."

The elf made a repulsed face. "Violence."

"Not everyone has your squeamish foibles," the detective said flatly. "Not everyone can afford them."

The inspector couldn't shake the feeling that there was something off about the whole conversation. Talus verged on unreadable, but the thief's emotions seemed all over the place. Hardly in line with what he would have expected.

"All right, hurry it up," Virdon said.

The thief's eyes flicked to him and she bit her lip. "I just… want to know: why me? Why come here?" she asked finally.

"You break the rules of society. You flaunt the order of things. Did you imagine that could continue forever?" Talus snorted delicately and stepped right up to the bars. "They treat you better here than I would, thief. If it were up to me, they'd throw you in a shadowed hole and forget you. I'd do it this very night."

"You're too clo–" Virdon started to warn the Thief-Taker.

It was too late. The thief's eyes had gone wide. She lunged forward and seized the sylicate through the bars. They struggled back and forth, a clumsy battle between two smallish creatures.

Virdon heaved a sigh and strode forward. He separated the pair with forceful shoves, getting the sylicate back over towards the wall and the elf back further into her cell.

"Enough!" the human said. "Don't make your situation

worse," he snapped at the elf. Then he turned to Talus. "And you! This is beneath you. Leave, if all you've come to do is harass her. She has enough problems."

Nalea just stood, panting. Talus cleared their throat and retrieved their top hat from where it had fallen to the ground.

"You are quite right, sir. I apologize. I will be on my way." The sylicate turned and departed without another word.

The elf was staring after them with narrow eyes.

"Are you all right?" asked the inspector.

"Yes… I… yes. Just leave me alone." She turned away and climbed back into her bed.

Virdon sighed and turned away. His shift was almost done anyway. At least this was over.

Night had come, bringing darkness to the jail. Nalea lay in the cot in her cell. She had been here for hours. It had started as pretending to sleep, but she was still so exhausted and overwrought that she had actually slumbered after a while.

She had waited all this time to examine the item. Quietly, tucked up against her body, she retrieved the tiny thing from her sleeve. It looked like nothing so much as a gemstone button in a golden circle. She peered at it as unobtrusively as she could.

The sylicate had slipped it to her during their fake scuffle. They had used the right phrases throughout. It had convinced her to follow along, to surrender and to pretend to attack them. They had even suggested she not use it until tonight.

Now was the moment of truth. There was no telling what pushing the button would do. Silence her somehow, keep her from drawing too much attention to Shadows? The alternative was a long, long time in a cage.

Nalea sighed and pushed the button.

It hummed and shimmered, but for several seconds nothing seemed to happen. Then golden mist began to pour out of the tiny device. It washed over her in a wave. She scrambled to her feet in alarm, but it clung to her. The whole world vanished in the haze.

Then it cleared all at once, and she was standing on a road out in the open air. Farmland surrounded her and the starlit sky was above. She took a deep breath, and released it. She was free.

Someone cleared their throat behind her, and she nearly jumped out of her skin. She whirled and found Ruvyn standing there with a flightcycle parked nearby. A few bags hung from the ramshackle vehicle, which appeared to have been pieced together with scavenged tech from a dozen sources. The other elf held up his hands soothingly and offered her a smile.

"Hello, young one."

Nalea blinked at him. "Ruvyn… so Talus was Shadows, after all? Was this whole thing a guild setup?"

The fence shook his head. "A guild course correction, more like. You had drawn a lot of attention to yourself, young one. Sooner or later, you would make a mistake and the hubbers would catch you. Then you'd be in a spot for real."

"But Talus is famous for catching thieves!"

The elder elf chuckled. "For certain. It's useful. The ones like you, who belong, they can help. The ones who don't belong to Shadows, well, who needs the competition?"

"Won't they trace this back to them? I didn't really have

contact with anyone else," she asked.

"No. The night guard owes a few favors to the right people. The footage will be erased. A master thief slips away in the dark under mysterious circumstances." Ruvyn shrugged. "Stranger things have happened. And – this is the key part – she's never seen again in Hub City, so no one has any reason to fuss about it." He patted the flightcycle.

"Ah." Nalea deflated a bit and looked off down the road. She could see the city there, a mass of lights in the distance. Her home. At least, it used to be. "What do I do now?"

"You're a smart one. You'll figure something out. I heard Quantum City is a lovely place." Rubyn stepped out of the way. "I took the liberty of packing up what you will need from your home."

"What about the bits you owe me?" she asked.

He smiled slightly. "Consider it a fee for services rendered."

With a sigh, Nalea nodded and went to climb aboard the flightcycle. She settled into the seat and got comfortable, then looked the other way down the road. Her spirits were starting to rise, just a little. Hub City was full of variety, it was true, but the wonders of the Crucible were never ending. Who knew what adventures were there to be had out in the world?

"Oh, and Nalea?"

She blinked and looked to Rubyn once more.

"Do try to be more subtle this time. The best thieves, you never even know they were there."

Nalea grinned at him. "I'll see what I can do."

Then she gunned the flightcycle and shot off down the road towards the horizon.

USEFUL PARASITES
M K Hutchins

Taryx had once removed a broken tooth from the maw of an æmberdrake that could swallow him whole. He'd set the legs of ether spiders. He'd even treated an entire school of piranha monkeys for stomach aches after they'd devoured a pack of cyber rats – flesh, fur, bolts and all. He did dangerous, difficult, complicated things all the time.

And yet something as simple as gathering the motivation for a morning shave seemed impossible, however much he needed it. Digging his root-like toes into the bank, he leaned out over the water. He didn't just have lichen shadowing his face; moss grew in tufts on his bark-like skin. If he left it for a week, it'd cover his face and start moving down his neck and up his forehead. Still, he wondered if he shouldn't just go back to bed and deal with it tomorrow. It wasn't like he planned on talking to anyone today.

A crash broke the quiet of the forest, sending a flock of screeching sparrows into the sky, where they lived up to their name. Taryx spun around. Some creature was almost certainly hurt. And it would need his help. The melancholy that usually weighed him down dissipated as he catalogued what kind of creature it might be and what treatments it would likely require. Taryx put his obsidian shaving blade in the pocket of his cotton robes and ran. His two dozen long, whip-like toes were perfect for sprinting over uneven terrain.

In under a minute, he covered a half mile of ground. There, on the other side of the woodchip bed where he grew sky cap mushrooms, he spotted a twitching wingtip. Cresting the woodchips, he stared down at a being he'd never seen before. Its purple-magenta spherical body and tangle of black tentacles looked like something a school of piranha monkeys would cough up. Its body couldn't be much bigger than that of a jewel-footed heron's, though its thin tentacles looked like they might be nearly as tall as himself.

He had absolutely no idea what it was. Taryx could hardly claim to know about everything that lived in the Lesser Uncanny Forest, let alone on the whole of the Crucible, but his stomach still sloshed with unease. There was something deeply unnatural about this one. The *wrongness* of it seeped up through his toes and oozed into his gut, like he'd rooted himself near a toxic gurgle pool.

It pathetically twitched a tentacle and let out a whimper of pain.

Unnatural or not, Taryx's patients had rarely lashed out at him, however huge or ferocious. If a creature had the instinct to find Taryx's house for help, it had the good sense not to gobble him up afterward.

Taryx approached slowly. It was obviously injured, with an oozing cut on its round body. "Hello. I don't know if you can understand my language, or any language, but I'm here to help you."

The thing reached towards Taryx with the feathery end of a long, tangled tentacle.

Taryx flinched back, then curled his toes in shame. What was wrong with him today? Just last week, he'd patched up a lost human bureaucrat; no creature could be more terrifying than *that*, surely. This thing wasn't going to try to drive him insensible by talking in acronyms.

It gave a whimpering, burbling coo. Taryx knelt and held out his long, thin hand. "I'm sorry. You startled me. That's all."

It reached out once more, laying its feathery tentacle on Taryx's palm.

"Brmbrm," it purred.

Taryx's panicky unease melted away like slush under a bright spring sun. Yes, this thing was incredibly ugly, but that somehow made it cute again, in the same way that the scrunched-up faces of interdimensional bats were adorable. Taryx gathered it up in his arms, gently draping the tentacles over his shoulder. "Let's take you inside and get you patched up, shall we?"

"Brmbrm," it agreed, nestling against his chest.

Taryx eased the door to his home open and laid the creature on his spare cot. He put a few slices of dried quickbalm mushroom into his ever-hot kettle – a gift from Minerva, a former patient. It was the only piece of advanced technology he owned, powered by a chip of æmber in its base. He picked it up, and moved it to the far side of the room.

His home was made of a dozen rib bones from something as large as an æmberdrake, staked in a circle to form a dome.

The lower half of the walls were wattle and daub, but his roof was made of cheerful, living red æmberflowers. Instead of facing the sun, they turned their blooms toward any source of æmber.

Taryx didn't know if the æmberflowers had been bred to seek out æmber, or if they'd evolved that way, perhaps to soak up the æmber itself? Or to lead useful pollinators towards it, who would then flourish and propagate the æmberflowers?

In any case, as he took the kettle from the center of the hut, the flowers rustled and turned and snaked over the ribs of his home, opening a large skylight directly east, right where the sun was brightest at the moment. Taryx needed good light to treat his patient. A few of the flowers turned their faces to the injured creature, suggesting it, too, had a bit of æmber inside. That didn't surprise him; plenty of species absorbed æmber into their bodies for a multitude of reasons.

Taryx poured some of the quickbalm tea over a clean cloth and used it to dab at the wound. With a dozen thin, many-jointed, branch-like fingers on each hand, Taryx could do delicate work with great precision. The stuff that seeped from his patient didn't quite seem to be blood. Some kind of ichor? It was an awful shade of magenta, with a strong whiff of sulphur. The creature gave a few soft whimpers as Taryx worked, but didn't seem overly distressed.

"This tea is both a disinfectant and a mild anesthetic. I'll have you cleaned up in no time, little guy."

And then he'd have to burn these rags. Whatever he was cleaning up, it didn't belong in the compost pile – that was for certain.

After enough of the ichor was cleaned away, he could

examine the wound. Two deep gouges gaped between its wings. Perhaps it had been raked by claws? Whatever had happened, the poor thing had clearly been struck from behind.

"What got you, eh? I don't suppose you know if it was poisonous?"

The creature whirred noncommittally. It probably couldn't understand him, but Taryx always talked to his patients. They seemed to be calmed by his tone, if not the content of his words.

Taryx mixed the tea with cool water until it was pleasantly warm, then poured it all over the wound. Poisoned or not, flushing the cuts couldn't hurt. They were deep enough to show black bone beneath. No – not bone. Wiring.

"You're part cybernetic?"

It lazily flicked one of its tentacles. Perhaps the quickbalm was making it tired. Or its wounds. Or both.

"Well. It doesn't look like anything metal actually got harmed in here." If it had been, he might need to call Minerva. Wires and processors and the like weren't his expertise. He got out some spider silk thread and stitched the wounds. Then he covered them with a thick layer of honey salve. The stuff helped powerfully in healing, and wouldn't harm any creature that licked their wounds.

Taryx frowned. Did this creature even have a tongue? He looked his patient over. A few of its tentacles had three-pronged attachments, but they appeared to be hand-like, with no mouth in sight. Taryx couldn't find one anywhere on it. Perhaps all those magenta panels over its spherical body gathered in solar energy? Or maybe it absorbed æmber and used that to power itself.

"I don't know nearly enough about your kind, whatever you are," Taryx whispered, "but I hope I've done enough that you can mend and make it back home, wherever that is."

All of his patients eventually made their way back home. It was what patients did. Even if it took this tentacled orb years to recover, it would move on some day. Taryx was just a healer. That was his role. His niche. Nothing more. Even Jani had left him, in the end.

Thinking of Jani made the air inside suddenly feel too thick to breathe.

"I'm going to step out for just a moment and let you rest. I'll be back shortly."

He left the creature drenched in sunlight, in case it really was solar powered, and ducked outside. His bark felt too tight, like it was about to crack and start peeling.

Taryx turned to his garden. To those who didn't know how to look, it would appear to be just another part of the forest. Berry bushes grew in the understory, mulched by the nut trees above. Herbs grew here and there in patches of dappled light. Trees lay where they had fallen, inoculated with mushroom spawn – some of the mushrooms blooming in glorious pink and blue frills, others dormant for the time being. Numerous other mushroom species grew in his woodchip beds and around the bases of living trees in balanced symbiosis.

Taryx filled in the hole in the woodchip bed where his guest had crash landed. Then he walked over to his herbs and pinched them back, encouraging bushy growth. He breathed in the freshness of them, their brightness. He marveled at the scalloped edges of the leaves and their bright, new-green color. Then he turned his hand over and let them drift away to become part of the mulch.

Most things in the world were temporary, ephemeral. Leaves grew, then withered. Trees soared to the top of the forest, only to become a home to mushrooms. Jani was gone. And one day, Taryx's sorrow would dissipate, too. He hoped.

Taryx only wished he could make it happen faster. But even if you heaped leaves into a compost pile, even if you turned them every day, they would only crumble so quickly. He couldn't simply burn his grief away like it was a flush of invasive mushrooms. He couldn't prune it off. Or carve it out of himself. Or keep it at bay with a well-made salve. Grief was more persistent than foot-lichen. And it annoyingly insisted on being composted one painful day at a time.

Taryx sighed at himself, then took a quick stroll through the rest of the garden. All was in order, so he returned to check on his patient.

The second cot was empty. Panic swelled in Taryx's throat. That creature hadn't been in any condition to fly. He started for the door, but then he glimpsed part of a wing sticking out from under his own cot, in the shade.

"Are... are you there?"

It burbled unhappily and tucked its wings all the way into the dark shadow under the cot. Taryx frowned. Usually he didn't have any difficulty understanding the needs of creatures, but this wasn't exactly a natural being. Perhaps that's why he'd found it so unnerving at first. Even its flesh might have been grown in a vat, if it was some kind of probe designed by Minerva's people. It could even be one of the faeries of the forest – made by the Architects themselves to help keep balance in the world.

But Taryx had glimpsed faeries before. They tended to be lithe, graceful creatures, and his patient was neither.

"Is the light bothering you?" Taryx picked up his kettle and moved it back to the small table in the center of his room. The æmberflowers rustled and spread out to better stare at it – replacing shafts of sunlight with green shade.

His patient shuffled out from under the bed, pulling its spherical body forward with those long tentacles.

"You're not solar powered, then. Are you some kind of cave-dwelling faerie?"

It didn't say anything. It just climbed back onto the cot and lay shivering silently in the darkness.

On its second day, the creature began to explore, walking on its tentacles. By the third day, it was flying. It followed Taryx as he harvested and sliced mushrooms to dry for various healing compounds. It watched – if it could watch, without any eyes – as Taryx drilled holes in a newly fallen tree so he could hammer in wooden plugs he'd already colonized with quickbalm mycelium.

The creature clumsily picked up a drill in its tri-pronged tentacles and tried to create a hole, too. The poor thing was still shivering, even on a warm day like this. Occasionally, a purple-black spark spluttered from the end of one of its tentacles. Maybe it was still injured somewhere in its wires? Taryx was no expert when it came to technology. If the creature worsened, he'd call Minerva; there was a button for that on the control panel of the kettle.

Already, though, Taryx liked having its company. How

could he not find the creature endearing, with how earnestly it was mimicking him right now? It wasn't so hard to get out of bed in the morning when he woke up to the comical sight of this creature poking at the teakettle, as if trying to decide if the kettle was alive or not.

But patients weren't meant to stay. "You don't need to help me. Or try to repay any sort of debt. Your life is your own. Now that you can get about, you should return to your own kind. You'll recover better in your native environment, wherever that is."

It wrapped a tentacle around Taryx's arm and whimpered in that whirling, burbling way. "Brmm, brmmm."

Taryx sat on the log and stroked the top of its spherical body. "You don't have to go today. But you should start thinking about it."

It nestled closer against his chest and purred like a cat. A winged, tentacled cat.

The creature didn't leave the next day. Or the next. It followed Taryx around, sometimes lending a tentacle, and burbling unhappily anytime Taryx tried to shoo it away.

Had something bad happened to it among its own species? Something that looked like itself couldn't have inflicted those two deep gashes on its back, but if it had been manufactured, perhaps its creator had attacked it? Or perhaps it no longer had a home to return to.

Taryx reminded himself this was only temporary. Still, couldn't they be friends for now? An ephemeral thing. Like the solstice flowers that bloomed once a year, and only for an hour at that.

Taryx had a skein of yarn lying about – a gift from one of

the elves who lived nearby, after Taryx treated her for a nasty viper bite. He'd meant to make a sling out of it in case he needed one, but instead, he had knitted a hat. Then he put it on top of the creature. "There. That might keep you warmer. I'm not really sure. Do you like it?"

"Brrm, brrm," it burbled happily, stroking the hat. It didn't seem to be shivering quite so badly now, and only emitted one or two little purple sparks. Taryx was no master knitter, but his lumpy hat and the round creature seemed perfect for each other.

"I can't keep calling you *it*. If you don't mind, I think I'll call you Burble."

It showed no signs of hearing. Instead, it picked up the teakettle and started flying slow laps around the house, making the æmberflowers rustle every which way. It had done that before – it seemed to be the creature's favorite game.

Taryx sighed. "Well. I don't know if you can even understand me. But you don't seem to mind. Burble it is, then."

The next morning, a tri-deer staggered into the clearing in front of Taryx's house, snuffing and grunting in pain. Its three horns flashed green and yellow in warning to other tri-deer, and the tufted ends of its three whip-like tails thrashed in the air.

It held one of its dainty hooves off the ground, where it dangled at an unnatural angle. Taryx approached slowly, hands held low and spread wide. "You've found help. You'll be all right now."

He reached out, laying a finger on the tri-deer's face. It

calmed a little. "Good job. You're safe. I'm going to fix your leg. Let's have you lie down."

He made some quickbalm mushroom tea and gently trickled it over the leg. The edge of the bone was just sticking out of the skin. A compound break. This wouldn't be easy to set. He readied his splints and bandages, then he tried to ready the deer. He fed her a whole dried cobalt mushroom – as much as was safe. It would make her less than lucid, but he never gave patients enough to knock them out entirely. Most creatures who fell asleep from eating the cobalt mushroom didn't wake up again.

She blinked sleepily. Her flashing horns slowed to a heartbeat tempo, pulsing yellow green, yellow green. Her tails flopped this way and that.

"All right. I've numbed you as much as I can. But setting this still won't be fun. Breathe deep, if you can."

The tri-deer obeyed. But as soon as Taryx wrapped his fingers around either side of the break, she kicked out with her good leg. Her hoof thudded solidly into Taryx's side, deeply gouging him. Taryx grunted as sap pooled around the wound. He proceeded, tightening his grip – but the deer flailed her broken leg. Taryx had to drop it, for fear of doing her more harm.

"Brmm brmm." The familiar sound seemed sad to him. Taryx stepped back from his patient and turned to meet Burble. It passed him a bandage.

"Thank you." Taryx wrapped the bandage around himself. He'd have to tie the deer up next, unfortunately. He rarely needed to restrain patients, and he hated doing it. But, well, tri-deer were good at panicking. Prey animals often were.

Those instincts had kept her alive, and she couldn't readily set them aside.

Burble floated up to the doe. She didn't even notice it, with her eyes glazed over blue, thanks to the cobalt mushroom.

"She's injured. She didn't mean me harm," Taryx clarified, though Burble didn't seem angry. Perhaps curious? A tri-deer might be as strange to it as Burble was to him.

Burble gently reached out one of its feathered tentacles, laying it on the side of the deer's face.

Her horn slowed, then stopped flashing all together, turning a neutral brown. Her tails stilled. She breathed deeply and steadily, blinking slowly.

Taryx stared. "How… what did you do, Burble?"

Burble gave a self-satisfied coo.

Taryx hurriedly knotted off his bandage and moved to check the deer's pulse. It was strong and steady, just like her breath. She wasn't panicked any more. "Did you inject her with a drug? Was that some kind of hypnosis? Or did you stun her?"

Of course Burble couldn't answer.

Well. What was done was done. Sitting around wouldn't make things any better for the doe. Taryx laid his long, multi-jointed fingers around the delicate leg. She didn't move. Taryx set the break – quite nicely, given that the doe didn't flinch the entire time. He splinted and wrapped the whole leg.

"Well. That much is done. You should come back every week so I can check on it until you're healed."

She licked him with her small pink tongue. Taryx sat by her for the next hour, until the cobalt mushroom wore off. Her eyes turned from orbs of deep blue to the pale blue of the sky, to their usual white-and-brown. She scrambled up onto three legs, blinking like she was a little disoriented, but no worse for wear. Moving fairly well on her uninjured legs, she walked away, disappearing between the trees.

Burble's wings buzzed energetically. Instead of sending out a few sparks, it let off two small jets of celebratory flame, then flew in excited loops over the house.

That same afternoon, a brightly colored male bumblebird arrived with a gouge in his back. Something with a sharp beak had tried to eat him for lunch and failed. Taryx hadn't even gotten the quickbalm tea ready when Burble lovingly laid its soft tentacle on his delicate wings. The bumblebird relaxed entirely.

With such a still patient, Taryx used his thin fingers with extreme precision, cleaning out the wound and packing it with salve. When Taryx had finished, the bumblebird buzzed and stretched, casting rainbows with his iridescent wings. Then he flew out the opening in the æmberflower roof.

Taryx stared at Burble. Was it some kind of doctor-faerie? He could think of no other easy explanation for why it was so capable at sedation. There were plenty of predators who might use poison to stun their prey, but Burble didn't *eat*.

"You're a marvel," Taryx whispered.

Burble burbled happily in response.

Over the next three days, Burble helped treat two more patients, putting them into a relaxed, distant state while Taryx worked. He almost wanted to get his friend Minerva out here to analyze just how Burble was doing it. She'd come if he called – like all good Logotarian scientists, she loved a good research project. But, however much he'd like his curiosity satisfied, it felt wrong to subject Burble to such scrutiny. Especially since it was in such good spirits. Burble no long shivered. It could fly faster, quicker, with more precise turns. The thing was a feat of engineering, or nature, or both.

Taryx headed out to burn back a stand of cobalt mushrooms growing on his sky cap bed. Burble followed. With its hat hanging askew, it looked like Burble had its head curiously cocked.

"The cobalts are useful, but invasive. If I didn't burn back their colonization efforts, they'd take over my whole garden," Taryx explained, gesturing at the half-dozen brilliant blue mushrooms sticking out of the woodchips. It was a slow process – first wilting the cobalts with his torch, then smoldering the area around them.

Burble approached the nearest flush of cobalts and lowered one of its three-pronged tentacles.

A jet of flame shot out. In a heartbeat, the mushroom crumbled into white ash. Burble turned toward Taryx, as if waiting for approval. Taryx hurried over. The mushrooms were gone, along with the mycelium underneath the surface – cleanly and neatly burned out.

"Would you mind doing that to all the rest of the blue mushrooms on this woodchip bed?"

"Brrm brrm." With incredible precision, Burble incinerated each and every one while Taryx stood back and watched in awe.

Burble wasn't just a doctor-faerie. It was like it'd been made specifically for Taryx. First sedating patients, now incinerating the cobalt mushrooms. Was it possible that the Architects had designed this creature of flesh and filaments for him? For this forest? For the tri-deer and the bumblebirds and all the others who'd benefited from its help?

If that were true, Burble wasn't just a patient. And it didn't have some other home to return to. This was where it belonged.

Taryx might never need to worry about being alone again.

The next morning, Taryx woke before the sun. The sky outside was blue-black and freckled with stars. One moon was full, the other crescent, like it was winking at him. On the other cot, Burble lay still, a dark round shadow against the faint light.

"Burble. Are you still sleeping? Maybe you don't even sleep. Anyway, I'm going for a stroll to one of my favorite places. Would you like to come?"

Burble rolled up on its tentacles and responded in that peaceful, familiar, "Brrm, brrm."

"Excellent. Let's head out."

Burble had done so much for the forest already. He ought to see the best view it had to offer. If the Architects had crafted Burble just for the Lesser Uncanny Forest, surely they'd given it some way to appreciate the beauty here.

They headed east first, then turned north and forded a shallow stream.

A harsh voice cut across the pre-morning stillness of the forest. "What new invasive horror have you adopted, Taryx? At least the last one was an elf."

Gaalm, the leader of the elves who lived this way, stepped around a tree, hands planted on his hips. He had pale blue skin, the color of icicles, and eyes that shone gold from lid to lid.

Taryx had never much liked the brash elf, but he still politely turned his palms outward in greeting. "Hello, Gaalm. I should be asking you what you're doing out so early."

"Fishing, of course." He held up his spear. "Not that it will do me any good, now that you've scared the fish away. What is that *thing* following you?"

"Its name is Burble, and it's a faerie, thank you very much."

"What kind of mushrooms are you growing, Taryx?" Gaalm asked. "That thing's no faerie. It doesn't belong here."

Arguing with Gaalm was worse than arguing with a rock. Rocks, at least, didn't insult your friends. "Thank you for your opinion. We'll be going now."

Gaalm grumbled about the fish and about things that did and didn't belong in the forest, but he didn't stop them. Taryx kept a good pace, the faster to leave him behind.

"Well, I'm sorry not all the neighbors here are friendly."

Burble wasn't paying the least bit of attention. It had found a stand of whistle grass and was brushing its tentacles over it, eliciting pipe-like tunes. Around the next rise, it found the sentient fog. The fog tended to lay low in one of the depressions near the path. It never spoke, but if you got close to it, it would form a face to mirror your own.

Looking at Burble confused the fog a great deal. It stretched one way, then the other, eventually deciding on becoming a ball.

Taryx had needed to point such things out to Jani. The elf had always looked upward, noticing rope bridges, nests, and which trees had moved since their last visit.

A whir startled Taryx. For a heartbeat, he thought

something was wrong with Burble, but then he spotted the real source of the sound – a leaf faerie, sputtering between the trees like its mechanisms were damaged. Did faeries have someone like himself to go to when they malfunctioned? He took a step toward it, but it disappeared as quickly as it had come. Faeries were like that.

Except Burble. Burble didn't flit away. All the other faeries he'd seen had two legs and two arms, in a vaguely bipedal shape. And that leaf faerie was small enough to fit in his palm, its metal shell painted a natural-looking green.

But given all the things that existed in the Crucible, Taryx really shouldn't be surprised that the Architects made at least one very unusual faerie. The sky was lightening. "Come on. We should hurry now."

Hurry they did, but it wasn't far. Taryx made it to the open top of the hill just as the sun crested the horizon. Below them spread Cobweb Grove, with webs from all kinds of spiders hanging between the trees. This time of day, dew ornamented those silken ropes. When the sun hit them, they shone like living æmber.

Taryx had seen it hundreds of times, but it never failed to move him. The spiders hadn't been creating art. Neither had the dew. Or the sun. And yet there it was – a symphony of colors that was ephemeral and permanent, lasting only a few moments a day, but recreated day after day after day.

Jani had loved this moment, too – always noticing the clouds and the different hues of the sky.

"I wanted to bring you here," Taryx said, but his voice was tight.

He hadn't been here since Jani left. He thought coming

with Burble would only mean a new, happy memory. But he still felt like his insides were made of weak, knotty wood. Jani would have had a way to describe the colors of this sunrise that would make it even lovelier, even more real.

Taryx tried, but he couldn't come up with such sentiments on his own. His shoulders sagged. He was a gardener and a healer. Not a poet. Not a child of the sky. He could imagine Jani smiling, Jani laughing, Jani saying something profound, but he couldn't actually recreate the words, the laughter, the feeling of being next to someone who was comfortably familiar, yet unpredictably spontaneous, whimsical and wise all at once. Memories and imagination were no substitute for the real, living Jani.

Not for the first time, Taryx wished he could simply stop thinking about Jani altogether – that he could burn his grief away as easily as Burble burned back cobalt mushrooms. Taryx ought to be enjoying this moment for what it was instead of mourning what it was missing.

"I'm sorry. I'll go down first. I… I forgot to do something at home."

Burble raised his feathered tentacle toward Taryx, but he shook his head and brushed it away. "I'm fine. I promise."

Burble's tentacles all twitched. In agitation, Taryx thought. Faeries probably didn't like being lied to any more than anyone else. But missing Jani didn't seem fair to Burble, especially when Burble was right there. Taryx wasn't lonely any more. He wasn't.

But his wounds hadn't scabbed over as much as he thought they had, either.

• • •

Two days later, Minerva flew in. The teakettle beeped that she was near, so Taryx was waiting for her in the clearing outside his front door. She swooped down in a flash of bronze-gold wings. They gave off a soft glow, as if the metal itself had been infused with æmber. Taryx had never asked; even if Minerva wanted to explain the technicalities of how she'd augmented herself, Taryx didn't have the expertise to follow such talk. A lattice of wires of that same gold-bronze color covered both her exposed arms, contrasting sharply with her steely gray hair.

She grinned fiercely at him. "Taryx! You're looking much more yourself since the last time I saw you."

She'd come only three days after Jani left. Taryx had been standing out in the rain, toes rooted to the earth, pretending to actually be a tree. He wished he could make her unsee that. He could hardly have looked worse.

"I'm doing just fine. And you?"

Minerva frowned and rubbed her shoulder. "It's just not right, Taryx. I should be able to formulate something to ease this joint pain instead of relying on your remedies, but nothing I've tried works. And I've tried a lot. I even worked on growing your sky cap mushrooms in my lab."

"Do you need help getting them to flourish? Indoor cultivation can be tricky, but sky caps grown that way should be just as effective as the ones I harvest here."

"Ah. I meant I tried synthesizing the mushrooms properly in a petri dish, nicely monitored and standardized. Not like this," she waved her hand at the woodchip beds and fallen logs. "It's so *messy*. So many *variables*."

"But it works."

She sighed. "Yes, it does. A frustrating bit of data. If any of my compatriots ever make their way to you, don't tell them you know me. I'd be a laughing stock for this."

"You're the only Logotarian scientist who's crash-landed here, I promise," Taryx said. It had been quite the shock to him – he'd expected a roc, or an æmberdrake, or really anything other than a half-mechanical woman that day, ten years ago, when he woke to a booming thud outside his house. Minerva had still been perfecting her wings. She'd had to stay two weeks before she was able to fly out again.

During that time, Taryx had liberally covered her wrenched shoulders in a liniment of honey and sky cap mushrooms. Now and again her shoulders still troubled her, and she came to get more medicine.

"Are you sure it's not something more than soreness?" Taryx asked. "If you've already gone through the jar I made for you last time, you've been in pain every day."

"Well, I thought it would be good to have some extra on hand, if you don't mind," Minerva said innocently.

She hadn't come for the liniment. She'd come to check on him. "Minerva. You saw the worst of it. I'm better now."

"Gaalm snuck into your house two days ago and called me on the kettle. Said something about you going mad and keeping an abomination as a pet."

Sneaky little elf. "And you believed him?"

Minerva snorted. "Of course not. But it did interrupt my work, and that made me realize I should have dropped by some time ago."

"I'm *fine*." He'd even shaved this morning – not a trace of lichen or moss on his face anywhere.

"Jani was like a brother to you and he left barely a month ago. It'd be downright strange if you were *fine*. If you let me put stress-monitoring nanites in you, I could prove it with numbers."

Jani hadn't been like a brother. Brothers and sisters all drifted far apart from each other, claiming their own bit of sunlight to grow in. At least in Taryx's species, family didn't remain close. Aspen-kin or birch-kin treewalkers might cluster together in communities, but juniper-kin treewalkers like himself lived apart. Some of his kind formed close bonds with members of other species, but more often than not they lived alone, often choosing remote and difficult-to-access places to build their homes.

For decades, Taryx had comfortably enjoyed both his work and his solitude when there were no patients to treat. He never thought he might prefer to live otherwise.

And then Jani had stayed with him for over two years. He'd told Taryx about forests all over the Crucible, from the Valley of Jewels to the forest around the World Tree.

Taryx had never had someone next to him day in and day out before. He'd told Jani how unfurling mushrooms were so beautiful, it sometimes made him weep. How he was afraid of heights. And how compost made him philosophical. One foggy afternoon, he'd even laid out his fears of what would happen to his garden when he, too, rejoined the earth.

Jani had been his *friend*.

But in Minerva's culture, everyone accepted the loss of friendship as normal. Friendships lasted months, perhaps years, but rarely lifetimes – everyone seemed to expect that changes in common interests or proximity would cause friendships to fade as inevitably as summer gives way to autumn. Friendships were generally less permanent and less important than family, in Minerva's world. He shouldn't have been surprised that Jani felt the same way.

"No nanites. I don't need to be monitored."

She frowned. "Well. If you don't want nanites, my offer on the infrared implant for your eyes still stands too. You ought to have some bit of technology to help you out here in the wilds."

Taryx sighed. "*Minerva*, you promised."

"Fine, fine. I won't bring up eye implants again."

"Or?" he demanded.

Her shoulders slumped in defeat and she mumbled, "Or install some while you're asleep."

"Thank you." Taryx opened the door to his home. Minerva might not be fond of organic environments, but even she smiled at all those cheerful æmberflowers thatching together to make his roof.

Taryx glanced around his shelves and drying racks, and under the cots. "Burble must have gone out. It loves flying zig-zags between the trees – like the whole forest is one giant obstacle course."

"So Gaalm wasn't lying about you adopting a pet?"

"Well, I think it adopted me. But it's *not* an abomination."

She smiled, brushing her fingers along the petals of an æmberflower. "A pet. I actually think that's a marvelous idea. There have been over four hundred and twenty research papers showing that pets can–"

"*Please* don't quote research at me."

"Research is useful, Taryx. What kind of animal is it?"

He pulled his jar of dried sky cap mushrooms from a shelf and began grinding a few down in his mortar and pestle. If he told her that Burble was probably a faerie made by the Architects just for him, she'd think he was becoming delusional. "Ah. I'm not sure. It's got a lot of cybernetic parts. Maybe it's even a lost Logotarian probe of some sort." That could be true, if his theory about the Architects was wrong. "Do the Logos ever make exploration probes with social tendencies?"

"The Logos rarely generate *scientists* with social tendencies. At least, not at my research facility."

Taryx drummed a dozen fingers on the table. "Hmm. Well, Burble's very friendly. It doesn't want to leave. It follows me around like a puppy."

"I, for one, am simply glad you're not all alone. Maybe a faerie nudged it here. Sometimes the Crucible takes care of its own." She stretched her shoulder again. "I, unfortunately, need your mushroom liniment to take care of me. I think I should put some on sooner rather than later. It's a good flight from here to the research facility."

She always called it *the research facility*, as if no other Logos labs outside of Macro-Research Facility 47μ really counted.

"Of course." Taryx turned to grab the mortar and finish his work. When he turned back, Burble was floating in through the ceiling. "Ah. There you are. Minerva, this is Burble. Burble, Minerva."

Minerva turned. Her eyes flickered as they searched some unseen database. Her polite smile shifted into horror. "Taryx! That thing was made by *demons*. I hate to say that Gaalm was right about anything, but your 'Burble' is dangerous."

Taryx had, of course, heard rumors about the soul-eating demons who lived somewhere beneath the crust of the Crucible. But Burble hardly looked nefarious, flying there with its hat askew. "Really?" Taryx chuckled uncertainly, like Minerva had just made a bad joke. "Aren't demons supposed to have spikes all over and wear scary iron masks?"

"It's an imp. A servant to a demon. They send them to the surface to collect the pain and suffering of creatures, so they can feast on them down below." She'd stepped back toward the door. She was actually nervous about being in the same room with Burble.

"I thought demons were supposed to eat souls."

"Do you really want to quibble over semantics right now? Whether you want to say it eats souls, or eats the suffering of souls, or uses psycho-reactive æmber to capture emotional energy to later digest, the conclusion is the same: that thing is dangerous. Has it been feeding off you?"

"Of course not. Burble's harmless. It's been helping me in my work."

"Taryx!" She turned to him. "You can't let that thing near your patients!"

While she wasn't looking, Burble shot out its two longest tentacles, the ones with the feathery ends. It laid them on either side of her face.

She opened her mouth as if to scream – but then she relaxed instead. Taryx thought Minerva might even faint. He reached out to catch her, but she caught herself on a rib of the doorframe.

Burble released her and politely flew back into the shadows of the house.

Minerva rubbed the side of her face, like she'd just woken up and didn't quite know where she was. "The pain ... it's gone. My shoulder doesn't hurt. That thing. It ate up my suffering."

Taryx glanced between the two of them. Was that actually how Burble had been helping his patients? "That's amazing!"

Minerva frowned. "No. It's not."

"Why? Because you have some notion that it's evil? Burble took your unwanted emotional waste product – agony – and turned it into food for himself. He's like one of the birds that eats gnats off the back of a sabertooth tiger, or the bugs that clean the forest floor. People often think of scavengers, decomposers and the like, as loathsome and disgusting, but every living thing has a role to play in the ecosystem of the Crucible."

Minerva rubbed the side of her face, her frown lines deepening. "But it's not a natural, living thing. It's ... I know it's bad." She blinked, like she was trying to clear sleep from her eyes. "I was so frightened for you a moment ago. And now I'm having a hard time remembering why. Can you make it leave?"

It wasn't like Minerva to overreact like this. Usually if she got upset or excited about something, her reaction was to study it – not push it away. But he supposed stories about demons could bring out superstition even in a Logotarian scientist.

"Burble, will you make sure the log we inoculated the other day isn't drying out? It might need a bucket of water."

Burble obediently wandered off through the skylight in the roof. Taryx had no idea if it would actually do as he'd asked, but with it out of sight, Minerva relaxed somewhat.

"Demons are bad news, Taryx," she said. "Even the servant of a demon. They eat emotions."

"That one just anaesthetized you very nicely. You came to me for a liniment. I don't see how it's different."

"The liniment actually heals."

"Well, now you're pain-free and can apply the liniment without complaint. Do you have any idea how useful that kind of numbing is when you're trying to set a broken bone? Burble's eased a lot of suffering around here. My mushrooms are amazing, but they can only do so much. I wish Burble had already been here when I had to relocate your shoulder."

Minerva shuddered. "That, I can remember with perfect clarity."

"And wouldn't it have been nice not to feel it? I can't believe I'm trying to get you to be *more* rational."

"I am being rational. That thing isn't a medical tool." Her eyes flickered, searching her unseen data network again. "If this is accurate, your pet is an ember imp. It's a dangerous parasite."

Some of his best mushrooms were parasites. Sure, people liked the decomposers better, and everyone loved the *mycorrhizal mushrooms* that interlaced with the roots of trees, benefiting both organisms. Those fungi cleaned the forest and promoted tree health – but the parasites were useful, too, thinning out weak specimens of plants and allowing healthier ones to grow. "Parasites aren't evil."

"Well this one is. Ember imps can shoot fire, Taryx."

"Actually, the fire comes in quite handy when I need to keep the cobalt mushrooms in check."

Minerva groaned. She really didn't look well, her golden

wires shifting to a blanched silver.

"I'm being a bad host. You should lie down."

"No. I don't want to stay. Not here. Not where it is. I know that much. But I'm worried about you. At least, I was *very* worried a moment ago. You can't keep an ember imp as a pet."

"Not very long ago, you said it was sent here by the Crucible for my own good."

Minerva shook her head, then rummaged in one of her pockets. She pulled out a thin coil of bronze wire. "You put it over your finger. When you make a fist, it'll activate."

"What is it?"

"A circuit disruptor. If you activate that within five feet of the imp, it should go limp. Not dead, mind you – just offline."

"Minerva, I don't need this." He wasn't about to do anything that might hurt Burble. He tried to hand it back, but Minerva closed his hands around her gift.

"I hope you won't need it. But I'm leaving it with you anyway."

Watching Minerva fly away never used to be hard. Now it reminded him of Jani disappearing into that same blue sky.

Jani's tribe had only left him behind because they thought he was dead. He'd broken his wrist radio – along with his arm, his leg, and four ribs. Minerva was able to fix the radio, of course, and Taryx saw to the bones. When his tribe's airship came in range of the signal again two years later, Jani hadn't even hesitated. Elves tended to put their tribe above all else.

Jani wouldn't stay. And Taryx couldn't survive on an airship, away from the earth.

When he thought about Jani, he still felt all knotted up

inside, his bark papery and too tight. But there was no wood-cracking pain running through him. The sharp edge of his heartbreak had dulled a little. He hadn't composted his grief yet, but it was not new, either.

Having Burble around was certainly helping. Demonic monster, indeed. People were so eager to slap scary names on things they didn't understand.

Burble came bobbing back toward the house, its flight still a little uneven. It was a shame Minerva had spooked so badly; she could have used one of her fancy scanners or something to check Burble's interior wiring. It swooped up to Taryx and tilted to one side, as if curious. Or concerned? Perhaps he was reading too much into Burble's actions.

"I'm a little sad. That's all." He glanced up at the sky in time to see Minerva's golden wings disappear behind the trees. "Nothing's wrong."

Except of course something was wrong – Jani wasn't here. And right now, Taryx remembered just how much he missed Jani's whistling, and his jokes, and his fearless grin. Apparently, all their time together meant more to Taryx than it had to him.

One day, thinking about Jani wouldn't hurt, Taryx promised himself. He just wished that day could be today. He wished he could instantly compost all of the memories that made him ache for Jani into nothing more than fond, old memories of someone he'd once known.

Burble stroked Taryx's face with a sympathetic tentacle. The tightness in his chest eased and his pain became watery and indistinct. Yes, he'd liked having Jani around. But Jani was gone. Taryx was just scared of being alone. Nothing more.

"Thanks, Burble. Having you around cheers me up."

Burble's wings buzzed with excitement. He flew loops around trees, burning stray cobalt mushrooms with gusto as he passed over them.

Taryx leaned back and watched Burble in action. Minerva had been right the first time – the Crucible sometimes looked after its own. He'd been more than lucky that Burble had found him.

For the next three weeks, Taryx worked seamlessly with Burble, treating everything from blisters to bronchitis, in patients ranging from chameleon foxes to a giant sloth. Burble really did have a gift, taking away their pain and suffering. And in turn, Burble grew stronger. It could fly higher and smoother, and it could flame brighter and bigger than before.

Minerva hadn't had anything to worry about. Burble had found its niche.

With all the good Burble was doing, Taryx should have realized that sooner or later Gaalm would come by to complain about it. He pounded on Taryx's front door, then called, "I've heard you're still harboring that unnatural thing!"

Thankfully, Burble was off hunting down stray cobalt mushrooms to incinerate. Taryx had been knitting spider silk bandages, using his own long fingers as needles. Reluctantly, he set the delicate work down and stepped outside. He didn't invite Gaalm in. "We live on the Crucible, Gaalm. Nothing's exactly *natural* on this world, is it?"

Gaalm had the unique talent of glaring *up* at people and seeming taller for it. "Don't play word games with me. Do you think you're more in tune with the forest, just because you bear a superficial resemblance to some of its trees? The forest requires balance. The forest requires harmony."

The forest certainly wasn't what had dragged Gaalm's self-righteous backside over here. Gaalm's only joy in life seemed to be annoying his neighbors.

"And to find balance, everyone needs to listen to you and do what you say? Is that it?"

Gaalm quivered like a leaf in a gale. "You can't play with an æmber imp without getting burned. You have to take care of that thing, or everyone who lives here will pay the price."

"Like the improved medical care Burble's providing?"

Gaalm's golden eyes went wide. "You *named* that abomination?"

"It's a creature. Not an abomination."

"Fine. It's a *predator*, and it *eats souls*. A jackalope wouldn't welcome an æmberspine mongrel into its burrow, now would it? You're doing the same thing here. Bringing that monstrosity into everyone's home and pretending it's here to help keep house."

Taryx's jaw tightened as he curled his toes into the dirt. The disrupter from Minerva hung heavy in his pocket. He hadn't thrown it away yet. But he should have – long ago. "The only being that needs to leave my property is you."

Gaalm spread his hands wide in a gesture of peace. "Taryx, Taryx. Do you remember when you welcomed Jani into your home? When I told you a skyborn elf had no place in the forest? That he belonged with his kin? I was right. He followed the nature of an elf, and returned to his tribe. Your imp will follow its nature, too. I know you're sad about losing Jani. But that's no excuse to endanger all of us with that abomination."

Taryx blinked. Had he been sad? He remembered Jani on that rope ladder, climbing aboard the airship, high above the trees. He remembered Jani waving goodbye. Watching until Jani was a dark purple speck. Until the ship was nothing more than a dot on the horizon, indistinguishable from the birds. He'd stood there for three days, just staring up – until Minerva found him and brought him back to his house.

But he didn't feel any pain thinking about it. He felt… nothing. Nothing at all. "Sad?"

"Heartbroken. Morose. I'm not a thesaurus, Taryx. The point is, that imp will hurt everyone. It's not enough to send it away. We need to put it down."

Anger rushed into the space where the hollow not-sadness had been. "I won't put up with threats, Gaalm. You should go, now, before you say more things you'll regret."

Taryx took a step forward. He only meant to show he was serious and chase Gaalm away, but Gaalm went blotchy white, like cumulus clouds had suddenly covered his blue skin. He scuttled backward. "You- you keep that thing away from me!"

Taryx glanced over his shoulder. Burble hovered behind him. How long had it been there?

"We have to kill it! Stop it, Taryx, before it eats us all!"

Burble darted in front of Taryx and blasted a dart of fire at Gaalm. The elf stumbled back and raised an arm, shielding his face. He screamed. Even from this far back, Taryx could see that his sleeve had turned to ash and his arm was red and blistering.

"Burble!" Taryx thrust Burble back, putting himself between it and Gaalm. "That stupid elf was just leaving! I'm not going to let him hurt you!"

Gaalm screamed, "See! It's dangerous! I warned you!"

"Of course it is!" Taryx snapped. "If you threaten a creature, don't be surprised if it bites you! Burble, you stay here. I'm going to see to Gaalm's arm, then he's leaving. All right?"

Burble bobbed sulkily lower to the ground. Taryx sighed. Burble had actually *hurt* someone. Gaalm would never shut up about it now, never mind that he'd instigated the whole mess. Taryx turned and strode toward Gaalm.

The elf tried to scurry to his feet, but fell in the underbrush. "I don't want your help. Stay back! I'll leave. Please. Please keep it away. Please–"

"I don't force anyone to get treatment. If you want to leave, you can." Taryx reached a hand to help Gaalm stand, but a tentacle reached Gaalm first.

Annoyed, Taryx turned to find Burble just behind him. "Burble. I asked you to stay back."

Burble touched Taryx's face with his other feathery tentacle. Taryx's annoyances, worries, and fears all dissipated. It probably helped that Gaalm had stopped screaming. Taryx glanced at him. "Are you sure I can't bandage that arm?"

"I… I suppose you can. Why did I think that was a bad idea?"

Because he was a stubborn fool, but Taryx wasn't about to say that out loud. At least with his pain gone, Gaalm was starting to think straight. "Come on."

Taryx got him to his feet, put an arm around Gaalm's shoulder, and led him to one of the cots inside the house. Burble followed. Without Taryx even asking for help, Burble moved the kettle to the side, opening up the æmberflower roof for the best light.

Usually, Taryx worked slowly and carefully. Usually there was a knot of empathy in his gut, worrying over the wellbeing of his patient. Today, that didn't seem so important, not with Burble rubbing his back.

Taryx washed the wound roughly. He slathered on a poultice, not taking care to mind the blisters. Then he wrapped it. Analytically, he knew that Gaalm should be screaming and thrashing at such hasty treatment. But he didn't. Burble was touching Gaalm's shoulder, its wings beating faster and faster. Occasionally, it let out a satisfied, "Brrm, brrm."

Taryx was glad Burble enjoyed assisting him. Burble was such a helpful creature. Gaalm left without any further harsh words, he was so touched by Burble's efforts.

Taryx woke in the middle of the night. He hadn't moved the kettle, so part of the roof remained open, letting him see a swath of stars.

Jani was out there somewhere. Along with uncounted interdimensional bats. And æmberdrakes. And clouds. None of those things seemed especially more important than the others. Thinking about it left a sour taste in his mouth, and he wasn't sure why.

He hoped Gaalm wouldn't return. Taryx could deliver the salve to the elven village and let Gaalm treat himself.

Only then did he think about the way he'd cleaned Gaalm's wound. The way he'd bound it without pity.

Taryx had unnecessarily hurt a patient.

He thought he might be ill. Burble lay in the cot next to him, its round form gleaming in the starlight, its knitted hat hanging askew. It would be so easy to blame Burble, to call it a monster like Gaalm and Minerva had insisted he should.

But this was clearly all Taryx's own fault. He'd been upset. Burble had tried to help. Taryx had never explained that it was vital to only numb the injured person, not the healer.

Blaming Burble would only be a frail attempt to shift responsibility and numb his own guilt. He didn't want to be numb to that. Taryx needed to take responsibility for what had happened so it didn't happen again. Next time, he would be more careful. Next time, he'd make sure to be clear with Burble. He could and would do better for his patients – even patients like Gaalm.

Taryx stared back up at the stars. Jani had come from that sky. Taryx wanted to mourn him. He wanted to feel like Jani had been special and that his loss was something special, too. He wanted to curl his heart around that aching sorrow. But there simply was no pain any more. Inexplicably, and without warning, that grief had left him, just like Jani had left him. Here one day, gone the next.

Taryx's stomach turned. He glanced at Burble laying in the dark next to him. Minerva's words echoed back to him: *Has it been feeding off you?*

Today, Burble had eaten his emotions. Taryx could feel the strange emptiness where his shock, horror, and concern over Gaalm's injures should have been. And it was the same kind of emptiness he felt when he tried to think about Jani. If Taryx had actually composted that pain, he ought to feel *something* in the space where his sadness had been. Peace. Acceptance, perhaps. But there was just a gaping nothingness inside him. Only the fear of being alone remained.

Burble had just been trying to help, Taryx told himself.

It had wanted Gaalm to stop being afraid, not hurt him further. It had wanted to ease Taryx's heartbreak, not leave him empty. Tomorrow, Taryx would clearly explain that Burble should only take away the pain of patients in dire need of help. Then there wouldn't be any more problems. Burble hadn't acted out of malice or greed, after all – because if it had, Taryx would have to send Burble away. And then he couldn't fall asleep to the soft whirr of Burble's inner workings. He couldn't wake up to a happy flurry of tentacles. No one would bob along beside him as he worked.

Before Jani came, Taryx had never been lonely. He hadn't known what it meant to be alone.

The second time Taryx woke, it was to the smell of smoke and the screams and bleating of wounded, frantic creatures. The sun shone red through his skylight. Burble rolled upright, balanced on its tentacles.

"You stay right there," Taryx said and ran outside.

More than a dozen beings crowded in the clearing in front of his home. Two elves – part of Gaalm's tribe, though Gaalm himself was nowhere to be seen – along with tri-deer, briar grublings, an angora spider, and a number of other forest creatures.

All of them had burns. On arms, on faces, on flanks. Taryx swallowed, his bark going papery-dry. Burble couldn't have. Burble had been home all night. Hadn't it?

"There's a fire," one of the elves said. "Gaalm's got crews organized fighting it. But plenty of us have gotten caught. You'll help, won't you?"

"Of course." A forest fire. Just an ordinary forest fire. This had nothing to do with Burble.

Though Burble could have easily have started such a fire, creating a feast of pain for itself to devour. Surely Burble realized though, that if it injured its hosts too badly, they'd get rid of it? Burble could be fed for a lifetime as Taryx's assistant. It didn't need to cause a catastrophe.

But Taryx had never met an imp before. He knew practically nothing about them. He wanted to find excuses for Burble simply because he liked the creature. Animals in the wild exhibited similarly destructive behaviors – like a halacor, inciting a stampede near a cliff so it could climb down and gorge itself at its leisure.

Gaalm had just told him yesterday that if he kept an ember imp around, they'd all get burned. And here were so many of his neighbors carrying burns on their bodies. Burble had maneuvered him to hurt Gaalm yesterday. It had stolen his feelings for Jani so he couldn't even compost his grief, leaving a gaping, hollow hole Taryx wasn't sure would ever heal.

Burble nudged the door open, wings buzzing. It gave out an excited coo. At least, it sounded that way to Taryx. Excited and hungry.

Taryx had no proof that Burble had caused this. There was every likelihood that it had. But he didn't have time to think about that – not with so many patients to treat. He'd keep Burble away from everyone and decide what to do afterward. "Go fetch more water, Burble. We'll need plenty of water today."

Its tentacles drooped, but it grabbed a bucket and flew off toward the stream. Taryx quickly surveyed the group. Despite the frantically flashing horns on the tri-deer, it was the cracked carapace of a briar grubling that demanded immediate attention.

Taryx picked the creature up, speaking softly to it. He washed out the wound with quickbalm tea. Then, with his thin, dexterous fingers, he painstakingly dripped oil infused with blood-blooming mushrooms into the crack, to encourage the cuticle to clot. Bandages didn't do this kind of injury much good, so he finished up by boiling the resin of a darkwater tree and painting a thin layer over the wound. The stuff dried quickly, cementing the carapace together. That would give it some stability as it regrew from the inside out. In about six weeks, the resin would wash away on its own.

"All done. Let's find you a shady spot to rest while I help the next patient," Taryx said. His fingers were cramped, but it was reassuring to know that he was still a competent healer. One unfortunate mishap with Burble didn't change that.

Burble, for his part, obediently hauled buckets, never touching the patients. It could – and would – listen to him.

He treated an elf for a nasty wound on her leg that had only gotten worse with waiting. Taryx popped blisters and drained the purple pus from them. Gently. Delicately. With fingers that were only growing more cramped as his bark turned papery-dry with anxiety. Two patients down. But four more had arrived and joined the waiting crowd while he was tending them.

He set wings and treated burned-raw skin, fur and scales. A half dozen elves arrived from the crews Gaalm had arranged to fight the fire. The fire was out, they reported, but they'd still suffered from its effects. All of them needed to inhale medicated steam for their lungs and get slathered in balm for their chapped skin. At least he had the ever-hot kettle. He got the herbs and mushrooms for the steam going, tossed one of the elves a jar of balm, and set to work on a young elfin man with a burned foot.

By then, Taryx's hands shook so badly he dropped his jug of quickbalm tea. It crashed to the ground, cracking open and dampening the dirt with its contents. The blisters on these feet were like the blisters on the tri-deer, on the elfin woman, on the chameleon fox who'd turned purple-red all over to match her wounds.

Taryx stared down at the broken pieces of the cup. He needed to get a new cup. He needed to make more tea.

But he felt rooted to the spot, his fibers as slow as the actual trees around him. He couldn't do this. He couldn't help everyone.

Just then, Burble appeared through the roof with a bucket of water for the kettle.

If Burble took his exhaustion, worry, and frustration away, Taryx could keep functioning. Not perfectly. But that was better than not functioning at all.

Burble extended one of his feathery tentacles, as if in question. Taryx reached out and took it. The horror of the injuries and the stress of having so many more to treat was siphoned away. Taryx picked up the pieces of the broken pitcher, chucked them out the skylight, and got another one.

The elf watched Burble, his golden eyes wide. "Can that thing really take away my pain?"

"Yes. After a fashion. Though there's a chance it's not a wise idea."

"Please," he begged in a voice as frail as a wind-battered

autumn leaf, "please, let it help me."

Taryx didn't stop Burble when it reached out for the elf. Why had he thought this was a bad idea? Almost immediately, the pain drained from his patient's face. The elf looked a bit dazed, yes, but that was better than being twisted up in agony.

Taryx kept working, numbly plodding through treatments. It was not careful, skilled, caring work. But it was getting done, bit by bit. After the elves, he got the tri-deer buck laying on its side, revealing a nasty gash it had probably gotten trying to run away from the flames.

"Burble. The quickbalm, please."

Burble passed him a jug. Taryx splashed it on. The buck spasmed, but before any sound could escape its mouth, Burble was there, eating up the pain. Taryx sniffed at the jar.

"Burble. This is *vinegar*. I need quickbalm," Taryx grumbled, and fetched it himself.

Burble made the same mistake with the next patient. And the next. Correcting its mistakes every time was annoying.

At least Burble was always ready to soak up the excess pain, so no one felt the mistakes for long.

By the time everyone was finally treated and sent on their way, evening was coming on. Taryx sent Burble to fetch more water for tea – just for drinking, this time. Then he slumped into his cot.

Taryx knew he hadn't been the best healer today. He needed to thank Burble for allowing him to function. Or condemn it for starting the fire in the first place.

Keeping Burble around felt like betraying the forest. But sending it away felt like second-guessing his own feelings.

Burble might not be the most skilled assistant, but it had stayed to help the entire time, even if it had sometimes handed him the wrong thing.

Taryx blinked slowly. Burble hadn't just passed him vinegar once. It had done it over and over again. Taryx simply hadn't cared, with Burble eating away his emotions.

The vinegar wasn't an accident. Burble had deliberately tortured his patients and slurped up their agony.

Taryx had allowed it. He'd helped. His sap felt like it had crystallized.

Burble was quickly turning him into something other than a healer.

He'd resisted all Minerva's offers of cybernetic upgrades, feeling they were too artificial. But he'd found something else that could turn him into an unnatural automaton. One that would roughly treat patients and ignore whatever Burble was inflicting on them in the meantime.

Had Burble done this before today? Taryx racked his memories. He didn't think so. Burble was getting bolder, perhaps.

But torturing a patient even once was too much. No one today had threatened Burble; the vinegar was no act of self-defense. He'd used the trust that Taryx had with the rest of the forest to do harm.

Taryx reached into his cotton robes. He found that cold, metallic disrupter Minerva had handed him weeks ago and slid it over his finger.

Burble came in through the front door, wings buzzing faster than a bumblebird's. Taryx made a fist, bending the coil. Burble's wings and tentacles went limp. It hit the floor with a dull thud and rolled to the side, its hat falling off.

Taryx had no idea what to do now. He wasn't as bloodthirsty as Gaalm. He wouldn't hack Burble into pieces. Slowly, Taryx scooped it up in his arms, just as he had on the day they met.

"Well. Shall we go see if you started this fire?" Taryx asked. "I don't know if there'll be any evidence, but I can look. I feel like I owe you – and everyone else – that much."

Burble, of course, did not respond. Taryx strapped it to his back and headed east.

Taryx wasn't sure what he expected to find. A sign that said *Burble was here*? A streak of its magenta ichor on the ground? Twenty acres of forest had burned before Gaalm's people put it out. The ashes under his long feet itched, and the soil was baked hard. Skeletal trees jutted from the ground.

Forests needed some amount of fire to make way for new life. To clear dead plants. All things had their place, even destructive flames. But Taryx couldn't remember a fire scarring the forest like this before. It wasn't natural. He felt it in the fiber of his being. Just as he'd felt something unnatural about Burble the first time he saw it, laying prone on the woodchips.

Taryx walked over the acres, as if he needed to personally see every inch that Burble had destroyed. He needed to witness what its actions had caused. And then he had to decide how to get rid of Burble.

As he continued in long, slow strides, he almost tripped over something half-hidden by charred brush. Taryx easily cleared that away – it was mostly cinders now.

In a black circle of what had once been dried grass lay one

of the faeries of the forest. The green patina over its metal exterior had bubbled and melted in places, and its leaf-shaped wings were bent. One foot kept twitching, sending out a spray of sparks. It looked just like – and probably was – the faerie he'd spotted on their hike to see the sunrise over Cobweb Grove.

Taryx surveyed the burnt acres. He wasn't in the exact middle of them, but given the way the wind had been blowing, it was entirely likely that the fire had started here. With a malfunctioning faerie. Not with Burble at all.

The ember imp hung heavy on his shoulders. Burble hadn't caused the stampede of patients. But he'd still tortured them intentionally, gorging itself on their fresh agony.

Perhaps he could explain to Burble why that was wrong. Perhaps, in time, they could have a trusting partnership. All creatures, from the predators to the parasites, played their role in nature.

But Taryx's role was to heal. Whatever his hopes for Burble, he couldn't promise himself that he'd never let another patient be unnecessarily harmed. Not when Burble was around.

He stared down at that poor, broken faerie, sparking and senseless. It had been designed to help and had caused great harm. Burble had been designed to inflict and devour pain, but it had helped in healing so many.

Taryx carefully gathered up the broken faerie. He wished Burble had actually been one of these robotic caretakers of the world, crafted by the Architects themselves. The forest could have used Burble's unique abilities.

But the Architects weren't the only ones who knew something about biomechanics, Taryx thought as he strode back home across the ashes. Thanks to an unexpected crash landing a decade ago, Taryx happened to know a scientist with no small skill in the matter. Perhaps the Crucible really did take care of its own, on occasion.

Taryx set the imp and faerie side by side on his cot. With a little tinkering, something good might still come from all of this. He pressed the button on the kettle and called Minerva.

It took Taryx a day to walk to Macro-Research Facility 47μ carrying Burble and the faerie. It took another day to get cleared to enter. For the next three weeks after that, he stayed in Minerva's lab while she worked on the project he'd proposed. Taryx was largely useless, but he insisted on staying and watching every step of the process anyway.

Now that it was finished, he couldn't peel his eyes away from the glass lab table strewn with spare bits of Burble.

"That ember imp was the creation of a demon," Minerva said, her expression as steely as her hair. "A robotic probe designed to gather and return with emotional energy for its master to feed on. We didn't murder anything."

"There are sentient robots."

"Well, I promise you this one isn't. I've seen it inside and out now."

She could say that, but did anyone really understand how demons worked? Perhaps it simply had its brain in an unusual place. Or configured in a way they didn't understand.

Taryx wished that Burble could have simply been his assistant, but the imp was like a cobalt mushroom – potent and deadly, unless prepared carefully and used in small doses. And sometimes, Taryx had to burn back cobalt mushrooms so they didn't take over his whole garden.

"I've run this new model through thousands of simulations," Minerva said, taking Taryx's elbow and pulling him away from her workbench to a glowing suspension chamber.

Inside sat a hybrid drone. It had the faerie's wings, legs, and arms, and Burble's spherical body. Minerva had, according to her own tastes, plated the whole thing in swirling gold. It wasn't ugly-cute, like Burble had been. Just shiny.

"I maintained its ability to pull out emotions, but it can only do it to one subject at a time now. It can't numb you *and* a patient any more. And it can't feed on that energy. Instead, I installed a liquid æmber battery, which shouldn't run down for the next hundred years. The battery is sufficiently shielded that I don't think your æmberflowers will take much note of it."

From a demon and a faerie, Minerva had crafted a true medical assistant. Taryx could help his patients better than ever before, without worrying about losing his own soul in the process. He knew he should be thrilled beyond words that Minerva had been able to make this happen.

But it didn't look like Burble. It wasn't wearing a knitted hat. It didn't make that cooing, whirring sound. Taryx's eyes drifted back to her glass work table, to the black and magenta wings lying there among purple wires, bolts, and cogs.

Minerva shook her head. "Stop being morose and looking at the leftover screws. What you have now is infinitely better."

"Of course. Thank you so much, Minerva." Taryx put on a smile for her, because he was grateful. She'd let him keep this useful part of Burble and made it safe for everyone. But the grief remained inside him, as crisp as an autumn frost. In time, the pain would fade, composting into an old memory that was simply a part of him, instead of something sharp and bitter.

But for now, it was a relief to let that bittersweet regret churn through him, to see it and acknowledge it. It meant that the process of grieving hadn't been stolen from him. It meant he was feeling something.

THE PERFECT ORGANISM
C L Werner

A crimson light beat down upon the parched landscape. Though two centuries had passed since the region known as Nova Hellas had been transplanted from Mars and added into the Crucible's impossible skein, it stubbornly maintained the properties of the Red Planet, almost as though defying integration into this new world. The atmosphere remained thin and discolored by the red dust that filled the air. Gravity was weaker than elsewhere on the Crucible, retaining the reduced pull of Mars. It was a place where only the martians themselves could flourish. The martians... and the creations born in their vast laboratories.

Briilip strove to maintain the cold and studious demeanor befitting a Martian Elder while they gazed into the observation disc and the holographic images it presented. Perhaps if there'd only been the saucer's crew of stunted martian soldiers there would've been no need for such restraint, but the presence of another Elder made Briilip cautious. It wouldn't do to have a report filed that Briilip was exhibiting irrational excesses of individualism. Any question of independent attachment subverting loyalty to the Martian Empire was to be avoided. Briilip didn't want a reprimand affecting their record. Or worse still, an appointment with a reeducation pod.

Just the same, there was a thrill that raced through Briilip's veins as they watched the scene projected onto the observation disc by the flying saucer's exterior sensor arrays. The desert with its wind-lashed buttes and boulders stretched away in every direction. Faintly on the horizon the Elder could see the Spire, but the gigantic structure at the Crucible's geographical pole wasn't the focus of their attention. The cause of Briilip's excitement was a colossal shape that scurried across the sand.

The beast was rodent-like in its form, though its body was armored with great plates of cellulose, lending it a waxy appearance that recalled an agriponic vegetable more than anything animal in nature. Ten spidery legs stretched out along the creature's sides, each tipped with thorn-like talons. A mass of thin root-like appendages dragged after it as the thing scuttled through the desert, the yellow fuzz of the nettles that coated each tail replacing the dull green of the armor plates. The head, broad and flat, sported a set of massive mandibles and a mouth composed of octagonal segments sharp enough to chew through quantum-folded cobalt. There were no eyes, as such, but rather an assortment of nodes scattered about the creature's head that could shift beneath the armored plates. As they moved, patches of the cellulose would become transparent and enable the nodes to draw sensory input from the monster's external surroundings.

"Number 647 is a complex construction," Briilip stated as they stared at the hologram. "It represents the culmination of ten cycles of research and the refinement of approximately one hundred and three divergent theories of genetic manipulation."

"You have devoted considerable attention and resources to this project," the other Elder said. "Your focus on the needs of Mars is commendable."

Briilip caught an inflection they didn't like in their companion's tone. There was a suggestion of doubt there that provoked the scientist. They held themselves before offering comment until the anger was suppressed. Ghireen might be deliberately trying to elicit a response. Probing to find some sort emotional failing that would indicate a strain of errant individuality.

"My creation has surpassed all tests it was exposed to under lab conditions," Briilip explained. "Number 647 is the highest-performing organism to be vetted by the bio-weapons drome at Zyypzyar Primary." The Elder's eyes gleamed with pride as they turned their gaze back to the observation disc and the monster they had manufactured in their laboratory.

Ghireen tapped on their chin with their long fingers. "Commendable," the Elder repeated, "but a high performance isn't enough to satisfy the mandate we've been given. As a bioengineer, you're aware that the objective is to design the perfect organism. A weapon that will be equal to any obstacle that presents itself. When Mars expands the empire into the shards occupied by inferior civilizations, the margin for error must be eliminated." Ghireen shook their bulbous head. "A failed experiment can be overcome, but failure during a conquest will necessitate reeducation."

Briilip was too filled with confidence to respond to Ghireen's warning. "Number 647 will now face the ultimate experiment." Their eyes stared at the other Elder. "You don't recognize this region of Nova Hellas, do you?"

"I must concede that my researches haven't called for that particular divergence of study," Ghireen retorted.

"This is Anomaly Epsilon 54," Briilip said. They indicated the rock faces and then gestured to a jagged crevasse that snaked its way across the desert. More ominous were the half-buried wrecks that poked out from the red sand. A vast debris field created by dozens of downed flying saucers.

Ghireen nodded. "That explains why you requisitioned a stealth field for your craft. That was a risky choice. Stealth field technology hasn't yet been converted to æmber and the reserves of cavorite are dangerously minimal."

"It was the only way to linger in the vicinity of the anomaly," Briilip explained. "The Prime Director of our facility was impressed enough by Number 647's potential to authorize the use of cavorite. This will be more than a field test of my creation. Afterwards the vein of æmber beneath the anomaly will be available to our miners again."

"Then you're confident Number 647 can succeed?" Ghireen asked. The Elder's voice carried an unguarded note of awe and admiration that magnified the confidence Briilip felt.

"Today will be a historic moment," Briilip said. "We will observe the final destruction of the intrusive being designated

'Tyrant'. Today the monster meets a superior organism."

The martians watched Number 647 scurry nearer to the crevasse. A weird prismatic pulsation rose from the crack in the floor, a glow that had come to be associated with Tyrant's presence. Briilip considered the theory that the monster consumed æmber and that it was to feed on the material that it had appeared in Nova Hellas. Since its sudden arrival three years ago, no fewer than six military expeditions sent to eliminate it had been annihilated. Rather than squander further resources on a losing prospect, Mars simply surrounded the region with sensor arrays and left Tyrant alone under the theory that it would be content with the deposits in Anomaly Epsilon 54. The concession to pragmatism rested ill with many of the Elders, though none were so brazen as to openly doubt the decision. Briilip would alter that state of affairs when their creation annihilated the monster, as it was certain to do.

Nothing could prevail against Number 647.

Outside, the multi-legged creature warily advanced towards the pulsating glow. As it did, the air was filled with a rumbling growl. The sound issued from within the crevasse, a threat vocalization that had been recorded by every expedition sent against Tyrant. Number 647 didn't hesitate. Anything resembling a fear response had been conditioned out of the creature through brain surgery and gland blockers. It knew only aggression, and so returned the warning growl with its own buzzing ululation produced by vibrating its great mandibles.

Number 647's defiant challenge was soon answered. Another mighty growl rumbled up from the crevasse. The pulsating glow winked out as the monster producing it ceased to feed. The martians in Briilip's saucer held their collective breath, even the dullest of the soldiers anticipating what must come next.

Up from the crevasse heaved a colossal beast. It began its ascent by using a multitude of bristling suckers to drag itself to the surface, but once enough of its squamous bulk was exposed, a set of tremendous wings slipped free from pouches on its back. Unfolding to their full breadth, the wet, glistening wings pulled the monster into the sky.

"Tyrant," one of the soldiers muttered, unable to contain their fear. Briilip tried to note which of their underlings had spoken so that they could be sent to the reeducation pods, but the Elder was too much in sympathy with that fear to look away from the observation disc. Watching that enormous monster rise into the air, Briilip was quite happy that their saucer was both cloaked and surrounded by a forcefield.

The behemoth's body was serpentine, coated in a rough hide of craggy black scales. Along its belly ran columns of sucker-like appendages that were ringed with serrated teeth. Tyrant's head was surrounded by a cluster of sharp horns, its face tapering into a canine muzzle that bulged with interlocking rows of fangs. The monster's compound eyes protruded from the sides of its skull, each facet gleaming with the sheen of cut diamond and a fiery inner light. As it flew into the sky, a slim, bifurcated tail whipped into view, electricity crackling between its prongs.

"Today an enemy of Mars dies," Briilip declared, their hand gesturing to the hologram of Number 647 as the creature positioned itself to react to Tyrant's ascent.

The multi-legged organism gripped the desert surface with its talons and leaned back. The sensory nodes shifted about on its head so as to focus on Tyrant as the winged monster soared above it. The great mandibles clicked against one another, crashing and vibrating at great speed. A brilliant sphere of light began to manifest.

"Tyrant isn't the only creature that harnesses æmber," Briilip said. "Number 647 can absorb even the smallest trace particles from the air. It channels those particles through its body and then gathers them into a concentration around the mandibles." The Elder grinned as they glanced over at Ghireen. "Now watch how it uses that energy!"

The sphere of light expanded into a crackling nimbus. Number 647 continued to follow Tyrant, angling itself so that it was always facing the foe. When the martian warbeast decided the charge was powerful enough, it fired the concentration full into its adversary. There was a blinding flash of light as the deadly orb rushed towards Tyrant.

"Shield the sensors!" Briilip cursed the saucer's crew. Once the bafflers were in place the dazzling light diminished to a dull haze. Briilip felt their primary gastric pouch sour when they saw the revealed image. Tyrant had withstood the blast! From between its scaly plates, pulsating light exuded, completely surrounding the monster.

"Tyrant has created its own defensive field," Ghireen said. "It is utilizing the æmber it has consumed to protect itself."

Briilip could see that the monster was doing more than just protecting itself. Tyrant was absorbing the energy from Number 647's attack. It was feeding off the æmber the martian warbeast directed against it! No, more than that.

While the Elder watched, the flying abomination circled their creation. The fringe of horns shifted their positions and aimed down at Number 647. From the tip of each horn a lance-like beam of light shot at the plated creature, a hail of lasers that scorched through the cellulose and sent pillars of greasy smoke into the air.

"The fight doesn't appear as one-sided as you calculated," Ghireen observed.

Briilip bit down on a retort. "Number 647 isn't finished," they stated. "I've engineered it to feel neither pain nor fear. It will adjust its tactics and destroy the enemy."

The martians could see the warbeast's body tense for a supreme effort. While smoke continued to billow off its scorched armor, Number 647 braced itself for a tremendous leap upwards using its powerful legs. The hail of lasers streaming down from Tyrant abated as its foe sprang at it from the ground. The lunge brought the two colliding together. Number 647's vicious mandibles and taloned feet latched onto the monster's serpentine body. Unable to remain airborne with the added weight of its opponent, Tyrant plunged to the ground. The two huge beasts slammed into the desert, a great cloud of red dust exploding into the air.

Once again, the filters of the saucer's sensor array pierced the obscuring veil to show the martians what was unfolding outside. Number 647 grappled Tyrant and lashed it with its whip-like tails. The stinging nettles crackled with venomous fluids that steamed against the monster's scaly hide. The huge mandibles ripped and tore, growing slick with Tyrant's blood.

"Victory," Briilip boasted, a smile on their face. Then the smile faded. Tyrant was writhing in what the Elder had thought was pain, but which they now saw was a more strategic effort. It was slipping coils of its undulating body free from Number 647's grasp, then throwing them back to wrap around the warbeast, the suckers along its belly latching each loop of crushing flesh in place against the armor plates so that it was impossible for the enemy to break free.

"Tyrant will crush your organism," Ghireen warned.

Briilip had no response. At least nothing that wouldn't expose the fright that now hammered at their confidence. Number 647 wasn't reaching any vital spot of Tyrant's anatomy with its claws and mandibles. The monster, meanwhile, was delivering an annihilating force all across the warbeast's body. The Elder watched hopelessly as the mounting pressure from the constricting coils began to fracture the cellulose plates. Great strips of the fibrous material spilled away from Number 647 as it was crushed in the monster's grip.

"Mars Lives On," one of the soldiers in the saucer invoked the Empire's mantra. Creed, battle-cry and ideal, the martians invoked the words now as a show of defiance. A rejection of the defeat they were witnessing.

Briilip held out the illogical delusion of hope a little longer than the saucer's crew. When a pulpy slush from ruptured internal organs seeped away from Number 647's constricted body, even the Elder had to concede that their creation was doomed. Only a sense of obligation to see the very last caused them to order the saucer to stay on station. By the time Tyrant finally released Number 647, the creature had been squeezed to a third of its original size. For a time, the body twitched and quivered, but these were merely its subsidiary neural nodes shutting down. Number 647, the greatest of Briilip's creations, was dead.

Tyrant slithered back to the crevasse, battered but very much alive. It was too much to dare postulate that the monster's own injuries might prove fatal. Briilip had to concede to reality. Number 647 had failed, and by its failure so too had all the Elder's aspirations of designing the perfect organism.

"Return to Central Drome," Briilip ordered the saucer's crew. A glance at Ghireen told Briilip nothing of what the other Elder was thinking. After the assurances of success Briilip had made to gain access to precious cavorite reserves, Ghireen would have little problem advancing their own position by elaborating on the failure of Number 647. Briilip's fall would speed Ghireen's rise.

"Mars Lives On," Briilip muttered to themselves, trying to reassure themselves that whatever their own personal disgrace, the Mars Empire's knowledge would reap some benefit from it.

Briilip sat within their laboratory, staring at the hologram display and trying to concentrate on the chemical formulae they were trying to adjust. Number 647 had been the most remarkable creation to ever be developed at this facility. Even though the warbeast had proven unequal to facing Tyrant, the Elder was operating from the theory that a creation derived from the same biogenetic markers could prove superior. Strong enough to prevail where its predecessor had failed. By doing so, they hoped to increase their value and importance to Mars. Access to better facilities and greater resources so that they could pursue even grander avenues of research.

Such was the reward Briilip aspired to once they solved the problem posed by Tyrant.

It was difficult to focus completely on the problem, however. Two cycles had passed without any word from the Prime Director. Briilip had expected some manner of reprimand to be issued already. The longer silence prevailed the more anxious the Elder became. It was an indicator that extra attention was being extended to Number 647's failure. The more attention they warranted, the more severe Briilip expected their punishment to be. What, precisely, had Ghireen put into their report?

Briilip was still devoting a large measure of their awareness to that question when the hatchway to their lab fanned open and the subject of their speculations walked in. Ghireen came alone, no detachment of martian soldiers followed them. That was at least something to lessen Briilip's anxiety. Had the decision been rendered to remove them to a reeducation pod, a squad of soldiers would have been sent to enforce the command with ray guns.

"You're back at work?" Ghireen inquired as they marched to Briilip's workstation. Briefly they let their gaze sweep across the massive facility and the scores of martian workers attending the processing vats and biomass tanks.

"For as long as I'm allowed to be of service to Mars, it is my duty to perform to my utmost potential," Briilip said.

Ghireen looked around again, then lowered their voice. "In my capacity as observer I reported to the Prime Director on your field test of Number 647."

Briilip's mood instantly darkened. Their hearts slowed to a dull quiver as they braced themself for the decision of their superiors. Reeducation? The consequent reordering of their identity and the inevitable erasure of knowledge was a fate to be dreaded. Even being reassigned to some inconsequential outpost at the edge of Nova Hellas would be preferable.

"I explained in great detail the exacting procedures that culminated in Number 647," Ghireen said. "I reported the immense promise your experiment exhibited."

A flicker of hope squirmed in Briilip's being. "What was the Prime Director's decision?" the scientist finally asked.

"I prevailed upon the Prime Director to extend your contract and provide resources for further research." Ghireen nodded. "The development of your line of study shows enormous potential."

Briilip stirred from the dejection that had gripped them only a moment before. "Number 647 was the highest performing organism to be tested at Zyypzyar Primary. I am convinced that the design can be furthered and improved upon."

Briilip's fingers flew across the controls of their workstation. The hologram shifted its display to afford Ghireen a glimpse of the new theories Briilip was exploring. "Number 647 was defeated because the organism was too rigid. This new design will not have that weakness."

A confident smile showed on Briilip's face as the display changed once again and showed the full design they were working on. "Let Tyrant try to squeeze *this* in its coils! Number 648 will use the monster's own tactics against it!

"This time there will be no question of victory!" Briilip boasted.

• • •

The rumbling roar echoed across the dry wastes of Anomaly Epsilon 54. This time the sound appeared to have no source, but rather erupted from thin air to cry its challenge to the barren desert. The pulsating light that shone from the depths of the crevasse flickered and winked out. From the pit an answering rumble sounded, so similar in cadence it might have been an echo of the first.

Up from the crevasse rose the serpentine mass of Tyrant. The monster's compound eyes gleamed in the sun as it stared across the landscape. A hiss of confusion rasped across its fangs when it found no source for the roar it had sensed. Instead of taking wing, it slithered out over the sands. From the sides of its canine muzzle, wriggling tentacles extruded and tasted the air for the presence of an enemy.

Too late did Tyrant detect its adversary. Hidden by camouflaging chromatophores, an abominable bulk heaved across the sands and threw itself upon the monster. The shapeless mass engulfed the gigantic worm-serpent, its tremendous weight bearing its enemy to the ground. As Tyrant struggled to free itself, Number 648 ceased to mask its presence and stopped producing the secretions that hid it.

Briilip's new creation was far different from its predecessor. The Elder had gone back to the very foundations of organic structure in designing the warbeast. The fixed rigidity of Number 647's armored frame was now replaced by an amorphous, pulpy essence. A formless flood of physical matter like a living mudslide. Its body, without the action of the chromatophores, was a colorless bulk, pale and leathery in appearance. Sensory nodes, limbs and bio-weapons all shifted and squirmed about the undulating muck, rearranging themselves to better suit the demands of the moment.

The Elder observed from his cloaked saucer the reaction of Tyrant as it strove to free itself from the smothering mass of Number 648. Briilip grinned at the monster's desperate efforts. "No, this time it is you who will be confounded," they gloated. "I've seen you in action now and the old tricks will no longer save you."

As they spoke, Briilip watched Tyrant throw its coils around Number 648. The monster tried to constrict and crush the warbeast, but as the pressure mounted, so did the syrupy mass ooze out from between the scaly folds. Number 648 seeped through Tyrant's grip and spread itself even wider that it might more quickly entrap and suffocate the enemy.

Tyrant's horns blazed with energy and sent lasers shearing through Number 648. The damage was inconsequential, like stabbing a pool of water. Unfazed, the martian warbeast sent waves of itself surging up over the monster's head.

Light flickered from between Tyrant's scales as Number 648 smothered it. Briilip noted the effect with some amusement. "Your protective field won't help you now," they said. The Elder thought Tyrant must be growing desperate to expend its waning vitality on such an empty gesture.

The next moment a flutter of alarm rushed through Briilip's nerves. The light Tyrant was exuding was different from the forcefield it had used to absorb Number 647's æmber beam. Concern in the martian's brain grew when the intensity of the glow increased. Something was happening that Briilip hadn't seen before.

Number 648 was now completely engulfing Tyrant. Were it not for the glow the monster was exuding, it would have been completely obscured beneath the pallid mass. That inner light, however, was shining through like an x-ray. The warbeast writhed, shifting its limbs around to tighten its hold on Tyrant in an effort to smother the growing light.

Briilip knew the glow was reaching a critical stage. The discharge, however, was more devastating than the Elder could have imagined. A pulse of gargantuan magnitude throbbed outwards from Tyrant's body with annihilating intensity. Number 648, completely surrounding the monster, was ripped apart by the tide of destruction. Fragments of its shapeless bulk were hurled in every direction, smoke billowing off the charred protoplasm of its flesh.

Tyrant lurched upwards, a victorious roar bellowing from its jaws. The monster slithered across the ragged debris of Number 648 and withdrew back into the crevasse. Briilip waited until its forked tail vanished from sight before snarling a command to the saucer's crew.

"Return to Central Drome."

"Your hypothesis to bypass Tyrant's tactics was a clever one. You couldn't anticipate that the monster had other powers it could use against Number 648." The words of encouragement came from Ghireen. The Elder stood beside Briilip at the latter's workstation. All around them the shorter worker caste of martians tried to look busy, diligently shifting materials across the laboratory. In truth there wasn't any work for them, not until the Elder settled upon a new course of research, but none wanted to risk an accusation of disloyalty by looking idle.

"It was a failure," Briilip groaned. "Number 648 showed

such promise, but Tyrant eliminated it even more completely than it did Number 647." They gave Ghireen a grateful nod. "Were it not for your intercession with the Prime Director, I should certainly have been reprimanded for failing in my duty to Mars."

"There has been no dereliction of duty," Ghireen said, their tone almost scolding. "You have put every mental effort into your experiments and committed all the resources at your disposal. To give everything for Mars is all any of us can do."

"Yet I have failed to kill Tyrant. The organisms I've created are dead while the monster still lives." Briilip waved their hands in a hopeless gesture. "I should almost welcome being deployed to a frontier outpost to study the growth of red weed in heavy gravity environments."

"That would be a mis-use of your abilities," Ghireen told Briilip. "You are obligated to do your utmost for Mars. Your expertise is in bioengineering and in that function you're most valuable to the Empire. Even if you can't see the importance of what you're doing."

Briilip rallied to Ghireen's words. "Mars Lives On," they said, determination in their voice. "The Empire wouldn't be where it is today if not for the unwavering loyalty of brilliant minds. You're right, Ghireen, I have already proven my usefulness. Number 647 was far beyond anything created in any other laboratory. Number 648 exceeded it in most every way."

"Now you must devote yourself to pushing even further with your research," Ghireen prodded. "Who else is there with the genius to finally destroy Tyrant?"

Briilip nodded. Their fingers raced across the buttons on

the workstation's console. The hologram shifted, altering its appearance. Now in addition to genetic codes and controlled mutation designs there appeared technical schematics.

"My error with Number 648 was in trying to bypass Tyrant's behavior patterns," Briilip said. "I tried to sneak around the monster's defenses. Since that effort failed, the solution must lie in creating a warbeast strong enough to withstand whatever Tyrant can throw at it."

Ghireen peered closely at the information flashing across the hologram. "You seem to already have a new design theory. This looks like a radical departure from what you've tried before." They gave Briilip a cautious look. "This isn't purely bioengineering."

"Science can allow no dogmatic scruples," Briilip returned, confidence beaming from their face. "To serve Mars we must follow our research wherever it leads, even if that means a fusion of disciplines."

"Do you think this will be able to defeat Tyrant?" Ghireen wondered.

Briilip grinned. "When next I return from Anomaly Epsilon 54, there will be no cause for you to offer excuses for me to the Prime Director. Tyrant will be dead and the supremacy of my design proven beyond all inquiry.

"Number 649 will be the perfect organism."

Starlight cast a somber veil across Anomaly Epsilon 54, transforming the region into a skein of scarlet shadows and black enigmas. Briilip had a difficult time detecting the advance of Number 649, even with its saucer's sensors telling the Elder where to look. There was only the faint distortion of motion to betray the warbeast's presence.

Number 649 drew the best features of its predecessors and melded them to a new cyborg design. Among those features was an ooze-like epidermis with light-bending chromatophores. Briilip had implemented a system of tiny perforations throughout the cobalt plates that encased the cyborg's body. Through these microscopic holes, the creature could extrude its gelid epidermis and coat its body with a camouflaged exterior. The Elder would have preferred a stealth device, but they knew they could never appropriate enough precious cavorite to power both the warbeast and the flying saucer. Priority demanded concessions and in this case a living epidermis proved a feasible workaround.

The prismatic glow shone from the depths of the crevasse. Briilip knew Tyrant was near. As before, they issued the command for Number 649 to lure the enemy out with a challenging roar. The serpentine monster wasn't long in appearing, nor did it allow the absence of a visible threat to keep it on the ground. The wings unfolded and the huge beast quickly rose into the sky. Its jaws opened in a menacing hiss as it circled the area.

"Number 649," Briilip said into their cyborg's audio command control, "beat Tyrant to death." The addition of vocal command response was another benefit of the partially mechanical design.

The Elder grinned as the warbeast responded. The cloaking epidermis was disrupted as panels opened up along its sides. From each hatch, a spurt of flame blazed into the night. The flashes drew Tyrant's attention and it turned towards the disturbance. The energy field it had used before erupted all around its body, but Briilip's design took this defense into account. The missiles Number 649 launched were engineered to pierce the forcefield without feeding any æmber back into the monster. The projectiles, sharp flechettes of tri-folded steel, sliced through the bubble of energy and stabbed into Tyrant's body. Its head reared back in a howl of pain.

"Reel it in," Briilip ordered. To the end of each missile a heavy length of chain was attached, connecting Tyrant to Number 649. As the chains were drawn back, the monster tried to pull itself free. The martian cyborg responded by sending electrical pulses sizzling along the chains to shock its prisoner.

Tyrant writhed in pain. It emitted its own pulse of æmber energy in an attempt to end the shocks lashing it along the chains. Though smoke rose from the cables, their coating of crystallized titanium endured the assault.

"Faster," Briilip prompted their cyborg. "Draw Tyrant down to you."

The chains accelerated Tyrant's descent. The monster flapped its wings in a desperate effort to stay in the air, but it was unable to defy the pull of its captor. Drawn closer to the ground, it produced another blast of energy. The chains continued to hold, but now Number 649 was within the radius of the destructive pulse. The gelid epidermis steamed away in columns of greasy smoke. The cyborg's camouflage was gone, and it stood exposed before Tyrant's vicious gaze.

Number 649 conformed in general dimensions to Number 647. A long, low body supported by ten clawed legs on each side. A blunt head with a wide mouth and shifting clusters of sensory arrays. Its tail, however, was a single long tube that, as the camouflage burned away, was quickly raised to arc up over the warbeast's back.

Tyrant's jaws opened wide and from its throat a stream of energy seared down at the cyborg. The regurgitated æmber billowed across Number 649's armor. Deflectors built within the carapace defused much of the intensity, diverting it in shimmering waves that rippled through the desert air.

"You're mistaken if you think it'll be that easy." Briilip smiled. "This time you're finished."

The chains holding Tyrant now brought the monster crashing to the ground. A huge cloud of dust erupted from the impact, momentarily blocking Briilip's view of the fight. When the saucer's display filtered the obstruction, it revealed Number 649 gripped by Tyrant's crushing coils. The enemy rushed the cyborg while it was hidden by the dust and tried to gain advantage over it.

Briilip's fist tightened as they sensed triumph was near. "Now I'll use your own tricks against you."

The coils winding around Number 649 brought obscene pressure to bear against the cyborg, but Briilip's design was equal to the struggle. The cobalt armor and the alloy skeleton at the core of the warbeast's organic structure could exceed the highest evaluations the Elder was able to extrapolate from the earlier battles. More, the creation had been engineered to exploit Tyrant's tactics.

The cobalt armor quickly began to grow hot. Number 649 was channeling its bio-energy to the metal shell that encased it. The plates shifted from a dull blue to a fiery red in a matter of heartbeats. Now it was Tyrant's time to burn. The serpentine monster howled in agony as the super-heated hull cooked its coils. Swiftly it unwound itself from its intended victim. Blood streamed from its seared body and broad patches of scales peeled away from its flesh, melted to the cyborg's armor.

One side effect of the attack was that the chains attaching Tyrant to Number 649 were at last compromised. They snapped as the monster climbed back into the sky, freeing the creature to maximize its ascent.

"Don't let it get away," Briilip commanded their creation. The order caused Number 649 to shift its tail. A green light grew inside the hollow tube. In a few moments a blinding beam stabbed up at Tyrant. A magnified ray cannon many times the intensity of the armaments affixed to martian saucers, the beam lanced through Tyrant's body and brought the hulking monster crashing to the ground once more.

Briilip grinned. They turned to observe the saucer's crew and assure themselves the soldiers were expressing a suitable amount of excitement. This was a stupendous triumph! The Elder's theories were proven. The Prime Director would have to admit that Briilip had created the perfect organism, the supreme addition to the arsenal of Mars.

Tyrant reared up, its body coiling around itself in a slithering spiral. The monster's bifurcated tail was outstretched, its tips shaking from side to side. A deafening whine screamed through the saucer before the exterior sensors reduced the volume they were relaying to the martians. Several of the soldiers were doubled over in pain. Briilip themselves staggered, a trickle of green blood falling from their nasal openings. The Elder recognized the effect as that of a sonic attack. Doubt crawled into their hearts as they focused again on the holographic display.

Number 649 bore the brunt of Tyrant's assault. The casing around the ray cannon mounted in its tail was shattered, exploded by the sonic vibrations. The destructive waves continued to pound the cyborg. One after another the cobalt plates of its shell were rupturing.

"Quick! Destroy Tyrant's tail!" Briilip ordered their warbeast, desperation in their voice. Number 649 scurried forwards, but it did so with far less speed than its predecessors. The weight of its mechanical components was now showing its negative aspect. The cyborg wasn't as agile as a purely biological design. The barrage of vibrations continued to ravage it as it trudged through the red sand. Ruptured plates opened like ghastly flowers all across its body.

With its main ray cannon destroyed, Number 649 opened up with the smaller batteries scattered across its hull. A fusillade of energy beams rippled across Tyrant, trying to distract the monster and stop the devastating sonic attack. The serpentine hulk, its thick hide compromised by the cyborg's assault, burned as the rays struck it. It soon drew upon its forcefield to shield it from the barrage. In doing so, it was forced to cease the vibrations of its tail.

Briilip felt renewed confidence when the sonic attack faltered. Tyrant couldn't block Number 649's barrage and maintain its own simultaneously. That gave the cyborg an opening. A chance to close with the enemy and bring its other weaponry into play. When the warbeast lunged at Tyrant and sank its claws into the bleeding flesh, the Elder was certain victory was only a matter of moments.

Tyrant undulated its body under the slashing talons of its foe. The long tail whipped against Number 649 with the fury of an avalanche. Had the cyborg's armor been intact it should have withstood the blow, but with its plates ruptured the strike buckled the damaged metal and sent its jagged edges stabbing inwards to skewer the warbeast's biomass.

Devoid of any sense of pain or fear, Number 649 fought on, oblivious to the havoc each blow from Tyrant was visiting on its internal constituents. The cyborg's metal jaws clamped down on the side of the monster's body and began to grind through the thick scales. At the same time a strike from the ophidian tail crumpled the plates behind Number 649's tail.

Dread returned to Briilip as they saw Tyrant squirm its body and arc its jaws down towards the now exposed neck. The combatants were in a race now, a contest to see which could pierce the other's defenses to reach a vital area. The Elder didn't know enough about the biology of the enemy to determine if the cyborg would hit a lethal area, but they were well aware of what Tyrant's fangs were within reach of.

"Impossible!" Briilip groaned. "Why won't it die?!"

Blood and chunks of meat sprayed from Tyrant's body as Number 649 ripped away at its foe. The monster wasn't distracted from its own goal. The rows of fangs tore through the remaining layers of plates and the softer biomass within. Buried in that biomass was the cluster of nerve nodes and computation relays that served as the cyborg's brain. A bright plume of fire erupted from the warbeast's neck when Tyrant bit into that brain. It reared back, nerves and wires hanging off the biomechanical mass locked in its jaws. Coolant and cerebral fluid dripped from the monster's fangs as it crunched away at its prize.

The removal of its brain caused Number 649 to

immediately shut down. So complex and vital was the control system, that Briilip was incapable of providing their creation with a redundant backup. The Elder could only watch in despair as their creation froze in place, as immobile as a statue. When Tyrant spat out what was left of the brain, a flick of its tail knocked Number 649 onto its side. Vengefully the monster battered the lifeless hulk, smashing it into a scrapheap of mangled metal and pulverized biomass.

"Commander, what should we do now?" one of the martian crew asked Briilip.

The Elder weighed their options. Number 649 had damaged Tyrant more than any other attack trained upon the brute since its arrival at Anomaly Epsilon 54. It was visibly weak and wounded, but given its ability to harness æmber to regenerate, that condition wouldn't persist long. Against this, Briilip weighed the fact they had but a single saucer at their command. The ray guns and weapons aboard wouldn't amount to even the force of a single barrage from the armaments of Number 649. To try to attack Tyrant on their own, even in its weakened state, was a losing prospect.

There was something else for the Elder to consider. How this latest failure would be received by the Prime Director. The prospect of reprimand and reeducation was enough to sour Briilip's digestive tract. Death in battle with Tyrant might be preferable, though doing so would mean squandering even more valuable resources.

"Our duty to Mars is to return to Central Drome with this saucer and its assets," Briilip told the crew. "Even in defeat, Mars Lives On."

As the saucer flew away from Anomaly Epsilon 54, Briilip

consoled themselves with the thought that Ghireen might again intercede with the Prime Director and allow the Elder to try again to design a creature capable of destroying Tyrant.

Ghireen watched as Tyrant finished smashing Briilip's latest creation into a pile of junk. The cyborg inflicted an immense amount of damage on the monster, but in the end it wasn't enough. Now the creature was slithering back into its crevasse to draw in the revitalizing æmber and heal its injuries. Judging by its wounds, Ghireen thought the thing would be in fighting shape within a few solar cycles. Regeneration was one of the principal strengths of its genetic design.

The Elder's saucer was hidden under the sand at the edge of Anomaly Epsilon 54. Near enough to observe, but not near enough to be caught in any of the fighting. Ghireen was too prudent to make reckless requests for cavorite from the Prime Director. Such things were bound to draw the curiosity of ambitious scientists and make them wonder why the scientist needed the precious resource. Much better to keep a low profile so that their experiments could be conducted with a modicum of secrecy.

"The other saucer has disengaged its stealth field," a martian soldier reported. "They're leaving the area. Course prediction postulates Central Drome as their most likely destination."

Ghireen nodded. "Briilip has failed and is returning to their laboratory to try again. I don't believe they can improve on this last design, however. I think anything they create now will simply be derivative and motivated more by desperation than innovation. A pity. I've profited greatly from Briilip's efforts. Yet I can in no good conscience allow resources to be wasted.

That would be to the detriment of Mars."

The bifurcated tail of Tyrant vanished into the darkness of the crevasse, leaving only the shattered debris of Number 649 on the desert floor. Ghireen studied the wreckage for a moment, their mind analyzing the details and adding them into the Elder's calculations.

"Briilip's utility is over," Ghireen decided. "I will suggest the reeducation pods to the Prime Director." They shifted their attention back to the crevasse and thought of the vanished Tyrant.

"It is to be regretted Briilip will never appreciate the service they have provided for Mars," Ghireen mused. "Their flawed creations have helped enormously to demonstrate the genius of my own design.

"Tyrant has proven itself to be the perfect organism."

WIBBLE AND PPLIMZ, INVESTIGATORS FOR HIRE

M Darusha Wehm

The sign on the door was written in an alien sigil I didn't understand, but before I could get my pocket translator on the job, some piece of technology or arcane spell must have recognized my species because the shapes shifted and words began to cycle through several human languages.

Wibble and Pplimz, Investigators for Hire, it read.

I reached out to touch the door, but before I could make contact, it slid open with a deeply disturbing organic slurp that I tried immediately to forget. I hesitated, then a mechanical voice came from inside the dimly lit room.

"Habla español? Français, ꜰ�ꝛꞁꞁ ꞁꓷ꞊ ꟼꞁ꞊ꓭꞁꞁꓱ?"

"Versal," I called back.

"Enter, human, or close the door!" the voice responded.

I stepped over the threshold, briefly concerned that I would step into a puddle of sapient goo or be sucked into some fifth dimensional vortex, but I entered a room that wouldn't have been entirely out of place in one of the human enclaves on the east side of Hub City where I lived. There was a large desk with a holo screen, a couple of chairs facing the desk, and a large humanoid robot seated on the other side. Some kind of iridescent bulbous light fixture floated in the corner, but that was the strangest thing in the small place. I felt the breath leak out of my body as I relaxed.

A voice came from the direction of the stock-still robot behind the desk. "Have you need of investigation?" It must be some kind of receptionbot, I thought. What I could see of it was nominally humanoid, with a thin torso between two arms, its "head" a thin rectangular screen. The screen illuminated and a vaguely human-like face appeared. The mouth didn't quite move along with the words and the eyes didn't blink entirely in unison, but it was close enough.

"Yes. I'd like to meet with Wibble. Or Pplimz. Or..." It occurred to me that Wibble and Pplimz might be a joint construct, and I'd just insulted them. There were no species or house affiliations evident in the office, so I had no idea who – or what – to expect. All I knew was that Wibble and Pplimz were who you went to when the authorities couldn't, or wouldn't, help you. Which was exactly where I found myself.

"Please sit," the robot said. "Do you require hydration?"

"No, thank you," I said and perched on the chair. As soon as I'd seated myself a series of whirring noises came from across the desk and the robot seemed to come to life. The screen face took on an even more animated appearance as its arm-like limbs sprang from its body and began fiddling with items on the desk. A note tablet and stylus appeared at the ends of its appendages and the entire body leaned in toward me. That's when I noticed that it – that *they* – were not a robot at all.

Organic matter peeked between the edges of dark metal, silicon, and polymer. I couldn't tell whether they were an organic being who had been profoundly technologically augmented or a machine that had been built with organic components. Either way, it was none of my business and would have been inappropriate to ask. Especially since I was pretty sure this was...

"Pplimz," they said, sticking a "hand" across the table to shake. "At your service."

I shook hands with the cyborg, and pulled a holochip from my inside coat pocket. I set it on the desk and the image of a dark-haired, smirking woman was projected into the space between us, slightly illuminating the room.

"This is my sister, Kristina Shallas. She is missing, and I hope you can help me find her."

The floating light fixture in the corner strobed a pale blue pattern and a series of low, mournful sounds emanated from its general area.

"I agree," Pplimz said, looking up toward the object. It must have been some kind of communication device. I tapped my earpiece to make sure it was on, then flipped open my translator to see if it could make sense of the noises.

"Well, have you?" Pplimz asked, as if I'd understood the message. The screen on my translator unhelpfully flashed *Language Pack Not Found*.

"Uh..." I looked from the cyborg to the glowing light and back again. With an unexpected *pop* the tiny blimp moved of what appeared to be its own accord to hover unnervingly close to my right elbow. It pulsed slowly, the color of its aura shifting through the pastel spectrum. I didn't even have time to wonder what was going on when it extruded part of its casing and enveloped my translator.

I opened my mouth to say... something, just as Pplimz said, "Wibble! What are you doing? Give this human back her material object this instant. You have no idea where it has been."

I stared blankly as the pulsing blob squeezed my translator back out on to the desk.

A series of low sounds came from beside me, but my translator had obviously been updated, as I also heard a kindly voice say, "I'm sorry, this just seemed like the easiest solution." The creature waggled its tail and floated over to hang near Pplimz. "I asked if you'd gone to the local authorities," it said.

"Uh..." I took a moment to reassess the situation. I lost count a long time ago of the number of alien species I'd met on the Crucible, but I'd never encountered anything like Wibble. They were shaped most like a whale, translucent like a jellyfish, and bobbed about like a helium-filled balloon.

"Please forgive my partner," Pplimz said to me, their screen face shooting Wibble an exasperated look, "she can be somewhat excitable."

"Oh, no, it's not a problem," I said. "Thank you for the language pack." Wibble dipped her front end in what I guessed was a gesture of acknowledgment.

"Well?" she said, her voice impatient in my ear and her body flashing between pink and yellow. "The authorities? Which have you informed?"

"Ah," I said. "None of them."

Wibble made a noise that I didn't need the translator to tell me meant that she was unimpressed. I tapped a keystroke on my handheld and the hologram on the desk went dark, then the holochip projected a low-res two-dimensional video message onto the desktop.

Kristina was running, the view from the camera drone in front of her jerky and unfocused.

"Don't come after me, Margie," she said, looking over her shoulder quickly at the blur of dark forms in the background. "I found something down here but now they've caught up to me. You know what they say: no one ever gets out of here. Don't follow me, I mean it. They're–" She left the frame of the video as if she'd stumbled, and the beings chasing her came into full view of the camera.

Terrifying bodies of various configurations, with appendages made of blades and mouths crammed with too many teeth, bore down on the camera's position. I could make out something that looked at least nine feet tall, in a shimmering black outfit that covered their entire body including their head. Prosthetic fingers, sharp like talons, reached out toward the camera, and the face mask twisted into a hideous grin under a headpiece that resembled horns. Another one of them unfurled a set of pitch black mech wings which blocked out all light except the otherworldly glow of their seven pairs of eyes. A terrible sound somewhere between laughter and screaming filled the room, then the video went dead.

"I see," Wibble said after a long pause. "Well, I suppose that explains it."

"Dis," Pplimz said evenly, as if there was nothing even

remotely terrifying about the underworld society of cybernetically enhanced demons.

"No authorities in Hub City are going to be willing to go after them," I said.

"I imagine not," Pplimz agreed.

"Well, this *is* interesting, after all," Wibble said, as if it were merely a particularly challenging brainteaser as opposed to a person's life we were dealing with. "Dis demons don't generally kidnap people. My understanding is that they don't particularly care for strangers in their environment. How very interesting, indeed!"

I replayed the video clip. "I don't think they kidnapped her, exactly," I said. "I- I suspect she was already down there when they found her. And now they just aren't letting her leave."

"Ooh," Wibble said, her body pulsing yellow and green, flippers waggling in what appeared to be delight. "Is your sister some kind of thrill-seeker, delving into dangerous territories for the fun of it?"

"Something like that," I answered.

"The rumors that no one escapes from Dis are gravely overstated," Pplimz said with authority, and I raked my eyes over their cybernetic body. I'm not naive. I knew full well that not all cyborgs are Dis demons. I also knew that Dis demons *are* cyborgs, or something close enough to be called such, and that I was sitting across the desk from a cyborg who seemed to know a great deal about Dis.

"We'll take the case," Wibble said before I could come to a conclusion about my misgivings. She floated over to the desk and, using some kind of invisible kinetic force, passed me a tablet with a contract ready to be completed. The terms were within my means, so I added my name and thumbed my agreement.

After I left their office, I spent the rest of the day clearing my schedule. I might have to miss out on some lucrative business opportunities, but getting Kristina back was more valuable to me than a couple of days' worth of work. If this was what it was going to take, so be it.

My communicator chimed with a message from Wibble, asking me to meet her and Pplimz at the edge of a nearby aquatic enclave that evening. There was a rather pleasant green space adjacent to the water, which made for a recreational area for non-aquatic species as well as acting as a base for the airlocks which allowed communication between the air and water realms.

When I arrived, there was a small crowd enjoying the evening. A group of squat, multi-armed beings with their heads entirely covered in colorful garments which fell to their first pair of arms sat on a picnic blanket talking loudly and ingesting glowing cubes of what I assumed was sustenance. Near the water, a bronze giant dressed in the most exquisite silken robes, as if he had never once seen battle, walked hand-in-hand with an armor-plated saurian, her wings trailing behind them in the breeze. Takes all kinds, I thought, as I scanned the park for the detectives.

I finally spotted Pplimz sitting on a bench facing the water, their long arms slung over the seat back. They were wearing a human-style fine silver and dark gray pinstriped trouser suit, tailored snugly to their thin body. A charcoal brimmed hat perched precariously atop their screen head, which distracted me enough that it took me quite a while to recognize Wibble floating next to them. I hadn't noticed in the dim light of their office how translucent Wibble really was – I could very clearly see Pplimz right through her.

I joined them on the bench, the three of us making just another motley group of beings enjoying a pleasant evening in the park.

"Have you learned where Kristina is being kept?" I asked, keeping my voice down.

"I have made a thorough examination of the video image you provided," Pplimz said, carefully staring out at the water as if not looking at me would make anyone watching believe that we weren't talking to each other. Whatever. I could play pretend spies if that's what they wanted.

"And?"

"And I was able to match some of the background footage to a known Dis area in the Lawless Zone," Pplimz continued. "I believe Kristina is not that far from here." Pplimz swiveled their screen head briefly in my direction, and cast their eyes downward before returning to look at the water.

"We're saying we think she's somewhere underground, right here in Hub City," Wibble explained enthusiastically.

"I see," I said, evenly. It wasn't exactly news to me – that's where I thought she was, too. But I wasn't prepared to share everything I knew with the detectives, so waiting to see if they could figure it out seemed like a good test of their skills. They passed, more quickly than I thought they might. Perhaps they were as good as their reputation implied after all.

"So, what's the next step?" I asked, as a splash from the

water caught my attention. A small, green saurian leaped out of the water to become half-beached on the shore. A pair of beautiful quartz sylicates walked over to the marinusaur, their rocky bodies surprisingly graceful as they moved. They sat down at the water's edge, and the three of them began to have an animated conversation.

"We'll just have to mount a daring rescue!" Wibble said, flippers waggling.

"I am quite certain that ichthyosaur is in no need of our assistance," Pplimz said, waving an arm in the direction of the beach. "That is an amphibious species, I believe."

"Not here," Wibble said, exasperated. "In the underground warrens beneath the city. To rescue our missing person, satisfying our client, and fulfilling our mission in a grand adventure!"

"Alternatively," Pplimz said archly, "we could leverage our extensive contacts in various areas in the city, and see if we can make a trade. I find it highly improbable that anyone in the house of Dis has a strong desire to feed and lodge a human for an indeterminate amount of time."

"Oh, we never get to have any fun," Wibble said, sulking.

"We are not here to have fun, Wibble," Pplimz said. "We are here to do a job."

"You're only saying that because you never installed that *Sense of Adventure* upgrade I suggested you get," Wibble said, floating out to face Pplimz. "I should just buy it for you for your next naming day."

"I do not have a naming day, as you well know," Pplimz said, turning away from Wibble, who then floated directly in front of Pplimz's screen, making sure she stayed in their view no matter where they looked.

"Anyone can have a naming day," Wibble said. "You just have to pick a date."

"I do not wish to have a naming day and I especially do not wish for you to be giving me personality upgrades as gifts on said naming day."

"This is exactly what I'm talking about," Wibble said. "You never let me do anything nice for you! I just want to–"

"Excuse me!" I interrupted. "Can you have your weird personal argument on your own time? My… sister is being held captive by demons and even you agree that they're not going to keep her alive forever. We need to do something!"

"We are doing something," Wibble said, sounding confused at my outburst. "We're planning."

"No, you aren't," I said, not bothering to keep the anger out of my voice. "You're ruining a nice evening at the water's edge by bickering. And you're wasting my time!"

"Perhaps you forget that I am not a being like yourself," Pplimz said, only slightly patronizingly, "who can conduct only one or two activities at once. While we are meeting here, I am also negotiating with several of my contacts in the Lawless Zone to effect what I trust will be an appealing bargain for the return of your sibling. I expect that we shall have a deal in place by tomorrow."

I had no retort for that. Of course, Pplimz was multithreaded, why wouldn't they be? What was the point of being more machine than organic matter if you couldn't behave like a computer?

"Of course," I apologized. "What kind of… item are you thinking you will need for the trade? I'll have to make some calculations to see what I'm … able to afford."

"I do not believe we will require anything additional from you," Pplimz said.

"Consider it all a part of the service," Wibble added.

"That's very reasonable."

"We will need to finish our enquiries, but we should meet again tomorrow," Pplimz said.

"You want to meet again?" I asked. "Why?"

"This is a human matter and, as such, it requires a human's involvement."

"Surely my presence is only going to make things more complicated," I said. "I'd just be in the way."

"Nonsense!" Wibble said. "We couldn't possibly do this without you. You're the client, you must be there."

"For once, Wibble is entirely correct," Pplimz said, standing, the meeting obviously over. "We shall contact you tomorrow."

I could tell that they were adamant, but I still didn't understand what possible use I could be – or why I'd have to put myself in a potentially dangerous situation.

"Just be there when we call," Wibble added cheerfully enough as she floated away, but I clearly caught the implied "or else."

The next day I woke early expecting to hear from Wibble or Pplimz, but there was nothing. The day wore on with no sign from either detective, and it was getting to be late enough that I started to seriously consider that I might have been hustled when my communicator chimed with a message: a time and a location in the Lawless Zone.

I'd spent some time in that area of Hub City before, so I looked over my self-defense collection. I selected a pair of stunner gauntlets that appeared at a cursory glance to be fashionable gloves and slipped them over my hands. I added my special boots with their hidden pockets to my outfit and headed out into the steaming evening to meet the detectives.

I followed the directions they'd given me to a nondescript door halfway down a dark and foreboding alleyway. A being quite a bit shorter than me but at least twice as muscular leaned against the wall by the door, utterly failing to look casual. His dark blue skin showed where he'd rolled up the sleeves of his tunic, which looked like it hadn't seen the inside of a laundry since at least three battles ago. A heavy-looking broadaxe was propped up next to him, but his hands were in his pockets, not on the hilt of the weapon.

I'd had a few run-ins with goblins before, so I knew not to underestimate him, but he only nodded at me as I pulled open the door. Either I didn't look like a threat or he really was just holding up the wall.

I descended a dank stairwell to find myself in a surprisingly cozy underground tavern. Beings of all kinds clustered around small tables, drinking, eating, arguing and playing games of skill, strength and chance. I scanned the room until I saw the tall, lean form of Pplimz. This time their suit was a natty plaid number, in the same silver and dark gray. The ridiculous hat somehow managed to stay perched on their head as Pplimz stood nose to nose with what I suspected was a spirit of some sort.

Their form was more or less humanoid, but that might only have been due to the shape of their containment suit: one head, two legs, and the same number of arms, one of which held a brightly glowing sword. It could have been one of any number of species inside there, except for the warm yellow light leaking out from every edge of the golden glinting articulated suit.

I recognized the armor. Could Pplimz really be menacing a knight of the Sanctum? I glanced down at the knight's weapon, wondering whether Pplimz was made of stronger stuff than I'd imagined. I'd seen one of those swords slice clean through a solid titanium door once. I very much doubted Pplimz's body could withstand that. But they calmly stared down the knight, who appeared to be cowering – as much as a being in a six-foot-tall suit of armor could cower. It made for a very odd tableau, but I suppose stranger things had happened in this place, given how little interest the other patrons were taking in the scene.

As I approached, Pplimz caught my eye, then kicked at the knight's sword, sending it clattering to the floor. The knight made no move to retrieve it, instead looking over to Pplimz's side. I followed their glance and made out Wibble hovering next to the spirit and pulsing deeply – purple through green. The spirit's voice came to me low and thunderous, but I detected a note of fear in it.

"What is this supposed to be," they asked, "some kind of 'good cop, bad cop' routine?"

Pplimz took a half step back and somehow seemed to grow even more rigid. "Absolutely not." They managed to sound appalled and hurt at the same time. "I will have you know that both my partner and I are excellent investigators with dozens of satisfied clients who will attest to that fact. Our references are impeccable, and our results speak for themselves. And to refer to us in the vernacular as 'cops', well..." This was said with as much distaste as a mechanized voice could manage. "We are not employees of any official agen–"

The spirit suddenly doubled over, letting out a pained grunt. Wibble had extruded a stiff fist-like section of her body and thoroughly walloped the spirit in the midsection. Their shiny armor had about as much effect as a thin sheet of cheaply fabricated material, and the spirit took their time straightening up. The dent in the middle of their armor was quite impressive.

"I'm the bad cop," Wibble said, and giggled. She grabbed the spirit by the chin and hovered only inches away from their face. "So, are you going to talk, or do I have to get rough with you?"

"Wibble!" Pplimz turned to face their partner, their screen face somehow managing to convey both outrage and amusement. "Injuring this being is not going to provide us with the information we require. How many times have I told you that this kind of behavior is both unnecessary and unbecoming...?"

The spirit moved then, extending an arm out to their right toward a dim hallway. "Fourth door on the right," the spirit wheezed. "The keypad pattern is an inverted star." Wibble let go of her hold on the spirit and they sank down to the floor.

"You were saying something, dear?" Wibble said brightly to Pplimz as she lazily waved her tail and floated off toward the hallway.

The cyborg made a noise that sounded very much like a sigh, then turned to me. "We will need to change our appearances," they said, then strode off in Wibble's wake. What could I do, but follow?

Pplimz carried a small suitcase upholstered in a pattern that matched their suit, and set it on the floor next to the fourth door on the right. They inserted a tiny implement extruded from their left hand into a mechanism in the case and, after a brief whir, flipped open the lid.

"You came prepared with disguises?" I asked.

"Only one disguise," Wibble said. "Humans aren't exactly welcome where we'll be going."

I wondered what technological marvel they had in store for me: a holographic costume generator? Some kind of mind-altering forcefield that would make me appear to be a Dis cyborg?

Pplimz pulled what looked like a large plain black cloak from the case and held it out to me.

"What's this? Some kind of invisibility device?"

"No," Pplimz said.

"It's just a cloak, really," Wibble added. "Should be able to hide all your human bits under there."

I held the thing out in front of me. It was nothing more than a big piece of black fabric with a hood.

"You're joking."

"Put it on, please," Pplimz said, staring at me as if vaguely disappointed, then they removed their suit coat and neatly folded it before carefully placing it in the suitcase along with their hat. I slipped the cloak over my head and had to admit that it did cover me completely. With the hood up, I could be anything hidden inside.

"What about you two?" I asked. "It's roomy but I don't think we'll all fit under here."

Neither of them answered, but a soft whirring came from Pplimz's body. Their arms, which up until now had been humanoid enough, began to sprout additional appendages. Sharp, deadly-looking appendages. Soon, both their arms resembled a devil prince's own multitool, with blades, knives, whirling saws, and laser swords sticking out all which way.

I'd been so focused on the weaponry sprouting from their arms that I hadn't noticed that Pplimz also grew nearly eighteen inches in height, bulked out horizontally, and now sported a countenance that would make the most hardened Brobnar giant run screaming home to their parent. I found myself scrambling back until I ran into the wall.

It was the teeth, I think. Far too many sharp teeth for one face.

"Better get used to it," Wibble said, brightly. "You're going to see a lot more like that when we get where we're going."

I swallowed hard and did my best to follow her advice. "What about you?" I asked, facing Wibble to try to stop staring at those teeth. "Can you change shape?"

"Sure," she said, her body popping into a perfect cube. "But I can't look like that." She waggled a flipper in Pplimz's general direction and stretched back out into her normal ovoid.

"So, what's your disguise, then?"

She shimmered, then settled herself into the suitcase. "I'm going as carry-on," she said and Pplimz shut the suitcase, closing her up inside.

"You are most certainly a burden," the cyborg said under their voice.

"I heard that!" came a muffled voice from inside the case.

"Please, Wibble, be quiet for once in your life," Pplimz said and hefted the case. "All right. Off we go."

It was dark and humid and it smelled like sulphur and fish. I held a thick wad of the fabric from the hood of my cloak over my nose and mouth and was silently grateful that this was the disguise they'd brought for me after all. The walls of the narrow corridor dripped with a noxious, sticky goo and I carefully picked my way along the path to avoid getting the stuff on my borrowed cloak while trying not to think about the state of my boots. Pplimz was easy to follow, their illuminated eyes casting an amber glow as we descended through the winding tunnel.

"Where are we going?" I whispered.

"Down to meet with the people who have Kristina," Pplimz hissed. "And do try to be quiet. Walls have ears."

I squinted at the slimy corridor. It wouldn't have surprised me one bit if Pplimz had been being literal. There were niches cut into the walls, but I could only see eerie decorations that appeared to be made of rough-hewn stone. No body parts of any kind. That was a relief.

I was beginning to think that this was going to be fine. I was in the company of professionals, and we were on our way to make a business deal. I was good at business deals. So what if it was a deal with devils in the bowels of a secret underground cavern? It was business. Surely even demons could see the value of a good deal when it came their way.

I couldn't tell in the gloom how far we'd gone, but it felt like we'd been shuffling along the passageway for quite some time when Pplimz abruptly stopped.

"I can see three, maybe four, individuals upcoming." The voice from the suitcase was muffled but clearly audible in the small space.

"How can you see anything in there?" I blurted out without thinking. No one could tell what I looked like under this cloak, but my voice would give me away as a human to anything that could hear.

"Echolocation. Obviously," Wibble answered in a tone that implied she was reevaluating her opinion of my intelligence.

"Are these our contacts?" I asked, more quietly this time.

"I think not," said Pplimz. "I was given a very specific location and this is not it."

"Well, whoever they are, they're definitely coming our way, Pplimz," Wibble said, with uncharacteristic urgency in her voice. "If you've got a plan, I suggest you implement it forthwith."

"Thank you for your ceaseless confidence, Wibble," Pplimz said frostily. They opened their mouth and projected a dim green beam which danced along the walls. The light played over the tunnel, illuminating the grottoes with their disturbing statues shoved into holes in the walls, trails of oozing slime slicking down, and something that looked suspiciously like a door.

"Here is our exit," Pplimz said, and barged straight into the wall, the door soundlessly drawing open as their weight crashed into it. "Follow me."

They stepped through the open doorway and I followed

as ordered. I suppose I expected it would be another tight corridor leading down a different way into the depths of the Crucible. Instead, the floor disappeared, and my stomach flew into my throat as I fell.

After the initial drop, I found myself on my back sliding down a smooth, slick, winding incline. I could tell I was picking up speed, but I couldn't see a thing in the pitch black. All I could hear was Wibble's gleeful voice from somewhere not far in front of me.

"Whee!"

"Wibble, really," Pplimz said, "have some self-respect."

I was starting to become completely disoriented sliding down the lightless corkscrew when I abruptly crashed into Pplimz. I was momentarily stunned by both the impact and the fact that it appeared that I had somehow avoided contact with every single one of the deadly implements of torture currently covering the cyborg's body.

"There's nothing wrong with enjoying oneself, Pplimz," Wibble said. "Especially when things are most likely about to become decidedly less enjoyable."

"Wh- what?" I blinked, trying to see something – anything – in the dim light.

"We have company," Pplimz said drily as a flame flared into life before us. "Keep still."

Wibble's previous suggestion that I prepare myself for terrifying sights was appropriate and accurate, but entirely insufficient. However, my natural reaction to the large group of enormous Dis demons surrounding us, their very bodies seemingly built of the most diverse group of instruments for injuring another being I could imagine, was to freeze. I couldn't have moved if my life depended upon it, which at the moment it seemed very much like it might.

Many pairs of glowing eyes raked over us, and a noise that made my spine ache rose from the midst of the group. It was like a human scream, a banshee's wail, and the sound of metal gears that had never seen the taste of oil grinding painfully against each other. Was this some kind of sonic torture device, I wondered, when Pplimz took a step toward the group.

They bowed their head toward the demons while the terrible noise echoed throughout the chamber. Was *this* how they talked to each other? No wonder beings avoided the underworld if this was how one asked for directions.

The screeching went on for a few moments, with no other sign of aggression from – who were these beings? Our captors? A welcoming party? A debate club meeting we'd literally dropped in on? Regardless, they weren't currently tearing us limb from limb, so I took a moment to calm down. I'd just about remembered how to control my body when movement from my left caught my attention. I turned to see one of the smaller demons move unnaturally quickly from the edge of the pack to slither right next to me.

They may have been small, but they made up for their lack of size with augmentations that appeared to have been designed specifically to terrify a human. Their jet-black body was an articulated serpentine form, with razor-sharp scales that rippled in the flame's glow. That might have been tolerable, except for their head which was dominated by a large set of slavering mechanical jaws that gave them a wolflike appearance. It didn't help that they were smacking those jaws as if in anticipation of a delicious meal as they wormed their way over to me.

I was aware of the several knives I had secreted in the specially constructed pockets of my boots. I knew, intellectually, that all I had to do was squeeze my hands in just the right way, and thanks to my gauntlets I'd be able to punch an electrically charged wallop that would fell a giant. But none of that planning mattered. Once again, I was frozen in place as the demon shoved their muzzle right up against the hood of my cloak, as if sniffing me. They were so close, I could see the spots of rust on the individual metal hinges on their jaws.

A scream was brewing deep in my lungs and there wasn't going to be anything I could do to stop it from coming out, when my attacker cocked their head, blinked their many eyes slowly, then abruptly slithered back to the group. As if all the muscles in my body suddenly lost their ability to function, I deflated like an airship with the stopper removed. Physically and emotionally drained, I found myself lying against Pplimz, who had stepped away from the group when the terrible screaming mercifully stopped.

Pplimz turned, dumping me unceremoniously into a heap. I scrambled to make sure the cloak still covered me, but Pplimz said, "There is no need to disguise yourself any more. They know who you are." The cyborg extended a refreshingly knife-free appendage down to help me to my feet, and I stood, confused.

"What's going on?"

Pplimz said nothing, instead opening the suitcase. Their

suit jacket floated out, the charcoal hat perched just above the collar, and it hovered in midair for a moment. The arms waved around limply and I'd just about come to the conclusion that it wasn't possible for anything else to startle me, when the hat and jacket fell to the ground. Of course, it was Wibble.

She turned in a lazy circle, her body pulsing with a yellow light which further illuminated the cavern we were in. There were weapons from all corners of the Crucible hung on the stone walls, what appeared to be skins, carapaces, and skeletons of various beings on display, and cauldrons of that nasty-looking bubbling goo. As I looked closer, I could see large chunks of pure æmber dotted in some of the niches. It seemed like the rumors I'd heard of a valuable cache of æmber down here in Dis might be true.

"It's delightfully gloomy!" Wibble said, her flippers waggling. "What an interesting aesthetic sense they have down here, don't you think?"

"What is happening?" I hissed, my eyes darting from one terrifying demon to the next. I leaned in toward Wibble and lowered my voice. "I think that snakey one wanted to eat me."

Wibble tipped her entire body in a pose that reminded me of a dog perking its ears up. "Oh, it probably *did* eat you," she said, cheerfully. "They feed on emotions, you know. The stronger the better. I suspect you were offering up quite the buffet!"

"Come on," Pplimz said, packing the jacket and hat back in the suitcase, then waving a sword-arm in the direction of the demon mob. I took a tentative step to draw alongside Pplimz when the demons before me parted. Three individuals came toward us out of the gloom: two large demons bristling with weapons on either side of a much smaller humanoid. Not just any humanoid – it was Kristina.

She slowly lifted her head, her long hair hiding her face. I couldn't tell if she was injured; the demons on either side of her could easily be the only thing holding her up.

"What have you done?" I shouted without thought, and tried to run toward her, but I was held back by an invisible field. Once again, I was rooted in place.

Kristina brushed the hair from her eyes and stared at me. "I told you not to follow me," she said.

My mind was racing. Surely these were the demons we were meant to be meeting. "I had to," I said. "I couldn't leave you here, not *my own sister*." I hoped she'd get the hint.

She laughed then, and I noticed that the demons weren't holding her after all. She was standing there, free as anyone, with the same look of defiance on her face she'd had the first time I'd met her in that Eastside bar.

"Nice touch, that," she said. "Telling them we were sisters. As if family would mean anything to you."

I looked at Wibble and Pplimz, but neither of them seemed at all surprised at what Kristina was saying. Something in the back of my brain was telling me that things had gone sideways, but I was too overwhelmed to make any sense of it.

"I told you not to follow," Kristina went on. "I honestly hoped you wouldn't, but I should have known you'd never leave a potential haul of all this æmber just because your thief went missing. You've always used people, Margie, and when you assigned me to steal from the underworld, I'd finally had enough. Nowhere is too dangerous for you." She looked back at the group of demons behind her.

"Well," she added, "it's never particularly dangerous for *you*. You're always safe in your Eastside office. But you're perfectly happy to send someone else to do the hard work while you take all the profits. That's not a very fair trade, now is it?"

I didn't know what to say. I was starting to realize that I had absolutely no idea what was going on.

I'd been running a crew of thieves out of Eastside for ages, but it was a hardscrabble life. We'd never gotten more than a few æmbits or barts from any of our capers, and it was barely worth the risk. I'd lost more than a few members of my crew to legitimate work over the years. But then I heard a rumor that there was a huge stockpile of raw æmber in the Dis underworld below Hub City. The story went that it was hardly even guarded, since everyone was so afraid of even setting foot in the place. No one escapes the underworld, they said. Well, we'd just see about that.

"A great reward requires a great risk," I'd told my team. Of course, I wasn't about to take any of the risk myself, personally. I was the brains of the operation, and if something happened to me then it was more than just this one job that was in peril. No, I'd stay behind and set up the deals. Someone else would have to go and actually steal the æmber.

I assigned Kristina to the job. She'd been with the team for a while and she was the best at sneaking in and out of difficult locations. I'd never known her to be unable to get out of a tight spot. And it happened that she had come to me only a few days before, telling me that she wanted out of the gang.

"Just do this one last job," I'd told her. I most certainly

was not threatening her; the sparks coming off my stunner gauntlets were entirely unrelated to our conversation. "Then you'll have enough to do whatever you want. It's a good trade, I promise."

I would have found some way to keep her on the team, of course. Someone able to get in and out of the Dis underworld would be far too valuable to give up. And I only half-believed she'd pull it off, anyway. They say no one escapes from the underworld and it might have been true. But I was the boss and I told her to go. So, she went.

That horrible wailing started up again, and Pplimz stepped toward the demons. A moment later the other cyborgs began to shimmy and shake in an uncontrolled manner. For a brief moment I held out a faint hope that Pplimz had unleashed some kind of cyborg weapon, and we were about to make a break for it, but then I realized the demons were laughing. The screeching went on.

I turned toward Wibble. "Is this – *noise* – demon communication?" I asked, my eyes wide.

She bobbed back and forth and her voice in my earpiece barely cut through the din. "No. It's a sonic cloak, so we can't hear them. Although, come to think of it, it might just be a clever ruse. They may not even use sound to communicate, there's really no reason to assume that they do. After all, many beings communicate in other ways. Why, I knew a lovely phyll once–"

The screaming abruptly stopped, which shocked Wibble into silence. Kristina continued talking as if nothing remotely unusual had just occurred.

"I made a deal," she said, a grin spreading across her face. "I would *not* steal the trove of æmber you sent me to get, in exchange for flushing you out of your safe backroom in Eastside. That you actually came all the way down here is just a bonus for my new friends here."

"But how?" I asked. "No one can communicate with a Dis demon. Only Archons and other demons."

"Well, now, it turns out that this is only partially accurate," Wibble said. "And wouldn't you know it, but your former associate here became acquainted with a very clever detective who happens to have a particular affinity for languages."

"Oh, Wibble," Pplimz said coyly, a flush coloring their screen face. The cyborg couldn't take a compliment, apparently. Their ego was not my problem, however. I needed to figure out how to get out of this mess.

"Fine, Kristina," I said, "what do you want? æmber? A stake in the gang? What?"

"You don't get it, Margie," she said with a look of almost sadness on her face. "I want out. And I want *you* out." With that, the two demons flanking her stalked toward me. I tried to move away, but I was still frozen in place. In no time, the demons were on me, their metallic jaws so close to my face I could feel their hot breath on my skin. One grabbed my arms with the pincers they had instead of hands, and the other waved one of its eight articulated legs in a gesture to the rest of the demons to come closer. I thrashed and screamed, but no one came to help me.

"Wibble!" I shouted, desperate. "You're not going to let them kill me."

"Of course not." Her cheery voice was soft, but I had no

trouble hearing her. I craned my head around to see that she was floating just behind me. It was Wibble who had me in her invisible iron grip. "Don't be ridiculous. No one is murdering anyone. But there's no point in letting all your delicious emotions go to waste when there are hungry demons to feed, am I right?"

"It is only logical," Pplimz added. "Waste not, want not."

The group of demons converged around me, crowding me so close that I was no longer able to make out any of their individual features. It might have been a kindness, if it weren't for the heat and the smell of them. I held my breath, waiting to see what they would do to me.

They didn't touch me other than to keep me in place, and I didn't feel anything physically happen. It was not dissimilar to when the serpentine demon had... tasted me earlier. They came in close, noses and tongues and fangs and beaks extending toward me. I squeezed my eyes closed and waited for what seemed like a lifetime and then it was over. My arms were freed, and I collapsed to the ground, exhausted. When I opened my eyes, Wibble and Pplimz were looking down at me.

"Now what?" I asked, feebly.

"Now, we take you back up to the surface," Wibble said, gesturing to an open door I hadn't noticed before. "It's over."

I got to my feet shakily, and looked back toward Kristina.

"We could have reaped a lot of æmber together," I said.

She shook her head. "It's not worth it. Not your way." She turned and walked away into the gloom. That was the last I ever saw of her.

• • •

"Up we go," Wibble said, as Pplimz ushered me through the door. It was a small room that, once the door swished shut, I realized was a lift. As we rode up in silence, I thought about what I'd do now. I'd have to forget about Kristina and put this all behind me. Sure, I'd need to lie low for a while, but soon enough I could get a new crew together and look for a score somewhere else on the Crucible. This was only a minor setback. Everything was going to be fi–

The lift doors opened, and I was assaulted by the light. My eyes had adjusted to the dimness of the underworld and I was utterly unprepared to see a group of golden-armored knights of the Sanctum waiting for us. Waiting for me.

The one closest to the door took my arm in a firm grip. "I'm afraid you're going to have to come with us," they said, then flipped up the face plate on their helmet. I blinked my eyes a few times, the light pouring from the helmet nearly blinding me.

"Aren't you … ?" A slight smile crossed the knight's exposed face and they shot Wibble a glance. It was the spirit from the bar!

"Don't we make an excellent pair of actors?" Wibble said to the spirit, gleefully. "You were completely convincing."

"It was rather fun," the knight said in a low, booming voice.

"I truly thought for a moment that Wibble had injured you," Pplimz said drily. "I am most pleased to see that it was part of the charade."

"Oh, I'd never hurt someone," Wibble said, "not unless I meant to. That dent in your armor was an excellent touch."

"Thank you," the knight said, shyly. "I am rather proud of that one."

"So, are you saying that this was all..." I looked between Wibble and Pplimz.

"It was no accident you were directed toward our offices," Pplimz admitted. "Do not be concerned, however. We will refund your fee."

"Seeing as how you were never really our client," Wibble finished, a rosy glow suffusing her body. She turned to the knights. "Well, my armored friends, I believe that we've made our trade."

The group bowed deeply toward the two detectives, and Pplimz reshaped their body back to the thin, non-demon form I'd first encountered. They opened the suitcase, slipped on their fashionable suit jacket and placed the hat, somehow, on their head. "Shall we go, Wibble?"

"Yes, Pplimz, we're done here," Wibble said. "Ooh, why don't we go skyhopping?! I heard of a lovely new airship for hire..."

"For goodness sake, Wibble, don't be ridiculous." The detectives went off bickering into the distance, leaving me to the not so tender ministrations of the knights.

No one explained anything as they dragged me off to whatever punishment awaited me. They didn't need to. I knew.

I *had* been hustled all along. Hustled by the best.

VAULTHEADS
David Guymer

Raymon D'arco pulled his ray blaster from its hip holster and fired. It made a high-pitched squirling noise, like an out-of-tune guitar string, and a microwave pulse leapt from the ribbed gun barrel to splash across the svarr mercenary's chest. The thin metallic wall rumpled as the elf threw herself against it and slid to the floor with a dramatic groan.

Ignoring her, the stormkin skirate continued out across the factory floor, faster than a walk although not quite running. At the last moment before reaching the downed elf, he dropped his shoulder and rolled into cover, avoiding the sight lines of the derricks, gantries, ledges and spaghetti criss-cross of torpid conveyer lines above him. The screeching vocals of *æmbersonic*, Hub City's most criminally underrated exotic metals wavecast, blasted at tremendous volume through his cochlear implant, and he nodded absently to the rhythm as he drew back against the near wall and hit the *recharge* key on his E-RAYzer. A variety of antennae and vanes flipped out from the pistol's stock to vent. Raymon's hands goosebumped in the little bubble of warmth, the rest of his body giving a not-at-all sympathetic shiver. Steam billowed out of his mouth. As thick as the discharge of a smoke bomb.

Pressing his finger in behind his left ear, he quietened the music. He pushed in. Something in his inner ear went *click*.

"Ribongun, this is D'arco. I'm in. Where are you?"

"*Coming up from beneath!*" Bursts of heavy, automatic fire ripped across the line, only slightly more frantic than the speaker himself. Ribongun spoke like someone completing a marathon as a series of fifty-yard sprints. "*The Director was expecting us!*"

"Don't get yourself killed. Not now we're so close."

"Wasn't planning on it. But! A little distraction would be nice."

"They don't know what's about to hit them."

He withdrew his finger from his ear and the link cut. Æmbersonic returned at its previous, punishing volume. Raymon winced, tapping rapidly on the side of his head until it became more agreeable. The svarr, spread out on the ground beside him, was still groaning.

What did she want: a medal from the Brobnar actors' guild?

"Hardpan," he hissed over his shoulder, and turned as the immense sylicate following up behind crunched herself into a rough crouch.

The vaultwarrior was almost twice his height and twenty times his weight. Her crust was hard, glossy, and black. Purple crystal formations sprouted from the backs of her hands and the sides of her head, projecting well above the cubicle wall of her supposed cover. A deep, geothermal glow seeped through the cracks in her duricrust. The scuffed walls and old machinery around her smudged and reflected it. Raymon shivered as her body warmed him through. Nor was the effect entirely physical. He smiled up at her, trying to give it the appropriate level of dash, but moved his eyes quickly on.

"Ribs is being pressed hard. It might be on us now." He nodded to the huge, harpoon-like weapon strapped across her back. "I hope you've been looking forward to using that."

The glassy facets of her eyes cut the wintry light into a thousand pieces as she turned her head to appraise the weapon. "I think… I have."

Raymon grinned. He'd been working up the courage for this for months.

He'd known she wouldn't be disappointed.

He'd hoped, anyway.

"Then get ready," he said.

"Where did you learn to fight like this?" she rumbled softly as she unslung the sharpoon.

Raymon wondered how much he needed to say, under the circumstances.

"Books. Magazines. Old reels. When I was younger, I went to Cirrus to learn the Stormkin martial art of skidad from the legendary skirate, Highblake Pontoon."

"Really?"

Raymon was offended. "Really."

"So how did you end up—"

"Follow me," he hissed before she could say any more.

He peeked out of cover, seeing no one, and then hurried across the open floor to the next partition wall. It rumpled as he pressed against it. The factory had been partitioned by a series of such walls, presumably to separate the various assembly processes, or perhaps as a maze to confound thieves and spies, or simply for the workers' amusement. Raymon had no idea what deviant research the Director conducted here. He didn't want to know.

Crouching on one knee, he whipped an æmberscanner from his utility belt.

Every skirate worth anything wore a utility belt.

The æmberscanner was silvery, crinkly as though wrapped in household foil, and fit snuggly into the palm of his hand. The readout displayed a pair of wavy lines, intersecting over a set of three-dimensional axes. He struggled to match it to the floorplan he had memorized earlier, looking up occasionally to find a reference point amongst the silent conveyers and creaking, ice-encrusted chains.

"Is that it there?" said Hardpan, peering easily over the top of the partition wall.

Raymon stared at the æmberscanner a moment longer before giving up. "What can you see?"

"An office. A control room, maybe. A central reservation. Lots of glass."

"Sounds exposed."

Hardpan grunted.

Raymon wasn't sure what to take from it.

"Any sign of the Director's goons?" he said.

The sylicate shook her head, grit trickling down her broad shoulders.

"I can't believe that that svarr is all he's got over his front door." Raymon took another look at the æmberscanner and nodded confidently. 'But this has to be it. Come on."

Gripping the now fully charged E-RAYzer, he peered out of cover.

A string of battened down assembler lines jigsawed their way through various steps, switchbacks and dangling walkways towards a wide flight of straight steps that led, presumably, to the control room that Hardpan had described. He rolled towards the nearest assembler platform.

Had he simply walked, then the blizzard of beamer fire that was waiting on him from the overwalks would have cut him to ribbons.

As it was, the volley of fire scolded across the back wall in an explosion of yellow sparks as Raymon clattered into new cover. Hardpan gasped, and Raymon glowed, as much at impressing the sylicate as at not being shot by a svarr N-72 pulse rifle.

"Is that all you've got, D'arco?" Shrill laughter raked down from the machine cradles above him. "So predictable. But then what do you expect from a skirate?"

"I'm not dead yet!"

Adjusting the E-RAYzer's focusing lenses to minimum beam width and maximum range, about twenty feet, he turned, half rose, and aimed upwards.

A torrent of fire put him back down again.

A svarr elf, small enough to hide amidst the detritus of the packed-up assembler lines, cackled as it let rip. The occasional beam found Hardpan where she was sheltering, diffracting through her head of crystals as though it was snowing rainbows. Gales of high-voiced laughter rang out from the assemblers.

"Damn it, we're pinned," he hissed.

"If we double back, can we get around them?" said Hardpan.

Raymon looked at his scanner. "I doubt it. They know what we're here for, and there can only be so many ways into the Director's offices."

"Then how do we get inside?"

Raymon slid into a fetal position with his back against the assembler panel and head between his knees as beam-fire scorched across the sloped terminal back.

"You're up!" he yelled.

"Me?"

"They're N-72s. Shadows mercenaries love them because they're quiet and cheap. They'd shred a human, but you can take it. Why do you think I was so insistent about bringing a sylicate along?"

Hardpan's face fissured into a deep smile. Purple light dribbled out.

"All right then," she said. "On three, two..."

On one, she rose out of cover like a Dis phantom, her sharpoon clutched in two megalithic hands. Beam fire scattered off her duricrust, followed by shouts of annoyance and the occasional cry of *"No fair!"* from the ambushing svarr. She moved towards the staircase. Raymon tucked in behind her, keeping low, his own aim loose, allowing the giant sylicate to soak up the mercenaries' heat.

They made it to the top of the stairs.

One mercenary left.

A giant, bulked out with the metal plates and thick muscle padding of an aggro-vest. He was a couple of inches taller than Hardpan. A steel buckler was strapped across one forearm.

The other held a sledgehammer. Behind him was what could only have been the Director's office, glass walled, raised onto its own sublevel on stilts to look down on the myriad assembler lines below it.

The giant planted his trunk-like legs and spat on the ground.

"I'm up..." Hardpan muttered to herself, then raised the sharpoon.

It wasn't really necessary to *aim* with a weapon like that.

When Hardpan pulled the trigger, the air surrounding the massive gun's heat exchangers gave a quiet little cry as the moisture was sucked out of it and heat expelled. The weapon was actually much less effective in the cold, something to do with the relative ability of hot and cold air to carry moisture, but an impressive six-foot long spike of solid ice slowly grew in the firing track regardless. Raymon would have loved to see what it could do in summer.

A second squeeze on the trigger loosed it.

The giant roared as the ice spear hit him in the chest, and punched the air in helpless aggression as he was pushed clear of the platform edge and fell the seven or eight feet to ground level.

Hardpan, meanwhile, was still moving, arms pumping, irresistible as an avalanche, the paneled flooring rattling in its housings. Raymon could have walked faster, but Spire, he would not have wanted to be anywhere close to in her way.

"That door's going to be locked," he said.

"May I?" said Hardpan, tectonic with excitement.

"Be my guest, only–"

The sylicate walked through the door without stopping. It shrieked free of its frame and went flying inwards. It crashed into the back wall with a *crunch* of glass and a shower of electrical sparks.

Raymon winced.

"–be careful," he finished.

He swung around to cover their withdrawal, taking low-power potshots whenever a head popped over a railing, but most of the svarr seemed to have given Hardpan up as a bad job and were keeping well down.

He backed in after her.

A bank of clunky, unlit monitors, now with a bent door sticking out of them, covered one wall. Broken glass littered a sweep of switches, sliders, and dials. A second door stood off to one side. The sounds of heated hand-to-hand combat rang from the other side of it. Nearer to there was a desk, and behind it, a chair. Ignoring the door, and the ongoing sounds of fighting, Raymon walked around the desk *and* the chair. In the wall behind them was a safe. He touched it.

The metal was icy with the cold.

"Trust the Director to be too cheap to heat even his own office."

Harpdan looked up. "Is it cold in here?"

Raymon covered his mouth and tried not to laugh.

"Is the æmber inside?" asked the sylicate.

Raymon checked his scanner. "Definitely."

"Then open it."

He grimaced. "Vaultcracking isn't my area."

He pushed his finger into the soft spot behind his left ear and waited for the *click*, but before he could say anything, the second door blew open as though thrown wide by a spirit entity of furious electronics and sparkler bombs. He backed away from the flash-bang after-glare as a goblin hustled inside. He was white faced, wildy red-haired, a pair of goggles covering most of his face. He was about four feet tall, wearing a trench coat that was fractionally too large, a pair of gloves with slightly too many fingers and so many belts, baldrics and bandoliers stuffed with tools that he jangled when he moved. A highly experimental jetpack was strapped to his back. Raymon had never yet seen it fly.

A robot rolled inside after the goblin. An armored footlocker on wheels. It was two feet high and about five long. Various colored bulbs decorated its "front", apparently to convey emotion, but someone had stenciled it with a pink smiley face that was both anthropomorphic and very, very disturbing. Strobes of gunfire lit up its ghoulish, painted-on grin as it unloaded its formidable arsenal onto the corridor, numerous arms telescoping from shuttered panels grasping a larger and unlikelier-looking weapon than the last.

The goblin hurriedly closed the door and leant on it.

The red bulb on the robot's indicator panel blinked on to indicate disappointment.

"*Beep,*" it said.

"Late as always, Ribs," said Raymon.

"I thought *you* were going to provide the distraction for *us*!" The goblin, Ribongun, or Ribs, eased off the door with some relief as its sensors timed out and fired heavy-duty locking pins into the architrave.

"They're getting wise," said Raymon.

"You know I hate change!"

"Beep."

"Not that it would have been a problem if X-TRM-N-8

here hadn't insisted on killing *absolutely* everything.'

"Beep."

A pink, happy, light blinked on.

Raymon was genuinely unnerved.

Ribs leant closer, forcing the taller Stormkin to crouch. "Where on the Crucible did you find that psychopath?!" he hissed.

Raymon shook his head quickly. That was a conversation for another time. Although he did worry that the robot was taking this whole thing just a little too seriously.

Meanwhile, the goblin had already capered around to assay the safe in the wall. His goggled eyes skipped over it, clicking and tutting under his breath.

"Can you break it?" said Raymon.

"Do I ask you if you can fly the ship?"

"Yes."

The goblin frowned. "Fair enough, then."

"Just get it done quickly."

Gunfire knocked on the other side of the door, and Raymon was very conscious of the fact that, courtesy of Hardpan's efforts, his own point of entry no longer had a door at all.

"*Beep,*" said X-TRM-N-8, deploying another bucketful of heavy weaponry.

Ribongun threw open his coat, selected a set of tools, and set to work.

"So how's she working out?" the goblin asked a moment later, muttering around the set of pins in his mouth.

Raymon looked over his shoulder and smiled absently. "A natural."

"Good luck explaining the door."

Raymon opened his mouth to protest when the safe gave with a *click*.

"Ta-dah!" Ribongun spread his arms with a flourish as the armored door eased open. A thin golden light trickled out, gilding all of their faces with one exception. Hardpan's glow was brighter.

"Well?" said Raymon.

The goblin turned to him. His baggy features loosened into a grin. "Make contact with the Archon, captain. Our business with the Director is done."

The rapid bass of indescribable phyll *glasshouse* music thumped through the Hub City tavern's thick walls. It vibrated through the polished wood of the bar and made the stools tremble like children lined up at the deep end of a pool. The air was aniseed and smoke. The carpets probably tasted of it. Paul Hendry, until about an hour ago Raymon D'arco, leaned on the bar, resting on his elbows. His loose, doublet coat was undone, the sleeves rolled up. His tricorn hat sat on the bar beside him. His utility belt looped over it.

A svarr elf patted him on the back. Given their relative statures, even with him sitting down, she was only able to reach about halfway up.

"Some good shooting back there," she said. "I never even saw you coming."

Paul raised his glass. "You made us fight for it this year."

The svarr wandered off to join the two dozen elves, humans, goblins, saurians and one frostbitten giant installed around the five large wooden tables. Most of them were still in mercenary attire, brandishing convincing replica firearms in the hands they weren't currently drinking with. About twice their number of animated, insectile krxix occupied the rest of the chairs and the standing areas around the bar.

Paul knew them all.

Except for the krxix.

They just knew a party when they saw one.

"A most profitable æmberheist, indeed!" Ribs shouted over the music.

Everything about the goblin's attire, like Paul's, was period specific. The trench coat was an exact replica of the one worn by their hero. The gloves had been hand-made, the designs culled from yellowed magazine articles and breathless contemporary reporting by the enthusiasts of the day. And so what if they had a few too many fingers for their actual hands? Accuracy was everything. The goblin had pulled their goggles up onto their forehead, revealing rings of green where the seals had pushed into the thick layers of white face paint to real skin. They held a long-stemmed glass in each hand, a piece of fruit floating in both, and eyed the gathering suspiciously.

"It's right that you don't carouse with the rank and file!" said Ribs. "There are parts of Hub City where that kind of fraternization would get a commander disintegrated." They struggled with their too-big gloves to bring the left-hand glass to their lips, and muttered into their cocktail. "Or so I've heard!"

"The game's over now," said Paul. "You don't have to stay in costume."

"Costume?" Ribs quickly reset their goggles, looking shiftily about the hired room. "I don't know what you mean!"

they said loudly and then, clutching their drinks, scurried off to find a corner.

Paul felt a smile break through.

He liked Ribs.

He had a lot of colleagues and acquaintances, most of them either here now, or through his day job as an aircab pilot, but not so many friends. He liked to believe that Ribs was one. Even if he didn't know their real name. They took authenticity seriously. At the time of the battle of Gregson's Vault, the insertion of Nova Hellas into the Local Group had still been a good five hundred years into the future and so there had been no martians around to take part. Paul appreciated that level of commitment. Why Ribs insisted on remaining in character and actually pretending to *be* a goblin even when they weren't role-playing was a mystery that Paul had given up trying to get to the bottom of.

An avalanche of gravelly laughter drew his attention from the unsolved problem.

Mica was squatting at one end of a long table and, having shed her Hardpan persona, had surrounded herself with krxix and costumed mercenaries as the very magnetic core of the party. Sylicates did not technically eat or drink, but this was Hub City, the civilized heart of the Local Group. If an establishment couldn't squeeze a few æmbits out of the more physiologically bizarre elements of its clientele then it wasn't going to stay in business long. Tasting bowls heaped with the salts of rare earths were scattered amidst the mercenaries' drinks. She reached for one. Her laughter rattled the full length of the table as a vaguely disinterested saurian in the long white coat, head mirror, and twitching surgical arm of a logos mender regaled her with a joke that Paul couldn't quite hear.

He thought seriously about getting up, going over there. Sipped his cocktail.

"Beep, beep."

"I don't know for sure," said Paul. "I think she enjoyed it."

"Beep, beep, beep."

Out of character, the robot, Smiles, betrayed a voluble side.

His rectangular unit was perched precariously on a bar stool, the various forces and counterforces at play subject to infinitesimal adjustments of his limbs. At the same time, apparently independently and carefree, one quadruple-jointed limb delicately tweezered the stem flute of a kettle bottom. Wherever the Twenty-One-Oh-Eighters met, week to week, to catch the latest vault battle, or admire one other's expanding collections of vault memorabilia, the robot always demanded the same drink: a kettle bottom. Failure to provide it could provoke… instability. It had come to the point that, as event organizer, ensuring that a venue had the requisite ingredients on menu had become an integral part of his working week.

The curiosity was: Paul had never seen the robot take a drop.

"I don't think she really gets it," he said.

"Beep, beep."

'We'll work up to that.'

"Beep, beep, beep."

"We work together. And you know the trouble we've had finding a sylicate to play Hardpan after Shail decided to take two weeks' vacation in Macis at Pearl's Spa right in the middle of battle season."

Various bulbs winked on and off.

"No. I don't think he ever did take this seriously."

"Beep, beep."

Paul sighed. "The owner wasn't happy about it, I'll tell you that. Even after I coughed up more than the price of the door by way of apology. I think we're going to have to find somewhere else for the æmberheist next year."

"Beep, beep, beep."

"Yeah, I know."

He lifted his glass and stared through it.

"Beep, beep?"

"Early shift tomorrow. A group of kids from New Horizon. Booked me for the whole day."

Paul wondered how it had all come to this. He had studied the old vault battles, read the semi-autobiographical *I am Raymon D'arco* fifty times, and run away from college to find a berth on a stormkin guncutter, only to be put back aground on Cirrus after a week in the air.

How had he ended up taxiing tourists around Hub City for twenty æmbits a half hour?

"Beep."

An arm telescoped from the robot's chassis and patted him on the shoulder.

With the exception of Mica, who wasn't really a member, at least not yet, Smiles was the most recent addition to the Twenty-One-Oh-Eighters, having found them about three months ago through an advertisement in *Vaultheads* magazine. Most who signed up that way weren't looking for anything more than someone to share a can and to watch the vault battle with, and either turned up infrequently or allowed their membership to lapse when confronted by the more… obsessive elements of the hobby. Smiles, however, had swiftly turned out to be one of the club's most enthusiastic members: a passionate collector, an earnest role-player, and ever reliable with an interesting titbit of vault trivia or an obscure stat. Before its membership of the Twenty-One-Oh-Eighters, the robot had roadied for the still anxiously remembered *Noisefest*, a Brobnar rock festival. Spent two hundred years following the rock star Spiretown free climber, Slazz the Indestructible, until her untimely death in a well-publicized mid-climb collision with a flying saucer. Been a member of the Emotional Landscape Free Ramblers Association. And, most recently, the Hub City Historical Society.

Whatever the robot was searching for, Paul was sure it had found it here.

The robot pivoted its chair towards the long tables. It waggled its antennae, blinked its lights.

"Beep, beep, beep."

"You really think I should?"

"Beep."

"You're right," said Paul, largely to himself. "It is what Raymon D'arco would do."

Paul downed his cocktail, took a deep breath, stood up, pulled the creases out of waistcoat and doublet, thought about the tricorn, left it, hesitating long enough to need a second breath and then finally made a decision. The robot made an encouraging "*Beep*," flashing him with his most strident bulb, which Paul translated as "*Go get her, skirate*," as he strode manfully into the crush of bodies.

Moving quietly through a crowd of krxix is next to impossible. Everyone wants to shake your limb analogue of preference and enquire excitedly after your day. Mica saw him coming a mile off, and raised a big, warmly glowing hand, like a set of landing strip lights to guide him down. He extricated himself from a trio of the breathlessly clicking insectoids before they could make firm plans for the weekend after next, and hurried over to join her.

The saurian she was with raised a glass in one tiny arm. The surgical implements attached to the other clicked and whirred. His vertically slit eyes narrowed as Paul crossed to join them. The saurian politely stood. Mica, sufficiently huge to deal with an upright man at eye level, remained seated.

"D'arco," he said.

"Director," said Paul.

The saurian's scales were the prismatic blue-green of the Photic Ocean carnosaurs. Paul had long suspected some kind of topical cosmetic behind their iridescence, although the saurian would stamp his feet and deny it even if Paul were to find the jar in his pocket. Even in the full logos pomp of whitecoat, mirror hat, and field specialty badges, he somehow managed to give the impression of *dressing down* for the benefit of the lesser species he indulged with his company.

Turquoise lips peeled back from a row of clean, white, very sharp teeth.

"Paul," he said.

"Alos."

"Mica was just telling me what she thought of her first vault battle experience," said Alos, his reptilian anatomy leaving behind only an odd *click* between vowel sounds and a trace of accent.

Paul turned to Mica, eager enough that he didn't even bother to point out that it hadn't, technically, been a vault battle. He could tell from the way Alos was fidgeting that the urge to do so was just about *killing* the saurian.

"The æmberheist of Director Sloane is one of the pivotal events in vault battle history," said Paul. "The penultimate encounter before the Battle of Gregson's Lot. Raymon D'arco and his companions broke into the Director's compound and made off with over a million æmbits worth of raw æmber, overcoming fifty hired guns of the DarkZone Shadowgangers to get it." He flicked Mica an embarrassed smile. "In case you were wondering, the club only has enough active members for us to put on about twenty. No one likes to get dressed up in the cold to play the bad guys."

Alos sniffed. "Arbitrator Taurex of the Piscus Letalis obtained *his* æmber without firing a single shot. He encountered an Inspired on the dark side of the World Tree and persuaded her to part with her æmber."

"Which always makes for a thrilling re-enactment," Paul muttered.

Mica masked a snigger.

"It is a little cerebral for most species' tastes, if that is what you mean."

"Yes," said Paul. "That's what I mean."

"Well, good."

Mica coughed politely. "Actually, I was just telling Alos how sorry I was about the office door. I hope I didn't cause you too much trouble."

"Don't worry about it," said Paul. "Happens all the time."

"Did Paul tell you about the time he got himself picked up by a pair of Rublex Bounty Hunters looking for a fugitive skirate matching his description?"

Mica clapped her hands in delight. "No!"

"He was halfway to Quantum City before they realized they had the wrong sentient."

"It's no great surprise really," said Paul. "I did fly with the stormkin, for a little bit."

'A *very* little bit," said Alos.

"Anyway," Paul shrugged. "It just goes to show how accurate this costume is, doesn't it? I'd like to see you convince a logos theorist that you're really an archmechanist in that get-up."

"What about the time I closed the Dis Library after telling the patrolman there was a snufflegator loose in the basement?"

"He thought the patrolman was Ribs in a different costume," Paul explained for Mica's benefit.

Alos shrugged.

Paul wished he could be that cold-blooded.

"I've watched plenty of vault battles on the screencasts," said Mica. "I've even seen a couple from the stadium zones."

Paul and Alos both nodded approvingly.

Aside from a re-enactment, the simulated experience of a properly outfitted stadium's psi-projectors was as near to the genuine vault battle experience as a committed punter could get.

"But I had no idea there were people who took it so… seriously."

"It's not *weird* or anything,' said Paul.

"It's history," said Alos.

Paul nodded.

"Actual real-life *scholars* study the Archons, you know," the saurian went on.

"Some people collect klaxon race cars," said Paul.

"Or old æmbit coins," said Alos.

"Building a modest collection of genuine vault battle memorabilia isn't so outlandish."

"It's archaeology," said Alos.

"I've heard that a lot of fans choose to support a single Archon," said Mica.

Alos looked sidelong at Paul. "I wouldn't say *choose*."

"Of course, there are casual fans in the stadiums, but it's not the same thing," said Paul. "It's not fun unless you pick a side."

He glanced at Alos.

Alos peeled his lips back over his fangs.

"You support Archon Thrurm, is that right?" said Mica, oblivious.

"Thrurm the Glorious," said Paul. "That's right."

Mica turned towards Alos.

"Ralleigh," the saurian said. "The Widow."

"That's its name?" said Mica.

Alos shrugged. "They hardly pick their own, do they?"

"Why do you follow them when neither one of them has fought a battle or even been *seen* in over a thousand years?"

"The mystery!" said Alos.

"The Battle of Gregson's Lot was listed in *Vaultheads* magazine, issue 2108, in the Local Group's Top Ten Vault

Battles," said Paul. He hesitated, reminiscing on a past, but still-raw grievance. "Personally, I think it deserved to be higher than eight."

"The writer was a fan of Kelroc the Remorseless," said Alos. "And you *know* how the magazine's sponsorship back then was tied up with Gilethlan the Golden Lady."

Paul nodded. "Dark times."

"So what was so special about this battle?" said Mica.

"About the battle itself?" said Alos.

"Nothing really," said Paul, and then grinned. "Except for how it ended."

"Or didn't end," said Alos.

"Or didn't end," said Paul, with an irritated glance at the saurian.

"What happened?" said Mica.

"Nobody really knows the answer to that," said Paul. "Both Archons had spent months, years, building their teams and acquiring the æmber they needed to forge their keys. They had brought them to the vault, ready to contest their rival for it in battle."

"It began at exactly 11:54, Hub Time," Alos interrupted. "The build-up had been well publicized. Not least by the director himself, who had spent the preceding weeks attempting to wrest his æmber back from Thrurm. But as you know, there's very little that even an evil genius can do to inconvenience an Archon." He cleared his throat, reining in his train of thought. "Depending on your source, somewhere between two and five hundred spectators turned up on the day to watch."

"The infamous Wrecker, Jim James, was trialing his Mk XII

Boundary Buster from Cirrus that same day," said Paul. "He attracted a lot of the live audience."

"More watched the psi-casts and flashbacks afterwards," said Alos.

Paul snorted at that obscene statement of the obvious.

"It began ordinarily enough," Alos went on. "Both Archons' vaultwarriors engaged with the vault's defenses, and with each other. But just as Ralleigh's warriors looked to be gaining the other hand and moving in on the Vault–"

"Pffft," said Paul.

"–just as they were moving in on the vault, both Archons suddenly disappeared."

"Raymon D'arco tried to keep on fighting," said Paul.

"Although, of course, without the Archons involvement there was really no point in carrying on. It was Arbitrator Taurex who talked him down."

"He told a *Vaultheads* reporter afterwards that he'd thought it was just another part of the vault battle. That's the thing about vault battles. And Archons. You can never know what might happen next."

"And neither Archon has been seen or heard from since," said Alos, with committed seriousness. "No one knows where they went. Or why they both surrendered the vault at the exact same time the way they did."

"Maybe they did it for the fame?" said Mica.

"I beg your *pardon?*" said the saurian.

"Smiles tells me they were both relatively obscure Archons before Gregson's Lot."

"It's not easy to try and guess at an Archon's motives," said Paul. "But it is half the fun."

Reaching into one of the all-weather pockets in his skirate waistcoat, he pulled out an image card in a clear plastic sleeve. The bright colors were bleached, but still showed a figure in golden armor and a crested helmet, light beaming from the wrists in place of hands and from the "T" shaped slit in the visor. A paragraph of heavily faded writing filled the bottom third of the card. A half dozen attribute stats ran down the side.

He showed it to Mica.

"Is this Archon Thrurm?"

Paul nodded. "An actual card from the time of his last battle. They can assume any form, but tend to keep to their known avatar when involved in vault battles."

Mica brought one slab-ended finger towards the card, but she had been long enough in the company of the Twenty-One-Oh-Eighters to know better than to touch it.

"What's this that he scores a ten in?"

Paul grinned, proudly. "Guile."

Alos arched his neck to poke his long snout over Paul's shoulder

Paul lifted the card to let him see it. "I got it from a dealer in Big Merch."

The saurian shrugged, then looked disinterestedly away. "Not bad."

"You have something better?"

"Not me. But I might have heard something."

"What?"

"Well…" Alos spread his small arms. "I'm not one to spread gossip, but I *might* have heard a rumor that Selxix has acquired something very special this year."

"Like what?"

"I don't know. It is just something I heard."

Selxix was a sentient spirit, said to have been one of the hundred or so spectators who had been in the crowd at Gregson's Lot that day. She was also the club's original founder. She had recently allowed a long-time human member called Tomar to help out with the running of the club. A few grumblers had suggested she was starting to lose interest, but Paul would like to see any of them maintain the level of enthusiasm she had shown for the last thousand years. Paul didn't know Tomar well. He seldom participated in events, with the exception of the big end-of-year re-enactments when he tended, but not always, to play Thrurm. He had been on the club's books for longer even than Alos, who, as the saurian liked to remind everyone, was otherwise the club's longest-serving fully material entity.

"Are you both looking forward to the battle?" said Mica.

"Always," said Paul. "Will you be there?"

Mica hesitated.

Paul opened his mouth to try and tempt her when Alos caught his eye and bid him to be quiet. A wave of shushing and quiet elbowing was making its way around the tables. One of the krxix scuttled over to the music box and obligingly dialed down the volume. Tomar strolled across the members' lounge, a cross between an aging rockstar and a retired holoflash presenter from an obscure channel, as if he had just wandered in from a larger convention in an adjoining suite. An oldish-looking man, he was dressed in a smart gray suit jacket over a black T-shirt emblazoned with the logo of the rock group, *Supermassive*, and a tie.

Paul wondered who or what the man was outside of the club.

No mere mortal should have been able to make any part of that combination work.

"Hallo," he said, hands up as though held amiably at gunpoint. "Hallo. Hallo." And everyone, whether human, elf, goblin, martian, saurian, or robot, or preternaturally chatty krxix seemed to understand and quieten down. "It's good to see everyone here. We're a few down on last year, but we've some new faces as well.' He nodded at Smiles, grinned at Mica. "And plenty of old ones still here." He looked wryly over a pair of gold-rimmed spectacles. "You all know who you are." Paul chuckled. He wasn't the only one doing so. Alos was hissing breathily, little arms wrapped over his chest. "As you know, the 1021st anniversary of the Battle of Gregson's Lot is coming around. And while Selxix and I have always endeavored to stage a better event than the year before, this year, as some of you will no doubt have already heard, we have decided to go all out with something extra special."

He glanced towards the back wall where everyone's winter coats hung.

Waited a moment.

Gave an embarrassed smile.

"*Ahem.* Any time now, Selxix. Please."

Another second of nothing elapsed. The vaultheads laughed uncertainly.

One of the coats suddenly inflated, and the laughter turned into gasps.

It was a woman's coat, ankle length, cut to a human's silhouette, dark green, with a deep hood and a fur trim. It fluttered down from its peg, filling up with emerald-colored light even as the coat tied itself up and pulled the drawstring tight to seal much of that light within. It drifted towards the nearest table, to more nervous laughter and light applause as those sat nearby scraped their chairs out of its way.

Tomar presented it with both hands.

"Selxix, ladies and gentlemen."

Once the applause had died down, Selxix's coat extended an arm. There was no hand at the end of it, just the outline of a shimmer, but in it, held as easily as Paul might hold a cup, was a small, pyramidal piece of delicately inscribed æmber.

Paul gasped in wonder.

"What is it?" murmured Mica.

"It's a replica of Ralleigh's Key. It's amazing. The best I've ever seen."

"It's *perfect*," said Alos.

"And, as if that weren't good enough..." With a showman's flourish, Tomar drew his hand from his jacket pocket to produce a complimentary piece of æmber. The fine detail of the inscriptions notwithstanding, they were identical. "As you know, the Battle of Gregson's Lot was abandoned before its conclusion. But both Ralleigh and Thrurm had with them an æmber key, forged and ready to be imprinted once the conditions to unseal the vault were met." He brandished the piece of æmber. "This is Thrurm's own, actual, key–"

"Oh, Boundary above me..."

Paul reached for the wall, suddenly afraid he might stumble. Alos was holding onto him. In that moment, neither cared.

"I have been holding onto this key for a long, long time," said Tomar. "Since before Selxix admitted me to this venerable old club. I was waiting for the right moment to unveil it, and now…" He gestured to Selxix's floating coat.

"No," Paul cried.

Alos raised his hands towards his mouth.

"Now we have Ralleigh's Key as well!" said Tomar.

Before Paul knew what he was doing, he was applauding, louder and harder than he had ever applauded anything in his life. He was an otherwise sensible man of thirty-seven years, but he jumped into the air and *whooped*. The presentation of the keys had galvanized the entire room. Whether it was some mysterious form of energy that flowed from the æmber or whether it was the other way around – Paul and his friends somehow empowering *it* – he did not know. He felt it fill him. Warm him. It gave him a voice that was stronger than his own, and he cheered with it, one long note in a standing ovation.

"Soon," Tomas said, without seeming to need to raise his voice, grinning from ear to ear, "we will fight the most authentic vault battle since Thrurm and Ralleigh themselves faced each other across Gregson's Lot."

"Raymon D'arco will be there!" Paul shouted.

"And Taurex Vor!" cried Alos.

"And Ribongun Red!"

"Beep Beep Beep!"

"And Hardpan!" shouted Mica.

The old man spoke for several minutes more.

Paul didn't hear any more. The words were irrelevant. The feeling was what counted.

The morning, suddenly, was inconsequential.

Soon, the vaultwarriors of Archon Thrurm would be going to battle.

• • •

Paul stamped his feet on the icy concrete and hugged himself. He huffed out a cloud of steam. He drew his wrist from his armpit, tugged up the doublet sleeve and, shivering, used it to wipe the condensation from the glass face of his watch.

11:39.

He covered his wrist again, hunched his head further in towards his shoulders and vigorously rubbed his arms. He'd thought long and hard that morning about wearing a heavier coat, before deciding against it.

He'd do this properly or not at all.

"Beep, beep, beep."

The robot's flat top was buried under a small mountain of snow. Just a pair of antennae poking out.

"Right!" said the small white lump shrouded in trench coat. "The battle was fought on a bright day! A bright, hot day! I have seen the pictures!"

"It's the mechanists in Micro-Research Facility 87θ," said Paul. "Tinkering with the climate."

"Do you think the First Among Us will have to shift the calendars again?" said Mica. A deep heat radiated off the sylicate's shiny black crust and the vaultwarriors, even Smiles, were huddled surreptitiously close around her.

"I doubt it," said Paul. "They'll just wait for another experiment gone awry to knock the seasons back where they're supposed to be."

"I hope so!" said Ribongun. "It is hard enough to keep track of the battle's proper anniversary date as it is!"

Paul checked his watch again.

11:42.

He eased his weight from foot to foot.

Gregson's Lot had been a parking lot 1021 years ago. It was still a parking lot now. The mythical "Gregson", sadly, had been long since lost to history. A few hover trikes and ground-scooters were parked in bays, just as it had been in Raymon's day. A thick white curtain of snowy sky obscured the famous glass and chrome skyscrapers of Hubcenter, and muted the garish displays of the Brobnar Clashzone and Central Stadium to a cold, neon smudge and a distant grind of noise.

He checked his watch.

11:44.

"Beep, beep."

"I know I'm not making it move any faster."

"Who'd leave their vehicle parked where a vault battle's about to be fought?" said Mica.

Paul's lips twitched, somewhere between an unconscious shiver and a smile.

She hadn't called it a re-enactment, a nerdgathering, or a geekstival.

She'd called it a vault battle.

"I'm glad you decided to come," he said.

"That Tomar…" she said, with a rumbling sigh that left Paul feeling awkward. "I've never met an organic who can speak the sylicate language like that. He spoke like a poet."

Paul frowned.

He couldn't remember Mica ever speaking with Tomar al–

"The weather hasn't dampened our enthusiasm, I see."

Paul bit his lip as Tomar crunched out of the snowfield behind them.

The old man was wearing a flannel jacket over another

Supermassive t-shirt. His white jogging shoes were ankle deep in snow. A bobble hat with floppy ear flaps was his solitary concession to the cold. For some reason the snow just didn't seem to settle on him. The flakes seemed to drift aside at the last moment rather than fall where he was standing.

He nodded towards Paul.

"Raymon D'arco."

Paul took a deep breath and straightened.

"We're ready," he said.

With great and terrible seriousness, Tomar brandished the key. Although it had never been imprinted with the emotional resonance required to unlock the vault, it was still æmber. It radiated power, its shape and color shifting to mimic the feelings of those in its vicinity towards that power. Under Raymon's regard it became the blue of open skies, of piracy and freedom, and feelings of nostalgia and want welled up in him so powerfully he could barely breathe.

"With this key shall I open the vault and liberate its treasures," said Tomar. "But to do that I will need you, my vaultwarriors, to vanquish the forces of the Widow and imprint upon it the emotion required to unlock this vault."

No one, except perhaps the Archons themselves, knew what it would actually take to activate their key and win the vault battle. That was part of what made them such thrilling spectacles.

Tomar – now Thrurm – lowered his face and raised up his hand.

Paul shivered with anticipation.

"But wait. I sense my rival's approach. Ralleigh has forged her own key, and brings minions of her own to challenge me.

Only one can activate their æmber and claim the vault for their own. I give you this last chance to go home to your lives. Or you can stay, and fight for me."

"Stay and fight!" Paul cheered.

"Stay and fight!" shouted Mica and Ribongun together, deep voice and high.

"Beep, beep!"

Smiles blinked furiously.

Paul checked his watch.

11:53... 11:54.

The snow between Ribongun's feet exploded as a laser bolt struck it.

The goblin screamed, igniting their jetpack and rocketing into the air.

They screamed some more.

Paul left his jaw behind as he tilted his head to watch his friend go.

"Spire..." he mumbled. "I had no idea that that actually *worked.*"

The other vaultwarriors hadn't been around long enough to see this as spectacular, and scattered. X-TRM-N-8 shook snow off its back like an aluminum war-dog and rolled sideways into the snow on its large wheels, emitting an increasingly shrill sequence of expletive "*Beeps*" as it struggled to de-ice its shutters and deploy its arsenal. Mica – Hardpan – lumbered on into the lot, further shots puffing up snow and ricocheting off cars as she advanced.

Only Thrurm seemed unmoved by it all, as awesome in his potency as any real Archon would have been. The æmber in his hand changed from blue-white to silver to gold and exponentially brightened, illuminating the old man's upper body fully, as well as a sphere of blizzarding snow. Paul averted his eyes from its sudden battle fury.

"GO!" Thrurm shouted, in a voice that had become so powerful that the ground shook with it and the snow around Paul broke up in midair. Paul wondered how he did it. "VANQUISH THE WIDOW'S VILLAINOUS DOGS, AND THE WEALTH OF THE VAULT WILL BE MINE TO SHOWER UPON YOU."

For a moment, it was so realistic that Paul could have choked on his own enthusiasm.

Drawing his E-RAYzer, he ducked low and hurried after Hardpan.

The sylicate was about thirty paces into the lot, the Widow's sniper laying down some heavy fire. The shooter was nothing more than a muzzle flash in the distance. Paul grunted as he worked out the distances and angles in his head. Outside of the battlefield. Technically cheating, then. But hadn't that always been the Widow's style.

"That'll be Mittlerad!" Raymon yelled. "Arbitrator Taurex's cmizz sharpshooter." The cmizz were just about the only race arrogant enough for a saurian to tolerate as equals. "A T9 Teleblaster! In the parking garage adjoining the lot." Hardpan continued her relentless advance, high-power beams blasting off chips of duricrust and punching dents into her torso.

The unbelievable realization occurred to him.

The weapon was real.

"A T9 would knock out a Sanctum Shieldship – get down!"

A single laser beam struck her hard. Bits of rock exploded

from her shoulder. The force spun her around and threw her onto the front of a car. She rolled off the dented hood, just as the vehicle's tamper alarm began to screech and a Pulsar stun cannon ratcheted up from a concealed rack in the roof. The pintle weapon tracked, and for want of an obvious vandal in its fire arc began blasting wildly. Electrical bolts spasmed across the lot like a laser shower at a music festival. Paul threw himself flat as one snarled across him. Another fried a truck parked about a hundred feet to his right. X-TRM-N-8 rolled into a lightning bolt without looking. Its entire rack of indicator bulbs exploded. Smoke coughed from its grille. The robot rolled to a complete stop with a piteous whine and sagged onto its wheels.

"No!" Paul yelled.

"The greater the struggle, the greater the prize," came Thrurm's voice. "We are far from finished yet, D'arco."

Paul could no longer see the old man for the snowstorm and the slashing of weaponsfire, but his voice inspired something in him to bring up his E-RAYzer and fire back.

The shot vaporized the car.

He looked at the ray pistol in his hand in horrified amazement.

His mouth hung open.

"Damn…"

It had never done that before.

A laser bolt smacked into the ground beside him. He dropped and rolled to the side, confident that he was as good as invisible unless the cmizz was packing seriously upgraded vision. He crawled towards the spot where Mica had gone down, as the sniper switched his Teleblaser to automatic and mowed the area with fire.

If nothing else, he had the elf's attention.

"Yaaaaaaarrgh!"

Ribongun was still screaming as their homemade, suddenly one hundred per cent functional jetpack carried them on a smoky parabola towards the multi-story garage on the other side of the lot, their arms and legs flailing like those of a panicked krxix. The goblin recovered something of their wits only as the cmizz turned her fire on them, the Teleblaser's turbocharged blasts bending around their prism field. The battery packs webbed to their chest gave off steam.

"Yaaaaaaarrgh-ha-hahaha!"

Drawing his own brace of pistols, he returned fire, the noisy, Bromdar-built bangpowder weapons finally forcing the cmizz from her vantage.

"A good play, Thrurm, but did you think it would be that easy?"

Selxix's emerald brilliance was a distant beacon in the snow.

Paul could not say why, or how, but her energy looked different. Purer. *Darker.* Less contained. She sounded different too. He had never heard her speak before, for starters. Even at past years' battles, she had always reprised her original role as a spectator.

"I know all your so-called tricks."

A pair of human skeletons with mechanical metallic wings flapped out of the snow. Raymon shot at them as they passed overhead. The range was too great for his E-RAYzer and they continued creakily after Ribongun.

Skeletimps.

He'd not seen anything like them in a vault battle since…

Not since...

"Boundary above," he muttered. "I'm fighting a real Archon."

A bullish roar dragged his attention to where it had been before Ribongun's dramatic overflight had distracted him.

Hardpan was hauling herself off the ground, one shovel hand to her shoulder, chin blunted where it had smacked the hood of the car.

The roar wasn't from her.

A massively up-armored ankylosaur pounded from the snowfield towards her. Cars a hundred feet away rattled with his footfalls. Dropping her hand from her shoulder, Hardpan smoothly unshipped her sharpoon and fired. The already cold air shrieked as it was drawn into the big gun's hoppers, hyper-frozen, and *twanged* from the track at twice the speed of sound. The ankylosaur dropped its head, icicles blasting off its heavy plate, and then rammed Hardpan's midriff. The sylicate weighed as much as twenty human men, but the running ankylosaur lifted her off the ground like a dummy, carried her about twenty feet and slammed her into the side of a parked truck.

Paul's breath caught in his mouth.

The Archons wouldn't allow any of them to come to lasting harm.

Would they?

"I'm coming, Mica!" Paul yelled.

He advanced on the ruined truck, gun up, the wrecked vehicle bucking like a wounded animal as the two combatants pounded one another with bone gauntlets and stone fists.

"Beep, beep, beep, BEEP!"

X-TRM-N-8 lurched suddenly forwards. Lights flickered back on. Flaps opened in the robot's sides as it began furiously unpacking weapons as though making up for lost time. It shook angrily, bristling with enough firepower to make the supreme commander of a small martian outpost blush.

And then loosed the lot.

Paul was sharp enough to throw himself flat as a blanket spread of flash bombs beat against the sky's anvil, sonically compressing everything ground-locked enough to be caught beneath it. Anything that wasn't already broken, broke. Snow exploded into puffy white clouds. Concrete slabs splintered through. Metal screamed, bent, snapped. Glass flew like faeries reprogrammed to kill. Vaultwarriors on both sides covered ears, tympana, and waveceptors, and writhed on the ground. Wild loops of scattergun-fire shredded a skeletimp and chased the other from the sky. Ribongun corkscrewed through blistering swathes of gunfire before crashing into a wall. The hyper-dense, impossibly black beam of a back-mounted gravicannon hit the Widow herself. The forced singularity rippled through her before demolishing the parking garage behind her.

It collapsed into a supermassive gravitic well and a tsunami of dust.

Paul looked up from the ground and gawped.

Ralleigh looked mildly irritated.

Then it rained missiles.

Paul buried his face under his hands as the world turned to fire. He stayed where he was for the longest time, not daring to move. Repeated explosions made the ground shake. He gritted his teeth, closed his eyes, waited it out.

And after the longest half minute ever recorded, it stopped.

A robotic voice, some distance away, gave an immensely satisfied "*Beep.*"

Paul lifted his face.

The movement was painful. The backs of his neck and arms had been burned. Flecks of gray dust fell lazily out of the sky instead of snow. Pockets of fire guttered where craters and the fall of assorted debris sheltered them from the cold and the wind. He coughed, atomized metals grating up and down his throat. His E-RAYzer lay in the half-melted slush where he'd dropped it. With one peeled and blistered hand, he reached gingerly out to take it.

A weapon clicked. He froze. There was a hum, pitch and volume increasing – the distinctive whine of a ray weapon dialing through the settings from stun to kill to disintegrate.

"Well, well, well…" came the sibilant reptilian voice behind the weapon. "Raymon D'arco. We meet on the field again at last."

Paul looked over his shoulder.

Arbitrator Taurex Vor held his neutralization ray at a spot between his shoulder blades. It was a Sanctum-blessed piece, white metal, stamped in emblems of peace and love. His long white Arbitrator's cloak rippled in the wind, citation laurels and gold leaf fleur-de-lis glittering. Frost crusted his blue-green scales, turning them almost white. Steam billowed from Paul's mouth, and he noticed that Taurex's breath, by comparison, was clear. Slowly, so as not to provoke, he turned onto his back. Taurex's aim followed him. Albeit sluggishly.

Paul's lips crept into a grin as his doubts and fears evaporated.

This wasn't a game any more.

It was better than that.

It was everything he had ever dreamed of having in life.

He *was* Raymon D'arco.

"Surrender, D'arco," said Taurex, ice splintering off his jaw. It was the cold. The carnisaur was struggling in the cold. He couldn't even shiver. "There's no rule that says these battles have to be to the death." Taurex shrugged. "I am a man of peace, after all."

"Never," said Raymon, and threw himself to one side.

Taurex fired, but the cold had left the saurian's reactions a fraction too slow. The neutralizer zapped the ground where he'd been lying. Knees under, he drove upwards and drew his combat weapon: a curved cutlass with a quantum-thickness dark matter edge. Too sluggish to do the same, Taurex parried with his bracer. The dark-matter blade struck sparks from the metal, and brought a tympanic jiggle from a low-level defensive field.

For a split second Raymon felt dizzy, one mind trying to inhabit two people, in two places, and in *two times* at once.

It was so perfect.

He could almost forget he wasn't fighting the real Taurex Vor.

The saurian turned his body with his parry, coat billowing, closing off avenues of attack as he whipped his white-bladed sword from its scabbard and countered.

Raymon deflected the thrust. Riposted with a rising slash from the left. Taurex skipped back, footwork drawing tracks through ash and snow, delivered a flurry of intricate blade-work that sent Raymon reeling back. He didn't press. The saurian backed towards the burning wreck of a hovercar. The heat loosened reptilian muscles. He lowered his guard and beckoned. Raymon grunted and charged, leapt the final half-dozen feet and brought his blade crashing into Taurex's. They spun apart, clashed together. Metal rang off metal. Exotic particles flew. Arbitrator greatcoats and flamboyantly sleeved doublets rippled with their increasingly energized blade-work and the hot breath of the fire.

The stirrings of a strange feeling began in Raymon's chest.

Taurex whirled back. He was almost glowing.

Raymon stepped after him, crisscrossing himself with short, threshing strokes of his cutlass. Rather than retreat, Taurex stepped in. The saurian's blade nipped along the flat of Raymon's. Then he caught Raymon's wrist and twisted, the cutlass popping from the stormkin's grip.

The knot in Raymon's heart became a spreading tightness as Taurex kicked him in the chest.

His armor was a soft fabric oversleeve to his waistcoat, designed to deflect ray blasts and beams. He felt it tear under the saurian's boot heel as he flew back to the ground.

The feeling was an emotional implosion, focused underneath his ribs.

Arbitrator Taurex stood over him.

His sword tip kissed Raymon's throat.

"I was always better than you."

Raymon bared his teeth defiantly. "And yet I never lost a battle."

At that moment, it didn't matter if he genuinely lived or

died. He'd been party to something incredible. He had seen a real Archon, two of them, in battle. In the same moment it dawned on him that the Battle of Gregson's Lot had never been abandoned at all. Ralleigh and Thrurm were Archons, and so what was a hiatus of 1,021 years in order to wait for just the right set of conditions to unlock the vault? The sizzling of warmth and pleasure spread from his torso, into his limbs. He had fought as Raymon D'arco in a vault battle. And not just any vault battle. *The longest recorded vault battle of all time!* It made the famous month-long Echo vault battle between Uriel the Crimson and Maxcorra look like a one-punch knockout. He had lived his dream, had been, for a few precious minutes, part of an event and a time that, although he had never personally experienced it, he had loved enough to color every decision he had made in his adult life.

His heart opened like a phyll pod, and a golden wave of nostalgia flooded him.

Suddenly, a vision of Archon Thrurm appeared before him.

The key in his grip exploded with power. Paul could feel his emotion exerting on the raw æmber, forging it to fill the shape of a lock that only an Archon could see.

"No!" Taurex cried, withdrawing his blade from Paul's neck and recoiling from the blazing Archon. "No, no, no! I was winning!"

Ralleigh hung her head, her brilliance fading from the field, leaving her followers confused and bereft as to what had just happened. Thrurm, however, burned with a radiance that outshone even æmber. There could be no doubt who had just been victorious. The Archon raised his key high, gigantic now, and inhuman, encased in metal plate armor with golden rivets.

Haloed in triumphant light.

A stunned silence lay over the bar, teetering on the back of something precious that no one who had briefly been permitted to touch it could quite describe or define. Paul breathed out, as though he'd been holding it in since the battle. Ribongun blew an unspoken agreement between their lips. Smiles clutched its kettle bottom, dashboard glowing contentedly. None of them spoke for a while. What was there to *say* after something like that?

"What do we do now?" Mica murmured. The sylicate had a dollop of Heal-X cement smeared across her shoulder, but she otherwise appeared none the worse for her ordeal.

"I can't wait to see the next issue of *Vaultheads*," said Ribongun.

Paul had never heard the martian speak so measuredly.

He thought back to the moment when the vault had opened. Light had spilled from the Archon just as it did in the holo-flashes. It had arisen from the Crucible itself, as if the ground and the air, and even Paul, had become æmber. He'd devoured so many stories of the legendary rewards of the vault. Some were said to shower triumphant vaultwarriors with gold or gemstones, rare metals or exotic plastics, weapons of the Architects or blueprints to the next great scientific marvel of the age. Paul had experienced nothing like that. Either Thrurm was keeping the vault's riches to himself, which he doubted, because what use did an Archon have for such trinkets, or the reward for his part in the victory had been something altogether different. Something more priceless and ephemeral by far. An enormous sense of satisfaction and pride had filled him, and it was a feeling that had remained with him even as he had stumbled, blinking, from the light. Nothing would ever be able to take it away from him, although the glow had already dimmed somewhat, leaving behind a sense of absence, and worry at how far that core of wellbeing might eventually diminish in time.

It left him wanting more.

"Do we just… go back to our lives?" Mica went on. "After that?"

Paul looked up as the door opened.

Tomar walked in.

Or *Thrurm* he should probably say, but could not, even in his own head. He wore Tomar's familiarly rumpled body and heroically mismatched attire. Paul's stool scraped on the floor as he stood. Ribongun jumped back off theirs. Mica looked up, her settled body creaking.

"*Beep,*" said Smiles, sagely, and Paul had never heard something so heartbreakingly profound, so succinctly put.

He threw a stormkin salute as though he had been waiting his entire life for it.

There was so much he wanted to say to the Archon, to thank him for. There was so much he wanted to be able to *ask*.

He knew he would never get the chance.

"Wow," said Thrurm, stuffing his hands in his jacket pockets and looking around. A single fzoont polished a glass about a foot off the ground behind the bar. He turned to Paul. "This place is so *dead*. I was just heading out to Brighthaven." He gestured equivocally towards the door. "If anyone here wants to join me…"

**RETURN TO THE
CRUCIBLE AND
KEYFORGE SOON**

CONTRIBUTORS

DAVID GUYMER is a scientist and writer from England. His work includes many novels in the *New York Times*-bestselling *Warhammer* and *Warhammer 40,000* universes, notably *Headtaker* and *Gotrek & Felix: Slayer*, and the bestselling audio drama *Realmslayer*. He has also contributed to fantastical worlds in video games, tabletop RPGs, and board games.

bobinwood.wixsite.com/thirteenthbell
twitter.com/warlordguymer

M K HUTCHINS is the author of the YA fantasy novels *The Redwood Palace*, and Junior Library Guild Selection, *Drift*. She is a prolific short story writer, appearing in *Fireside*, *Podcastle*, *Strange Horizons*, and elsewhere. A long-time Idahoan, she now lives in Utah with her husband and four children.

mkhutchins.com
twitter.com/mkhutchins

CATH LAURIA is a Colorado girl who loves snow and sunshine. She is a prolific author of science fiction, fantasy, suspense and romance fiction, and has a vast collection of beautiful edged weapons.

twitter.com/author_cariz

ROBBIE MacNIVEN is a Highlands-native History graduate from the University of Edinburgh. He is the author of several novels and many short stories for the *New York Times*-bestselling *Warhammer 40,000 Age of Sigmar* universe, and the narrative for HiRez Studio's *Smite Blitz* RPG. Outside of writing his hobbies include historical re-enacting and making eight-hour round trips every second weekend to watch Rangers FC.

robbiemacniven.wordpress.com
twitter.com/robbiemacniven

TRISTAN PALMGREN is the author of the critically acclaimed genre-warping blend of historical fiction and space opera novel *Quietus,* and its sequel *Terminus.* They live with their partner in Columbia, Missouri.

tristanpalmgren.com
twitter.com/tristanpalmgren

THOMAS PARROTT lives in middle Georgia, US, with his wife and three cats. He is the author of several short stories and an upcoming novel set in the *Warhammer 40,000* universe.

twitter.com/parrotttd

M DARUSHA WEHM is the Nebula Award-nominated and Sir Julius Vogel Award-winning author of the interactive fiction game *The Martian Job*, several SF novels, and the Andersson Dexter cyberpunk detective series. They have also written the Devi Jones: Locker YA series, and the coming-of-age novel *The Home for Wayward Parrots*. Originally from Canada, Darusha lives in New Zealand after spending several years sailing the Pacific.

darusha.ca
twitter.com/darusha

C L WERNER is a voracious reader and prolific author from Phoenix, Arizona. His many novels and short stories span the genres of fantasy and horror, and he has written for *Warhammer's Age of Sigmar* and *Old World*, *Warhammer 40,000*, Warmachine's *Iron Kingdoms*, and Mantica's *Kings of War*.

CHARLOTTE LLEWELYN-WELLS is a bibliophile who took a wrong turn in the wardrobe and ended up as an editor – luckily it was the best choice she ever made. She's a geek and fangirl with an addiction to unicorns, ice hockey and ice cream.

twitter.com/lottiellw

Defend the world from eldritch terrors in Arkham Horror

Countess Alessandra Zorzi, adventurer and international thief, sets out to steal an ancient petrified corpse from the Miskatonic Museum, but instead stumbles onto a nightmarish flesh-eating cult bent on invoking unearthly forces.

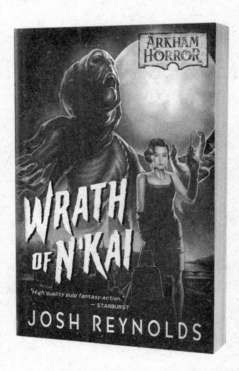

Charismatic surrealist painter, Juan Hugo
Balthazarr, enthrals Arkham's elite with arcane
illusions that blur the boundaries between
fantasy and reality. But is it just art, or does he
truly threaten to rip open the fabric of reality?

Venture into a land of duty and warfare, with Legend of the Five Rings

The mountainous border dividing the empire of Rokugan from the dark Shadowlands is perilous. Discovering a mythical city amid the blizzardswept peaks offers heroes an opportunity to prove their honor, but risks exposing the empire to demonic invasion.

Meet Daidoji Shin, a charming and indolent
Crane Clan aristocrat. When he's dragged away
from a life of decadence, he and his samurai
bodyguard discover a talent for detection, and
uncover a murderous web of conspiracies
in the Emerald Empire.